WITCHES RULE

URBAN FANTASY ROMANCE

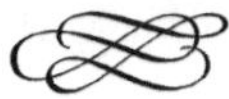

ANN GIMPEL

Edited by
ANGELA KELLY
Illustrated by
Sly Fox Cover
Designs

CONTENTS

WITCHES RULE

DEMON ASSASSINS, BOOK THREE

Urban Fantasy Romance With A Heaping Side of Hexes, Spells, and Magick
By
Ann Gimpel

BOOK DESCRIPTION: WITCHES RULE

Jenna's a special witch, sort of, when her magic works, which it often doesn't. One of three remaining demon assassins, she and her sister witches, Roz and Colleen, are Earth's only hedge against being overrun by Hell's minions. On the heels of Roz's and Colleen's weddings, Jenna is headed for the U.K. when a demon confronts her. Any other witch could teleport out of the plane, but not her. Frustration about her limited power eats at her. It would be pathetic to get killed for lack of skills a teenager could master.

Tristan is a Sidhe warrior, but his primary gift is attunement to others' emotions. He fell hard for Jenna, but hasn't had an opportunity to act on their attraction beyond a few kisses because she returned to Alaska, and he's been in the field fighting demons.

As seer for the Sidhe, Kiernan is haunted by visions, particularly an apocalyptic sending that seems to be coming true. A confirmed bachelor, he doesn't understand his attraction to Jenna, but it's so strong he can't fight it. After a while, he doesn't even try, despite recognizing Tristan's claim to her.

Startling truths surface about Jenna's magic, and then there's the problem that she's falling in love with two very different men.

At first she believes she has to pick one of them, but her spirit refuses to walk away from either. It's impossible to choose between a seer with dreams in his eyes and a beautiful man who intuits her every need. Standing on the verge of Earth's destruction, will she defy convention and follow the song in her heart?

This book found its roots deep in the southern ocean. Thanks to big seas and long days with my laptop, it was partially written when I got back from my first trip to Antarctica. In addition to my ever-patient husband, this book is dedicated to my fellow passengers aboard the Polar Pioneer who hung over my shoulder and read as I wrote.

CHAPTER 1

*J*enna Neil sank heavily onto her airplane seat and kicked off her high heels, shoving them beneath the seat in front of her. With a small sigh of relief, she rotated her ankles to take the pressure off her aching arches. She'd always loved heels—the higher the better—and insisted on wearing them, never mind they definitely lacked a comfort factor. Once she'd shot past six feet, she figured it didn't matter if she added a few inches to her already overbearing height.

A flight attendant leaned over to hand her a pillow and blanket. Jenna tucked the pillow behind her head as she listened to the safety briefing and estimates of their arrival time in London.

She closed her eyes, but it didn't ease how tired and gritty they felt, and smoothed her too-short denim skirt down her thighs. A red wool sweater and matching denim jacket finished off her outfit. She'd been so excited about getting out of Alaska and away from the layers she was forced to wear through the winter, she'd probably underdressed for the current jaunt. Less trendy clothes were tucked in her checked luggage, but they weren't exactly accessible.

The last few days hadn't offered much opportunity for rest.

She, Colleen Kelly-Regis, and Roxanne Lantry-Redstone—Roz to everyone who knew her well—were the last of the demon assassin witches. Having escaped Irichna demons by a ridiculously narrow margin—again—the three of them were on their way to the U.K. where they could do it all over again.

Jenna grinned ruefully. Demons running amok through the British countryside had thrown witches and the Daoine Sidhe together after two hundred years of enmity. It had also netted impossibly hunky husbands for her sister witches, but that was beside the point. Staying alive was a much more front and center problem.

Because Irichna demons had become so much more aggressive, everyone but her thought it would be best to travel separately. She hadn't agreed, but she'd been the one dissenting vote. As far as Jenna was concerned, there was always strength in numbers, but the others were convinced their current strategy would confuse the demons long enough for everyone to regroup on the eastern side of the Atlantic. Colleen and Roz were teleporting with their husbands. Niall, Colleen's Irish changeling familiar, was making his own way back home along with two Scottish changelings, Llyr and Krae. Jenna had never been much good at teleporting, so she'd opted to fly commercial. It would place her arrival at least twelve hours after everyone else, but she could live with that. At least the first leg of her journey, from Fairbanks to Seattle, and thence to New York, had been uneventful.

Thinking about Irichna made her shiver, so she unfolded her blanket and draped it around her shoulders. Demons didn't get much worse than Irichna. As Abbadon's chosen henchmen, they played for keeps, and Abbadon was the biggest and baddest of Hell's denizens, so nothing was off limits. Demon assassin witches had been a craw in his throat for a long time, and lately he'd upped the ante to get rid of them—permanently.

Them means me, and I'd do well not to forget that.

Jenna blew out a weary breath. One of her not-so-distant

ancestors had been forced into demon containment two hundred years ago by the Sidhe, breaking every rule that bound magic-wielders, but the Sidhe hadn't cared. In the intervening years, demons had managed to kill every single witch with demon-assassin ability—except for her, Roz, and Colleen. The Sidhe were primed to take back some responsibility for ferrying Irichna to the Ninth Circle of Hell where the gatekeeper locked them away, but that hadn't exactly happened yet.

She gritted her teeth and unclenched hands she'd balled into fists around the edge of the thin airline blanket. The aircraft backed out of its slip and headed for one of the many runways at JFK Airport. While it would be lovely to have help with the demons, working with the Sidhe held its own set of problems. For one thing, most of them were insufferably autocratic, which was how Jenna's great-grandmother had ended up being suckered into picking up the demon banner in the first place.

Even though Titania, Queen of Faerie, appeared marginally tolerant of Colleen's and Roz's marriages to Sidhe now, she'd given Duncan quite a bit of grief over his proposed marriage to Colleen at the front end of things. By the time Ronin, the *de facto* Sidhe leader, made it clear he'd set his sights on Roz, Titania had backed down a few notches, probably because they were beset by Irichna.

Jenna thinned her lips into a hard line. Hundreds of years before, Ronin's human partner had died in childbirth, and the child along with her. Apparently, both the Queen and King of Faerie made it clear Ronin had sunk himself by choosing to marry someone outside his race. In the face of their indifference, Ronin had carried his grief alone.

It's just like it is with humans. Everybody's got to have somebody to look down on...

Jenna tamped back a cynical grin. The Sidhe had made strides accepting other races, but they had a way to go before they moved beyond their intolerant past.

Jenna pictured her friends' husbands, and a small sigh escaped. Like all the Daoine Sidhe, Duncan Regis and Ronin Redstone were heartbreakingly stunning. Duncan's blond good looks and green eyes provided a counterpart for Ronin's dark hair and deep blue gaze. When Jenna scratched the surface and did a little soul-searching, she had to admit she'd never expected to find a permanent partner. Girls like her—well rounded and obscenely tall—weren't exactly in demand. Colleen was beautiful with her waist length auburn hair and pale blue eyes, and Roz was unusual and striking. Her Native American heritage and long, lean frame turned heads whenever she passed by.

Guess I'm the odd witch out these days...

Jenna pressed her lips together. It remained to be seen how her friends' marriages would impact their lives. Some things would have to change because she couldn't quite envision Duncan and Ronin simply moving in to her Fairbanks, Alaska, home along with their new wives. For one thing, all the Sidhe maintained amazing abodes in the U.K. Places that resembled castles more than houses.

Jenna reined in her thoughts. There were a lot of unknowns, but the main problem would be surviving the next few weeks. Once they got the Irichna on the run—if that were even possible—then she could figure out more prosaic things, like if she'd be the only one still living in Fairbanks and running their magicians' supply shop. Before the thought even finished forming, she knew that arrangement wouldn't work. She, Roz, and Colleen had to stay together, and if the others insisted on remaining in the U.K., well then she wouldn't have much choice in the matter. If she returned to Alaska by herself, she'd be a sitting duck for Irichna to swoop down and overpower her.

She shivered again and considered asking for a second blanket.

In an attempt to divert herself and maybe unwind, though it seemed unlikely, Jenna started to push her seat back and then remembered she wasn't supposed to quite yet. The plane's engines were revving, but they hadn't left the ground. She heard the captain instruct the flight attendants to prepare the cabin for takeoff and tried to relax in her plush first-class seat. If the goddess was good to her, maybe she'd catch a few hours of sleep before the plane landed.

A flurry of supernatural energy caught the edges of her attention, and Jenna's gut twisted into a sour knot. She sat up straight and craned her neck to scan the cabin, defensive magic at the ready. Her eyes widened in disbelief as Krae's unmistakable form shimmered into being, and the changeling bounded into the empty seat next to Jenna. Her long, bright red hair hung loose, and her eyes shone like emeralds. Krae's stocky body was draped in wide-bottomed green silk pants and an embroidered black tunic. As was usual with changelings, her feet were bare. The creatures drew their power from the earth, and Jenna assumed they didn't want layers of leather or rubber or neoprene between themselves and their magical well. With their three-foot height, broad shoulders, and longish arms, they looked like a missing link between humans and the great apes.

"What are you doing here?" Jenna kept her voice low.

"Don't worry," Krae replied, not exactly answering Jenna's question. "No one can see me except you."

"Where are Niall and Llyr?"

"Niall joined Colleen and Duncan, and Llyr is with Roz and Ronin."

Of course, why didn't I think of that?

Jenna cleared her throat. "Why did you make different plans?"

Krae cocked her head to one side and crinkled her gnome-like face, making her look even more outlandish. "We discussed it and decided you might need help." A corner of her mouth curved into a frown. "Personally, I thought it was a bit overdrawn, but Niall was most insistent about remaining with Colleen."

"Can he join her teleport spell after it's already set in motion?" Jenna was curious, but if Krae could teleport into this aircraft, maybe the other two could tap into a spell she'd always considered sacrosanct.

"Not directly, but he communicated with Colleen telepathically, and she altered her destination to pick him up. Llyr did the same with Roz and Ronin." Krae dusted her palms together and grinned. "Nothing easier." The changeling swept her agate-green gaze around the first-class cabin. "When will they feed us?"

"As soon as we pass through ten thousand feet, which won't be long since we just took off." Jenna paused for a beat. "If you weren't thrilled about the plans to get to the U.K., why didn't you speak up back in Alaska?"

"We did. No one listened to us. Roz and Ronin were so wrapped up in lust and pawing at each other, all they wanted to do was get to his manor house as fast as they could."

"Well, they did just get married," Jenna pointed out in defense of her friend. "And I don't recall anyone but me voicing concerns about splitting up to travel."

"That's because you weren't paying attention, either. Look, sweetie, if the Irichna win, no one will be tupping anyone." Despite being much shorter than Jenna, the changeling managed to send a withering glance her way.

"Point taken." Jenna shot an equally scathing glance back. "Next time, if you feel strongly about something and no one's paying attention, talk louder."

"Rehashing the past is a waste of time." Krae bounced up and down in her seat. Jenna considered telling her to fasten her seatbelt, but if no one could see her, there wasn't much point. "Be sure to take everything they offer foodwise," the changeling instructed. "I'm hungry."

"Shouldn't be a problem since I'm not." Jenna lapsed into silence.

"Why so glum, witchy girl?" Krae trained her ancient eyes, which probably didn't miss a trick, on Jenna.

"Oh, no particular reason." Jenna stifled a snort and rolled her eyes. "I find facing death several times a day downright exhil-arating."

A bell sounded, and the fasten seat belt icon winked out. Moments later, the first-class cabin flight attendant leaned close. "Are you all right?"

"Why wouldn't I be?" Jenna snapped and then winced at how surly she sounded.

"I heard you talking and thought maybe you needed some-thing." The flight attendant smiled encouragingly. Airlines had moved past using Barbie clones long since, and this woman was middle-aged with streaks of gray in her dark, shoulder-length hair, the beginnings of wrinkles around her blue eyes, and a kind expression.

"Food," Krae prodded, not bothering with telepathic speech.

"Thanks for being concerned." Jenna managed a genuine smile for the cabin attendant. "I am hungry, so snacks would be appreci-ated whenever you get around to serving."

"Of course." The woman smiled back. "I'm Suzanne." She tapped the nametag hanging around her neck. "Just press your call button if you need anything. Other than that, relax and enjoy your flight."

"You could've been a bit more assertive about our dinner," Krae complained.

"I'm guessing they can't hear you, either." Jenna switched to tele-pathic speech.

"Of course they can't." Krae blew out an annoyed-sounding breath. "Look, witchy-girl, draw a spot of magic and shield your speech. That way no one will bother us, and we can talk."

Feeling like an idiot because she hadn't come up with the idea herself, Jenna drew the requisite spell before she spoke again. "I was actually hoping to sleep."

"You can do that after we eat and talk."

Jenna turned to face the changeling and raised a quizzical

brow. "This is starting to sound bigger than you. Whose idea was it for the three of you to split up, and for you to join me?"

Krae's generous mouth twitched into a grin, and she jabbed a finger in the air between them. "Smart witch."

"You didn't exactly answer me."

"No. I didn't."

Jenna pressed her tongue against her teeth to manage her annoyance. The last thing she needed was a rousing game of twenty questions, so she trained what she hoped was a non-confrontational gaze on Krae and shrugged. "We have seven hours, feel free to take your time."

The changeling's green eyes sparkled with mischief. "You're burning up with curiosity. I can smell it."

Jenna didn't bother to point out she was so trashed from the past few weeks that she doubted she had enough energy to *burn up* with anything. Suzanne handed her a bottle of water and a tray with an assortment of appetizers. The flight attendant had no sooner moved on to the next passenger than Krae bent over the tray and dug in.

The changeling looked up after inhaling half the finger sandwiches and most of the nuts. "Sure you don't want any of this?"

"Help yourself." Jenna adjusted her seat so it tilted backward, twisted the cap off the water, and drank deeply.

"Beer, wine, or a cocktail, miss?" a masculine voice asked.

Jenna glanced up at a cabin attendant she hadn't seen before. He was tall and rangy with very blue eyes, white-blond hair, and a gold band on the third finger of his left hand. She swallowed a smile. With looks like his, he might have begun wearing the ring in self-defense, to slow the tide of women throwing themselves at his feet. He arched a brow and gestured toward the drink cart.

"Um, maybe a cup of coffee with a side of Irish whiskey."

"Excellent choice." He beamed at her, displaying very white, very even teeth. He may have winked, but she wasn't quite certain. "Would you care for cream or sugar?"

"Both."

Once he handed her drink over, she uncapped the small bottle of spirits and dumped a little into her cup. She'd traveled through so many time zones already, it scarcely mattered whether it was evening yet, and the liquor might have a salutary effect. The steward's gaze traveled up her body in frank appraisal before he moved to the passenger across the aisle. Jenna's face warmed a few degrees. What the hell? Was he sizing her up for a quickie in one of the plane's johns?

Krae twisted her head and stared at the man. The air glistened wetly where the changeling deployed magic. She wasn't particularly subtle, and the man's spine stiffened, but he didn't turn around.

"He felt that." Jenna pitched her mind voice just for Krae and shielded it to boot.

"Indeed he did." Krae narrowed her eyes. *"Do you know what he is?"* Jenna shook her head. *"Pity,"* the changeling went on, *"neither do I."*

"I don't think it's a good idea to send more magic his way," Jenna murmured. *"As it is, what you did tipped him off. How did you know something was wrong?"*

"How else?" Krae shrugged. *"I almost missed it, but something...odd drew my attention when he looked at you. If he'd been human, his gaze would have held more heat. Instead there was an...unnatural hunger."* She hesitated. *"More like he was relieved he'd found you rather than wanting sex."*

A shudder iced Jenna's blood. Unlike Roz and Colleen, she couldn't simply teleport off the airplane. Her heartbeat sped up. *"Maybe you should leave,"* she told Krae. *"No point in both of us being trapped."*

"Uh-uh. We hold our ground for now. It's possible his presence has nothing to do with you."

"Not very fucking likely."

Krae picked up another small sandwich and stuffed it into her mouth. Jenna snuck a peek at the steward just in time to see him disappear through the curtain separating first class from the remainder of the aircraft. Because she was desperate for information, she sent a tendril of magic snaking outward and yanked it back as soon as she determined the man wasn't an Irichna disguised as human. Duncan had run up against one masquerading as a priest near the Witches' Northwest Coven headquarters in Seattle. It had lured two female teenagers and would have drained them of life if Duncan hadn't intervened. As it was, he wasn't certain either had survived because he'd left them at a hospital and hadn't hung around long enough to find out.

Jenna ran options through her mind, not liking any of them. She didn't want to end up in a pitched battle inside the aircraft. Hell, they'd probably lock her away as a terrorist the minute the plane landed, and Irichna would pick her off from her cell.

"I was serious," Krae's out loud voice intruded. "There's at least a small possibility he's simply some sort of mage. He might have gotten a magical hit off your aura and was curious."

"What did you want to talk about earlier?" Jenna changed the subject because she could speculate about the mystery steward from now until he made a move against her, and it wouldn't change the outcome, other than making her more aware to watch out for him.

"How much do you know about my race?" Krae countered, answering Jenna by asking a question of her own.

"Mostly what I've gleaned from living with Niall for forty years. Why?"

Krae popped the last sandwich into her mouth, chewed, and swallowed. "We've always known we would have a key role to play in major battles against the Irichna. It's written in our histories, and we've prepared as best we could."

Jenna drew her brows together. "Niall never mentioned it."

"It's quite possible he didn't know. We've done our damnedest to keep that particular bit of knowledge quiet, so the Irichna wouldn't target us before the time came to play our part. Not that we didn't inform our people—and try to coach them—but Niall's been gone for a good many years."

Jenna rolled her shoulders to offset the iron bar of tension sitting between them. "You sound like a preacher threatening the latter days are nearly upon us."

"They are." Krae's expression turned deadly serious.

"More whiskey, miss?"

Jenna started at the sound of the steward's voice. He'd returned to the cabin so quietly, she hadn't heard him. "Um, no." She resisted the temptation to look at him. It would give her more information, but that was a two-way street.

"As you will, miss." He pushed the drink cart past her. It made quite a bit of noise, which led her to suspect he'd used magic to muffle his presence earlier.

How long had he studied her without her knowing?

Why hadn't Krae sensed him?

Worse, he'd apparently made his way back to the front of the plane, pushed the rattling cart past her, and served other passengers without alerting her to his presence. Not good. Jenna shielded her mind—just in case—and clamped her jaws together when he sashayed into the curtained galley alcove between first class and the cockpit. Her heart thudded against her ribcage, and her throat was dry. It was looking like she'd need to do something, but what would attract the least attention?

Krae uttered a muted expletive in Gaelic, bolted from her seat, and whisked after the steward. Jenna stared after the changeling with her mouth hanging open. She pushed upright, remembered her seatbelt, and fumbled with the clasp. By the time she was free of it, a flash of multicolored light practically blinded her, flaring above, below, and through the curtain. Heedless of the other first class passengers, who couldn't sense expended magic anyway, she threw her power wide open.

Jenna didn't realize she'd been holding her breath until it whistled from between her clenched teeth. She drew her lips back, hissing in satisfaction once she realized the blast of power had come from Krae, not the man. Balancing on the balls of her stocking-clad feet, Jenna strode forward and pushed past the curtain.

The steward was shaking his head back and forth, his face screwed into a mask of pain. Power flashed from the changeling's hands. "No more," he rasped, tottering from foot to foot. "I won't hurt either of you."

Jenna dragged an invisibility spell over all of them, layered a *don't look here* spell over that, and prayed to the goddess no one would enter the small, enclosed space for the next few minutes.

"What are you?" She shoved the question hard into his mind.

"I already figured that out," Krae said sourly. "He's a minor demon sent to keep an eye on you and report back."

"I already told you I hadn't," he whined. "And I won't. You can bind me with magic."

"That's not good enough," Jenna growled. "Demons lie."

"So do changelings and witches." He shot her a venomous look that belied his promises of non-interference.

"We're wasting time," Krae said and settled into a low chant.

A look of horror twisted the steward's handsome face into something unrecognizable. He tried to walk past them but clearly couldn't move. The air thickened, took on a blackish tinge, and stank of ozone just before smoke rose from the creature and he vanished.

Jenna drew back, impressed. Whatever Krae had done was magic well beyond her own abilities. Footsteps sounded on the far side of the curtain. Suzanne. Jenna recognized her energy and ducked into a passenger restroom. If Krae was powerful enough to banish the demon, shielding herself from the flight attendant should prove trivial. Kicking herself for being sloppy, Jenna pulled the magic from her spells to make the cramped galley appear as normal as possible.

"Paul," Suzanne's voice was pitched low, "your drink cart's here. Where are you?"

Jenna flushed the toilet and splashed cold water on her overheated face. She took her time drying off and settled her features into a bland expression before stepping out of the john. With a nod and a smile at Suzanne, she pushed the curtain aside and returned to her seat. Krae was already there, doing her best to mask a self-satisfied grin.

"Okay, I give up." Jenna eyed the changeling. "What did you do?"

"Teleported him outside the plane. Nature took care of the rest."

Jenna thought about it. "While it's good he's gone, how will we know he didn't report in somehow?"

"We won't," Krae said shortly. "Which means we'll have to be very careful not to lead the enemy right to wherever we're staying after we land."

CHAPTER 2

The rest of the flight unfolded without incident, but Jenna's nerves thrummed nastily from an overload of adrenaline. She picked at the array of food that materialized in front of her, all too aware Krae had saved her bacon. It was a relief when the captain finally announced they were starting their approach into London. She hated being stuck, and the airliner had started feeling like a flying deathtrap. She'd taken several walkabouts of the plane, magical senses on full alert as she checked out the rest of the crew—and the passengers. The crew were edgy, presumably because one of them had gone missing, but everyone else was exactly what they seemed.

"They've been a bit quiet about Paul's disappearance." Krae showed a mouthful of teeth, but it didn't resemble a smile, more like a warrior's deep satisfaction at having vanquished a foe.

Jenna shrugged. "They can scarcely announce *that* problem over the loudspeaker, now can they? And there's nowhere we can land since we're flying over the Atlantic." She pressed her lips together. "We may pay for what you did."

"How? They'll never figure it out. Paul—although I doubt that's his name—wouldn't have been able to contact anyone once his cells disintegrated. And that would've happened damned fast outside this plane."

"Mmph." Jenna tried for a snappy reply, but gave up. Likely, Krae was right, and there was no reason to flog a dead horse.

"Besides, we didn't have much of a choice." Krae looked askance at her.

"There's always a choice, just not good ones. He knew what we were. Regardless of his denials, he would've told whomever he reports to—if he had a chance."

Jenna furrowed her forehead in the kind of scrunchy lines that would probably make wrinkles as she thought about what Paul's presence meant. "What bothers me more is how many like him have been dogging Colleen, Roz, and me for years when we weren't aware of it." She sucked in a tight breath. "I always wondered how they knew exactly where to find us. I assumed the Irichna set spies from among their ranks. Never occurred to me they'd use minor demons."

"Why not?" Krae raised one red eyebrow. "Most organizations parcel out the shit work as low on the ladder as they can get away with."

Jenna grimaced. "It pains me to admit it, but I actually have very little idea about demon hierarchy, and now I'm scared to my bones that there's an entire dark army out there, all rabid for our blood."

"There is. What else is new? You've likely met most types of demons." Krae polished the last scraps of edibles from the food tray moments before a flight attendant picked it up.

"Return your seat to its upright position, miss," the flight attendant prompted and smiled.

"Of course. Thanks for the reminder." Jenna glanced at the youngish redhead. Her hair was cut short, and her dark eyes had smudges beneath them. "Where's Suzanne?"

"Serving the rest of the aircraft." A tightness beneath the woman's words matched how tense the crew had been since

Paul's disappearance, but the flight attendant moved past it and added, "We'll be on the ground in a jiffy."

Krae watched the woman's uniformed back vanish behind the galley curtain, a thoughtful expression on her face. "Back to demons," she prodded Jenna. "What do you know?"

"Let's see." Jenna counted on her fingers. "Beyond the Irichna, I recognize gnomes, bats, trolls, incubi, and succubi. When they take human form like Paul, it's harder."

"Not really." Krae pushed her hair over her shoulders. "If you look with your magical senses, there's a black tinge to their aura that's unmistakable."

The plane shuddered as it lost altitude. "That might work for Colleen and Roz," Jenna murmured, "but my magic isn't as strong as theirs. Especially Roz. That woman is a powerhouse. I can't keep magic deployed constantly. It would drain me."

"You don't have to. Just pulse it out every few minutes. You'll pick up ninety percent of what's important." The changeling twisted in her seat. "How do you feel about teleporting off the plane?"

"Fine, except I can't. That's one spell I never mastered."

"Not a problem. I can take both of us."

"Where?"

"It doesn't really matter, so long as we're away from the airport. If there's a greeting party—and I expect there may well be one since Paul dropped off the demons' radar—I'd just as soon not walk into their arms."

"Shit!" Jenna bit her lower lip, thinking about Roz and Colleen. "Do you suppose the others are in danger?"

"Maybe, but even demons don't like to create scenes. If they are laying for us, they'll nab us between exiting the plane and customs, long before we get anywhere near Colleen and them."

Worry about her friends stabbed deep, but Jenna pushed it aside. There wasn't anything she could do, and she was too far away to communicate telepathically.

"We'll need to do something so the flight attendants don't remember I was here, but that's easy enough." Jenna retrieved her shoes and slipped them on before slinging the strap of her shoulder bag over her neck.

"Excellent." Krae grinned. "You handle that part, and I'll do the rest. On my count of three."

"Give me at least ten," Jenna countered and went to work scattering a *forget I was here* spell.

"You got it. Starting now. Ten, nine…"

They came out in darkness, the air so damp it practically dripped. "Where are we?" Jenna asked.

"Couldn't risk someone seeing us, so we're north of town in a changeling lair."

Jenna sent power skittering wide. "I don't sense any more of you."

"Let's not worry about that. Follow me aboveground, and we'll figure out where Colleen and the rest of them are. When you and I don't show up at the airport, they'll be worried."

"Wouldn't it be safer to communicate from here?"

"Your magic would just bounce back at you, and your cell phone won't work. Our special places are shielded."

Jenna emerged into a sleeting rain and pulled her jacket closer about her. When she looked around, she saw an upscale neighborhood of country homes. Krae faded into the shadows of a grove of hawthorn trees, and Jenna followed her.

"Colleen! Roz!"

"Where are you?" Two mind voices vied with each other.

"North of town with Krae."

"Thank the goddess," Duncan cut in.

"Yes," Ronin added. *"When you didn't get off the plane and we realized one of the flight attendants was missing, we feared the worst."*

"How'd you figure that out so quick?" Jenna asked.

"I've been reading minds," Roz snapped, sounding so like her surly self it brought a smile to Jenna's lips.

"Pick us up at Worthington Green." Krae jumped into the conversation.

"On our way," Colleen said. *"Duncan will know where it is. Christ, but you gave me a fright."*

"Yes, well, it hasn't been much fun on my end, either," Jenna blurted and shuttered her power. She balanced from foot to foot as the chill from the cold pavement seeped through her shoes. "I don't suppose there's a coffee shop nearby where we could wait?" she asked.

"That would be a tea shop. Of course there's something, but we're safer out here." Krae sounded reproachful.

Jenna funneled magic to warm herself, but she kept it low-key in case someone was on the hunt for her. The net effect was she was still cold, but at least it was tolerable. "Thanks for all your help," she murmured. "Didn't mean to sound surly."

"No need to thank me." The changeling's voice sharpened. "What you need to do is develop a different attitude toward your power."

"Huh?"

"You're so used to seeing your magic as inferior, you've given up maximizing the gifts you do have. No two magic wielders are created equal. You could do a whole lot more with what you have than you do."

Jenna winced, grateful it was dark. The changeling had her number. About the only thing the creature hadn't pointed out was her tendency to feel sorry for herself.

"Colleen and Roz and I have been together forever. We came into our power about the same time, and the other demon assassin witches trained us as a group. Because my magic wasn't as strong, the other two took to covering for me." Jenna exhaled raggedly. "I suppose they've never really stopped."

"When you always work in a group," Krae said, sounding like she was choosing her words, "everybody does that. What you need is some time on your own to fully explore—and develop—the magic that's unique to you."

"Easy to say, but I don't see how we could finesse it. We need to stay together, or the Irichna will pick us off one by one. Maybe not so much Colleen and Roz anymore since they've got Sidhe backup through their husbands, but..." Her voice trailed off, and she swallowed hard, feeling glum.

Krae reached across the short distance between them and patted her hand. "We'll work something out once we're all together. Earth magic is your strong suit, just as it's mine. Maybe all you need is some time with changelings."

Jenna snorted. "Given that Niall lived with us for forty years, most of that in his cat form with us calling him Bubba, I'm still getting my mind around how powerful you are."

"Ah, but I'm one of the very few elders. Niall may be old, but he isn't nearly as old as I am. Magically, I can run rings about him." Even in the semi-gloom of the grove of trees, Jenna saw Krae smile, and it warmed her.

Headlights cut through the evening shadows, and a limousine rolled to a stop near where she and Krae stood, half-hidden by wet greenery. One of the back doors flew open. Roz jumped out and made a beeline for Jenna, with Colleen right behind her.

"Goddammit," Roz sputtered just before wrapping Jenna in a hug. "You cut a hundred years off my life."

"Mine too." Colleen wound her arms around her fellow witches. "Damn, but you're a sight for sore eyes. No more airplanes. Period. You have to learn to teleport. No more excuses."

"What the hell happened?" Roz straightened and looked hard at Jenna.

"It's a long story—" Jenna began.

"I told Roz and Colleen you were fine—" Niall bounded to them "—because Krae wouldn't let anything happen to you, but nobody believed me." He was a little larger than Krae, with coal-black, shaggy hair and dark eyes. Most changelings had his coloring, but a few were redheads like Krae.

"Thank you for the vote of confidence." Krae half bowed, her voice so serious Jenna's head snapped up. And then Duncan and Ronin and Llyr joined them, and everyone was talking at once.

"Back in the car." Colleen herded everyone toward the limo. "We'll all think better after a hot meal and a decent rest."

Jenna's legs felt shaky. She'd started for the sleek, silver, stretch Rolls Royce when a thought slammed into her. Tristan. Where was he?

She'd met him on her last trip to the U.K. He'd seemed interested in her, but they hadn't had time to do much more than exchange pleasantries and share a few meals.

And a few kisses.

She'd been disappointed when he hadn't come to Colleen and Duncan's wedding, but the world had pretty much gone to hell half an hour after they said their vows. There'd scarcely been time to think of anything beyond sidestepping Irichna long enough to stay alive…

More happy memories.

She rolled her mental eyes and wondered if she had *any* memories that weren't wrapped up in Irichna demons.

Jenna ducked into the car and tucked her teeth over her lower lip. Tristan's interest was likely her imagination. Just because he'd been kind to her didn't necessarily mean a thing. She wrapped her arms around herself to quell a sudden chill. She didn't often think about her lack of male attention because there wasn't much she could do about it. She'd had her share of lovers, but no one wanted to stick around afterward.

I could lose thirty pounds.

Yeah, but I'd still be six feet four…

The driver turned and gifted her with a dazzling smile. Not Tristan, but clearly another Daoine Sidhe. Rather than Tristan's tawny good looks and silver eyes, this man had dark hair and eyes the color of an ancient glacier. Classic bone structure graced him with a strong jaw and high cheekbones. Even seated, he appeared very tall with impossibly broad shoulders.

A warm smile softened the severe lines of his face, and he said, "You're looking a bit glum, miss. I'd say any day you stand up to demons and come out the other end alive would be cause for celebration."

"How do you know what happened?" she sputtered, nonplussed by his words.

He furled his brows. "It's about the only reason I can come up with for teleporting off an airliner. Besides, I read minds too, and the personnel pouring off that plane were brimming over with information."

Before Jenna could answer, the others crowded into the car, and the driver turned his attention back to the front of the vehicle.

Colleen didn't even wait for the car's engine to turn over before nudging her. "How about a full report?"

"Wait!" Ronin called. "Let's get rolling, and I'll shield the car from prying ears."

Jenna grabbed the opportunity to organize her thoughts, waiting until Ronin nodded in her direction.

"This won't take long." She focused on her hands, clasped so tightly the knuckles were white. "Things went fine—at least on the surface—until the flight from New York to London. That's when a minion showed up—"

"So it wasn't an Irichna?" Roz broke in.

"How'd you figure it out?" Colleen spoke on top of Roz.

"I didn't," Jenna said, her voice tight. "Krae teleported into the plane right around the time it took off. She guessed the drink steward was Mister Dark Side and teleported him into the airless void at thirty-five thousand feet."

"What aren't you saying?" Roz's voice held sharp edges.

"You know me far too well," Jenna grumbled.

"Indeed, but you didn't answer me."

"If Krae wouldn't have been there, I'm not at all sure I would have seen past the minion's gorgeous face and Chippendale body." Jenna blew out a disgusted breath. "Paint me shallow, but you should have seen him. He could've passed for one of the Sidhe."

"I suppose I might take that as a compliment," Duncan cut in, "but being likened to any of their ilk isn't high on my list."

Jenna muffled a snort. "Sorry, I didn't mean anything by it."

"He knows that," Colleen said.

"Of course I do." Duncan bent forward from his seat in the next row and laid a hand on her shoulder. "Just trying to lighten the mood a bit."

Krae spoke up. "Jenna needs time on her own, away from the two of you." She twisted from her spot in the front seat and pointed at Roz and Colleen sitting on either side of Jenna.

"That's scarcely possible," Roz gritted out from between what sounded like clenched jaws.

"Yes, we have to be together," Colleen snapped in a radical departure from her usual pleasant tone. "Our travel plans were incredibly risky for just that reason, but I was afraid if we were all in the same plane, it would've be all too easy for Irichna to take out an engine. We could have teleported out of there, but wading through the other passengers' panic wouldn't have been pleasant."

"The problem with playing Bobbsey Triplets," Krae went on as if Roz and Colleen hadn't said a word, "is both of you bail her out constantly, so she's never fully developed what she can do."

Roz opened her mouth, but Krae waved her to silence and said, "I'm not done. Every magic wielder has their strengths, including Jenna. Because the two of you command traditional magic, and it came easier for you than her, she's come to rely on you, and you automatically boost her power with your own. Since you're always together, she's never had a chance to optimize her skills."

"Your point?" Roz sounded as warm as an alley cat guarding a dead mouse.

"It's dangerous now. More than it's ever been before. You'll need to wring every last iota of power out of yourselves before we move into the endgame."

"Jenna could train with me," the driver said, "in that well-designed space beneath Ronin's castle. We're going to Ronin's anyway, so it would be convenient." He met Jenna's gaze in the rearview mirror, his blue eyes alight with obvious interest.

She thought she should look away, but his intense scrutiny warmed her, and she winked. He winked back and mimed blowing a kiss her way. His chiseled lips made her long for real kisses, and her belly tightened in anticipation of what might happen once they left the car.

"I'm not certain quite how that would work," Ronin inserted quickly. "We've never allowed anyone other than Sidhe in the arena—"

"If not the arena, there are always the gardens," the driver broke in, clearly not willing to let the subject drop.

The interchange triggered Jenna's temper, lifting metaphorical hackles the length of her spine. "Stop! Just stop!" She raised her voice, not caring if she sounded pissed. "Jesus fucking Christ! You're discussing me like I'm an object that's not even here. I'm so sorry I'm not worthy of the real practice area." She tried to reel in her sarcasm but couldn't. "Crap! No one knows my magical weaknesses better than I do. Or feels worse about them."

Her throat thickened, and to her horror, tears pricked, hot and bitter behind her lids. She gripped her hands tighter together, digging nails into flesh as she willed herself to find a calm center.

"Aw, sweetie," Colleen laid a hand over hers.

"Don't." Jenna forced the word out. "I don't want your pity."

"It's not—" Colleen began, but Krae interrupted.

"This is exactly what I mean," the changeling said. "You two have been taking care of her for so many years, you do it automatically. She'll never figure out who she is magically until she gets some distance from your sisterhood."

"That may have worked twenty years ago," Colleen spoke carefully, obviously measuring her words, "when there were a few more of us."

"I agree," Roz chimed in. "Splitting up is a luxury we can't afford just now."

"You haven't been listening." Krae spat each word individually.

"Yes, I have," Roz countered, sounding equally deadly. "I just don't agree with you."

"You're doing it again," Jenna shouted. "Talking about me as if I'm not here."

"I propose a compromise," Duncan spoke up. "But only if Jenna agrees."

"Really? I finally get a say in my own life?" The sarcasm Jenna had tried to squelch was back in spades.

"I didn't get a chance to introduce our driver," Duncan went on, not bothering to dignify Jenna's snarkiness with a comment. "His name is Kiernan, and he's the primary seer for our people. He also works with other Sidhe to strengthen their precognitive abilities. He's quite talented at bringing out the best in our people, and it's noteworthy he offered to help you." Duncan paused for a beat. "This is the first time in my memory he's proposed working with anyone outside our blood. It's quite an honor."

Jenna hunched her shoulders. What Krae said was true. She was overly dependent on Roz and Colleen. That dependence was a comfort zone—for all of them. Fear of the unknown clawed at her, but it wasn't nearly as bad as facing down an Irichna.

She cleared her throat and surprised herself by saying, "I accept, even if I can't train where the grownups do," in a voice that only trembled a little.

"But, sweetie," Colleen began, "we've been fine as a trio all these years."

"Now is scarcely the time to add something new," Roz cut in.

Jenna squeezed her eyes shut for a moment. When she opened them, she pried her hands apart and patted her two friends. "Thanks. I love you guys too, but I owe it to our partnership to shore up my side of things. We all know I've always been the weak link. Maybe there are a few tricks I could learn that would make all of us stronger."

"There's the spirit," Krae crowed. "You won't be sorry."

"If I am," Jenna muttered, "you'll be the first one I hunt down."

"Bring it on, witch. You'll find I only bet on sure things." The changeling twisted so she was facing forward again.

"Actually, I'm looking forward to it too," Kiernan purred, his voice like liquid honey. "And don't worry, we'll be sure to use the grownup's playpen." Something about those few words sent a shivery little thrill that started in her belly and radiated outward.

What about Tristan? her inner voice asked.

What about him? she answered back. *He's not here.*

CHAPTER 3

The remainder of the ride to Ronin's country estate on the outskirts of Penrith was relatively silent except for the three changelings chattering in the front seat next to Kiernan. They spoke Gaelic, so it was easy to let their words ebb and flow around her. Jenna wondered if she'd been hasty. Roz and Colleen had a point that they had a system they'd worked out over many years. Different magic might muck up what was currently a well-oiled machine.

On the other hand, it just might save my life—or theirs.

Her thoughts turned to Tristan. Before getting snared in all the demon crap with the minion in the plane, she'd been hoping the tawny-haired Sidhe would be part of the greeting party at the airport. There were lots of possible reasons he might not have met her, but the most likely was he wasn't interested in her—at least not *that* way.

Oh give it a rest. It's not like he's so much as called or e-mailed in the weeks since I left the U.K. I'll just embarrass myself—and look pathetic— if I ask after him.

Ronin had said something about Tristan being assigned to one of the garrisons dealing with Irichna, who'd been running rampant through the U.K. countryside. There was at least a slender chance he couldn't drop everything and show up to greet her. Worse, maybe he'd been forced into the *Dreaming* by a demon. Sidhe were immortal, but they could be compelled to leave the human world if they were injured badly enough.

The Rolls slowed at the carved, wrought-iron gates to Ronin's estate. Magic flashed, and they swung slowly inward. "It's just past ten," Colleen said. "What's scheduled for tonight?"

"Nothing in particular, but we do need to talk," Ronin replied.

"More to the point," Jenna spoke up, "what ground did you cover before I got here? Is there anything I need to catch up on?"

"Oh, that's right." Colleen turned toward her and cocked her head to one side. Like Roz, she was dressed in a fleece jacket, jeans, and lace-up boots. Far more practical clothing than Jenna's short skirt, high-heels, and inadequate jacket. "You told us your problems, but we didn't share ours."

A cold fist of fear closed over Jenna's stomach and squeezed hard. "I'm not sure I want to know, but what happened?"

"Well, we got here okay," Roz answered. "Not here, exactly. We came out above the Sidhe armory, closer to the center of town."

"Thought we'd pick up a few Seraph blades," Duncan noted. "Since we can't handle iron like you witches, the blades come in handy fighting Irichna."

Jenna cracked her knuckles in frustration. "Yes, but what happened?"

"What else?" Colleen made a sour face. "Irichna."

"How they figured out where we'd materialize will remain one of the mysteries," Roz growled.

Even though her words were angry, Jenna detected a hint of fear beneath them. She shook her head to clear an almost paralyzing fog from creeping in. What she'd been afraid of—that the Irichna employed minions to spy on them—was looking more and more real.

"How many?" she asked, her throat so dry it was hard to spit out the words.

"Fortunately, only three, but they didn't exactly lie down and cooperate," Ronin said. He focused his next words at the driver. "Just drop the lot of us off at the main house, Kiernan. It's probably best if we hash out a plan before everyone turns in for the night."

"Long story short—" Colleen picked up Roz's tale "—it took until just before we met up with the car and Kiernan to neutralize the demons and ferry two of them to the Ninth Circle of Hell. Ronin and Duncan annihilated the third one. We never did get into the armory to pick up blades for the men."

"Does that mean the U.K. problem is solved?" Jenna asked.

"Probably not," Duncan replied. "There are always more of those blasted buggers, no matter what we do."

"And they show up in different forms," Ronin added, "which makes it tough to know if these were the ones causing all the problems."

"It's not as if they're a static population," Roz said. "We've never been able to estimate their numbers."

"Isn't that the truth," Jenna groused as the car rolled to a stop in front of Ronin's home that looked more like a castle than anything else. Built from interlocking flagstones and huge beams of lumber, it soared five floors. Light glowed through leaded glass panes, adding a welcoming touch. Even though it was night and she couldn't see the grounds, Jenna remembered them to be immaculate. Sidhe didn't employ many servants. Most of the day-to-day tasks were accomplished with magic. She snorted inwardly. Maybe she could pick up a few housekeeping tips, along with whatever else the Sidhe taught her.

She exited the car behind Roz, and a thought struck her. "Aw, hell."

"What?" Roz drew her hands upward, preparing to draw power.

"Nothing like that," Jenna said. "My luggage. It's still at the airport."

"No worries." Ronin walked to Roz and draped an arm over her shoulders. "I'll send someone round to fetch it."

"Jenna will have way more to wear than us," Colleen pointed out, "since we teleported." She leaned toward Duncan and gave him a quick kiss.

"Easy fix, my love," he said. "We can shop for whatever you need tomorrow."

Jenna glanced from one couple to the other and hoped to hell no one picked up on the emotions running through her. She was happy for her friends. Duncan and Ronin were amazing men, but the surfeit of connubial bliss underscored how alone she was. Earlier, she'd told Roz and Colleen to hurry up and produce a child or two so she could settle in as a maiden auntie and spoil them shamelessly, but nothing like that was likely to happen anytime soon. Not until they got the demons on the run.

Niall surged to her side, along with Krae and Llyr. The changeling swept unkempt black hair out of his dark eyes and caught hold of her arm. "Don't paint the devil on the wall."

"Huh? When did you start reading minds?"

"I've always been able to, and Krae showed me an easier way where I don't have to use hardly any of my own power."

"Really?" Jenna stopped at the top of a dozen broad stone steps and skewered the changeling with her gaze. "How?"

He grinned like an imp. "Simple. I borrow yours."

"Thanks. It's not polite to help yourself to people's thoughts, though, or their magic."

"Maybe not polite—" Niall's grin widened "—but very interesting."

"Save your skills for our enemy," Jenna said tartly and pushed on the ten-foot-tall oak door carved with runic symbols. At first it didn't budge, but the air brightened around her hand, and then the door swung open. Someone, likely Ronin, had done something to countermand the warding protecting his home. Too tired to worry about who'd done what, Jenna stepped through into the foyer and made her way into the great room that spanned a great deal of the castle's lower floor.

Kiernan shimmered into being just ahead of her, a satisfied expression etched into his handsome face.

Jenna drew back, blinking in surprise. He'd obviously teleported from the driveway, but she wasn't used to squandering power so casually. Something drew her gaze upward. By the time she realized it was Kiernan's magic, she was looking into his blue-green eyes. They were cool, laced with mystery, but fire smoldered in their depths, as if in challenge. When she tried to look away, she couldn't. Jenna squared her shoulders, but the Sidhe was still taller than she by a good few inches was.

"Don't force me," she sputtered. "If you want something, ask first."

"I'll keep it in mind, witch." With a cross between a smile and a smirk, he turned and trotted deeper into the lavishly furnished great room.

Snug black pants fit like a second skin, outlining a high, tight ass. A faded, gray T-shirt strained across his heavily muscled back and arms. He was built like an ancient Viking warrior, with shoulders so broad she could almost imagine him at the helm of a warship, shaking his fist into the teeth of a shrieking tempest. Unlike Duncan and Ronin, who kept their hair long enough to braid, Kiernan's black locks were close-cropped, which emphasized his angular cheekbones and strong, clean-shaven jaw. Breath caught in Jenna's throat, and her belly tightened with a rush of sexual energy.

Because she couldn't tear her gaze away, she stared after the Sidhe. Coaxed by magic, lights flared on when he passed, and an assortment of plush leather furniture in earth tones came into view. Occasional tables laden with antique sculptures, cut crystal lamps, and other artistic pieces were scattered about. Jenna took a deep breath to ease the tingling in her nipples and then another, hoping her face wasn't as flushed as it usually got when she was turned on. To divert herself, she spun in a circle, taking in grandeur museums would have gone rounds to own.

"Where do you want us?" she asked Ronin.

"Back study," he said as he and Roz swept past, followed by Colleen and Duncan. "It's cozier, and we're a small group."

"Oh-oh." Niall nudged her. "Better watch it. I felt *that* flash of energy from twenty paces." Jenna stuck her tongue out at him, and he reached back to pinch her, edging out of the way before she could slap his fingers.

A swoosh of power behind her sent her heart into overdrive. She twirled, ready to shout at Colleen and Roz to come back and help, but the words died on her lips. Kiernan stood there beaming like a Cheshire cat. Despite the smile, he looked arrogant and dangerous, with a raw sexuality that practically held a life of its own.

Breath clattered from her lungs. "But you were ahead of me," she stammered. "Up there." She pointed and felt like an idiot, so she dropped her hand to her side.

"Observant of you."

He closed the distance between them until he stood scant inches away. The heat of his body eddied toward her, and it took all her willpower not to throw her arms around him and drag his mouth down onto hers.

"Do, er, did you want something?" Her voice came out high and squeaky, and she coughed to cover her awkwardness. As if drawn by invisible puppet strings, Jenna leaned toward him, so close her breasts brushed his chest, and her breath hitched uncomfortably. She clasped her hands behind her to reduce the temptation to touch him.

"I want many things, but most of all I want to get to know you better." He ran a finger down her cheek, leaving a trail of irides-cent motes that floated before her eyes. "Once we're settled in the study with the others, there wouldn't have been an opportunity to tell you that."

She opened her mouth to say something, anything, to break the sexual tension that overshadowed common sense, but he dissolved into nothingness, and she was left blinking at the after-image of where he'd stood. Jenna breathed deep to settle herself. If she was going to spend hours training with Kiernan, she had to get her libido under control, and damned fast. Otherwise, she'd be so addle-brained she wouldn't learn a thing.

DESPITE HIS DETOUR in the hallway, Kiernan Cliffert burst into the study well ahead of everybody else. He kicked himself for being a fool nine times over. Compelling the witch to look at him had been a huge mistake, but he'd wanted to gaze into her fascinating, multi-hued eyes. He'd caught glimpses of them in the rearview mirror while he'd been driving, and they shaded from green to gold to violet depending on how passing lights reflected off them. Beyond that, honey-colored hair framed her gamine's face, and he was having a hell of a time not imagining her naked with her full breasts and lush hips. As if that weren't enough, he'd waylaid her in the hall. If he had his druthers, they'd be on their way to one of the many upstairs bedrooms, not to a meeting.

He pushed his erection to a more comfortable—and hopefully less conspicuous—position and made an effort to normalize his breathing. He couldn't remember when a woman had quite this effect on him and understood fully why Tristan had raved about her.

Tristan.

Damn it! Kiernan blew out a tight breath. The other Sidhe had definitely staked a claim to Jenna, and it wouldn't be fair for Kiernan to take advantage of his friend and longtime associate being gone. Footsteps sounded in the hall, and he shielded his thoughts. Either he wasn't quite quick enough, or Ronin wasn't so besotted by his bride he hadn't picked up on the blast of lust that probably still hung in the great hall. The Sidhe leader quirked a dark eyebrow and shook his head as he walked past Kiernan.

"What was that about?" Roz asked, but Ronin didn't answer.

Kiernan made his way to a well-appointed liquor cabinet and poured himself a glass of mead. Fortified, he sank into an over-stuffed chair and summoned a spell to make himself less notice-able. From his vantage point, he studied the three witches as they filed into the room. Colleen, Duncan's bride, was lovely with pale blue eyes and auburn hair that hung in curls to her waist. Even though she was shorter than the other two, Colleen still had to be around six feet. Roz looked like a Native American princess with sharp bone structure, bronze skin, and coal-black hair braided into an intricate pattern. She was quite slender, moved with a simple elegance, and her astute, dark-eyed gaze probably didn't miss much.

Kiernan took a hefty swallow of liquor. No wonder Duncan and Ronin had been tempted out of long-standing bachelorhood. Sidhe women were lovely, but they lacked fire and warmth, traits the witches had in spades. Plus Sidhe lived forever, so even the best of them struggled with a certain world-weariness that came from having seen too much and from life having lost its mystery.

He directed his gaze to Jenna, pleased by the rosy tint in her cheeks. It hadn't been there before, so maybe she wasn't immune to the heat sparking from him. He settled deeper into his chair. Why had he been so quick to offer to entrain her magic? It would be sheer torture working side by side with her. Helping another find—and leverage—the roots of their power was incredibly inti-mate. It bound acolytes to their masters for centuries.

Perhaps that's just with Sidhe.

Even before the thought formed, Kiernan knew it wasn't true. Power was power. He couldn't hold back if he was to help Jenna. He was toying with the idea of delegating the task to someone else, or talking Ronin into doing the delegating to lessen the odds of being turned down, when his leader's voice broke into his thoughts.

"Kiernan!" Ronin's summons was pointed.

"Yes?"

"Stop hiding behind that deuced spell and join us. I don't know about you, but I'd like to spend at least a few hours in my bed tonight."

Kiernan scattered his magic. "Better?"

Now it was Duncan who shot him an odd look. "There's plenty of space on these two facing sofas for the six of us since the changelings prefer the floor anyway."

"Coming." Kiernan returned to the liquor cabinet and refreshed his drink. "Anyone else?" He waggled the bottle.

"I'd prefer whiskey," Jenna's rich, husky voice rang out, "but I can get my own."

"Fine." Ronin sounded tired. "Anyone who wants a drink, help yourselves, but be quick about it. Let's get this conversation started."

Roz whispered to him. He nodded, and she stood and wound her way to Kiernan and the mead bottle. He handed it to her and glanced at the couches. The only vacant spot, other than the one next to Ronin that Roz had just vacated, was next to Jenna. Hoping he didn't make an ass out of himself, Kiernan settled next to her, noticing she inched toward Colleen, who sat on her other side.

The slender slice of empty couch between their thighs called out to him, urging him to cover it so he could touch her. Before he could do anything, Jenna popped to her feet and strode briskly toward the liquor. She exchanged a whispered word or two with Roz before opening the cabinet and perusing its contents.

Drink in hand, she followed her sister witch back to the group, but instead of sitting next to him, she joined the changelings on the floor near the fireplace.

Kiernan's mouth twitched with the need to smile, but he controlled it as he wondered how the hell she'd manage to sit on the floor without shoving her already-short skirt up to her female bits. Apparently the same problem occurred to her, but she managed by first kicking off her ridiculously high heels and then folding her body toward the floor, knees bent and tucked beneath her thighs. She couldn't have been very comfortable, but she smiled brightly and gestured to Ronin that she was ready.

"I've given this some thought," Ronin said. "If anyone disagrees, speak up." He cleared his throat. "If we get lucky and the Irichna leave us alone tomorrow, I suggest we use the day to give Jenna time with Kiernan." Ronin moved his discerning, deep blue gaze from Jenna to Kiernan and jabbed a finger right at him. "Your task is to get as much done as you can. If she has access to magic she's not using, find it and teach her how to control it. She's far from an acolyte, so things should go quickly."

"I want to help." Krae jumped to her feet and went to stand in front of Ronin, hands on her hips.

"Any particular reason?" Ronin narrowed his eyes. Even though he'd invited the others to disagree, Kiernan knew how annoyed he was. As the Sidhe leader by default—no one else wanted the job—Ronin was used to the mantle of command, and he didn't run a particularly democratic organization.

"Her magic is closer to mine than yours, and time is short." The changeling's emerald eyes glittered with defiance, so apparently she was just as exasperated at being questioned.

"Fine by me," Kiernan spoke up.

"Indeed," Jenna cut in. "The more the merrier."

"Anything else?" Ronin glared at Krae.

"Nope." She dusted her palms together. "Got what I need Sidhe-man."

Niall and Llyr joined her in front of Ronin. "You have to stop underestimating us," Niall said.

"Aw, crap." Colleen rolled her eyes. "Not now. Please, just sit down so we can all go to bed sometime."

The changeling twisted to face her. "You don't understand—" he began.

"I do too," Colleen broke in. "Look, the Sidhe screwed us over too. They cut the knees out from under your magic and left us with the Irichna, but that's in the past. We have to move beyond it and work together."

"I agree," Roz said. "This stops here." She bent forward and laid her hands on Niall's shoulders. "If you can't do that, you probably should go back to your barrow in Ireland."

"Harsh. After all my years of loyal service," he deadpanned.

"Can it," Colleen snapped and turned her attention to Krae. "If you recognize the wisdom in moving on, say something. Llyr and Niall will listen to you."

Krae nodded. She linked arms with the other changelings, and they moved to a far corner of the room. Whatever she said was brief and to the point because they rejoined the group within a few minutes.

"Sorry." Niall focused a genuine smile Ronin's way. "I was out of line."

"Accepted." Ronin scanned the small assemblage. "Are we good to move on here?" Seeing nods, he continued. "I'd also like to take advantage of tomorrow to summon the Sidhe from where they're deployed around the U.K. Once they're here, they can provide a full report. If all our bits of intel are in the same room, maybe we can develop a strategy that makes sense, rather than being on the defensive all the time."

"Good idea." Duncan hid a yawn behind one hand.

"Why, thank you." Ronin inclined his head.

"What time and where in the morning?" Jenna asked Kiernan without quite looking at him.

"Is six too early?" Kiernan asked.

"No. Even earlier would be fine. We don't have much time."

Kiernan grudgingly offered her points for that. Rather than grumbling, she'd taken his gambit and given him one better. "All right, then. Five. Meet here and we'll teleport to our underground practice area." A corner of his mouth curved upward. "You know, the grownups' playpen."

"I'll be there," Krae said as if to remind them.

"Good." Jenna cast a warm smile toward the changeling before glancing at Ronin. "Where do you want me to sleep?"

"Good question. A few rooms are already made up on the second floor. Go upstairs and open doors until you find one that suits you."

Duncan got to his feet and offered Colleen a hand. "Unless I miss my guess, I do believe we've just been dismissed. I'll take my usual room here," he told Ronin. "In case you need me before morning."

"I won't," the Sidhe leader replied. "The manor house is well warded. It should be impenetrable to Irichna." He drew Roz against him. "Ready, love?" The strained lines in her face softened, and she nodded.

"Does that mean we can pick second floor bedrooms too?" Krae asked, her tone studiedly neutral.

"Absolutely." Ronin stood, along with Roz. "See everyone in the morning. Help yourself to coffee or tea. They're always brewing in the kitchen."

Kiernan headed toward the door, but Ronin called him back. "You might want to stay here tonight."

Kiernan pivoted to face his leader. "I'm planning to, but first I'll just teleport back to the airport and collect Miss Jenna's baggage."

"But that will take all night," Jenna protested. "Surely, someone can take care of it tomorrow."

"No, this will work out best. Hand over your luggage chits." He added a touch of compulsion to ensure she didn't refuse outright.

Jenna dug in her bag and dropped them on the table, rather than touching his outstretched hand.

"Thanks." Kiernan snapped them up and summoned teleport magic fast—before anyone could lodge a protest or call him back.

The walls of Ronin's cozy study shimmered and vanished.

Kiernan planned his egress behind a rubbish bin in a darkened carpark west of the airport and felt pleased when he hit the exact spot he'd aimed for. He needed time to think, and the drive back from Heathrow in a rental car would provide a perfect break from sleeping in a house with Jenna in one of the beds. He wasn't at all certain he could resist knocking at her door or simply barging in and letting the chips fall where they would. Tristan would be back tomorrow, along with the rest of the recalled garrison.

Maybe by then, Kiernan would have his lust for the lissome witch under better control.

Ha! Like hell I will...

Snorting under his breath, he strode toward the well-lighted airport, intent on getting in and out of there as quickly as he could.

CHAPTER 4

When Jenna wakened at four thirty, she found her suitcases just inside her door. Since she hadn't heard the door either open or close—and she hadn't slept all that well—she assumed Kiernan had employed magic to transport the battered valises into her room. Good thing, since her traveling clothes were woefully impractical for the kind of day she suspected lay ahead.

Rather than the dreams of Tristan she'd hoped for, what little sleep she'd gotten had been interrupted by hot, graphic images of Kiernan's naked body stretched over hers. Jenna swallowed around a suddenly dry throat. Somehow, she had to get through today without making an idiot out of herself. Krae could help with that. Jenna had been delighted when the changeling threw her lot in with them. If anyone could keep today's training session from drifting, it would be Krae. She took magic so seriously, it was both avocation and religion.

I should borrow a page from her book, Jenna thought ruefully.

It wasn't that she didn't appreciate and respect magical ability, but she'd always had so little, she hadn't consistently put forth her best effort—unless she faced an Irichna. Because they loved her,

Roz and Colleen were quick to step in and boost her efforts. That was about to change. Today she'd let herself run wide open and see where it got her.

Yeah, I get to see up close and personal just how pathetic my power really is.

Pawing through her suitcase, she pulled on black tights, a teal tunic that came down to her hips, and an old pair of river-rafting sandals. A glance in the mirror sent her scurrying for her hairbrush and a washcloth to clean her face. Nothing took very long, so she wandered downstairs to the appointed meeting place with plenty of time left over to go in search of a cup of coffee.

Krae was in the kitchen sipping a fragrant, herbal tea. She smiled approvingly and said, "Better early than late."

"What?" Jenna grinned. "No witchy-girl tacked on?"

"Not this time. Come on." Krae curved two fingers in clear invitation. "I've always wanted to see how the Sidhe do their thing."

"And here I thought you wanted to help me." Jenna followed the changeling to last night's meeting room.

"That too."

By the time they got there, Kiernan was waiting, wearing the same snug black pants from the previous evening and a beige T-shirt emblazoned with *Magic Rocks: Live the Dream*. Innocuous enough no human would question its message, the shirt clung to hard planes of muscle cutting through his shoulders, chest, and arms. Jenna realized she was staring and ripped her gaze away from the closest thing she'd ever seen to masculine perfection.

She smoothed the hand that wasn't holding her coffee cup down her body. "Thanks for getting my things. I needed something else to wear."

He half-bowed. "You're most welcome." A small, secretive smile tugged at his chiseled lips, almost as if he sensed the effect he had on her and it pleased him. He glanced from her to Krae. "Ready?"

The changeling nodded and angled her head to one side. "After you, Sidhe-man."

"I can't teleport," Jenna cautioned. "At least not very far or with much accuracy." A surprised look bloomed on Kiernan's face. He wiped it away almost immediately, but shame flooded her. It was hard being the only magic-wielder who couldn't master a rather basic maneuver.

Krae set her teacup down and stepped between them. "The lesson begins here." She turned to face Jenna. "You can teleport, but not the way you're going about it. Kiernan, send us an image of where we're going."

A large cavern with lights recessed into the wall at intervals filled Jenna's mind. When she looked closer, she saw a stone floor, rock walls, and an overflowing bookshelf with scrolls trailing onto the floor. A table sat dead center in the room with four chairs bunched toward one end.

"Got it," Jenna muttered. "Now what?"

"Forget about fire and air," the changeling said. "Draw earth power, feel it fill you, hold the image in your mind, and let the energy move you. Nothing easier. Don't think about it. Don't worry about it. Just do it."

"What are you, a Nike commercial?" Jenna snorted and plunked her cup on a nearby table.

"You're stalling." Krae's tone was deadly serious. "We don't have time for you to be a funny girl."

Jenna sucked in a tense breath. Here was where the rubber met the road. Was she up to it? She held the vision of the cavern in her mind and called earth power. Rather than only taking a small amount before mixing other elements with it, she kept drawing earth until she felt buoyant.

As if from a great distance, she heard Krae exhort, "Now."

Jenna loosed her spell. Moments later, she tumbled into the cavern. "Holy crap!" she gasped and scrambled up off her butt. "It actually worked." The changeling was just shimmering into view when Jenna mobbed her. "How did you know?" she demanded.

"Your magic is different," the changeling said as soon as she stopped glowing. "I sensed it in the airplane, plus I have inside information. Don't ask because I'm not saying any more about it."

Kiernan popped out a few feet away. "Hold up," he said. "If I'm going to be of any help, I need to hear this too, at least the parts you're comfortable sharing."

Krae drew her brows together. "I don't understand the why of it, but Jenna's magic is different than what I normally sense from witches."

"You have to say more than that," Jenna demanded. "If I'm not a witch, what the hell am I?"

"I didn't say you weren't a witch—" Krae held up a cautionary hand "—because that magic is in you too, but it's not primary."

"For the love of the goddess—" Kiernan strode close "—you're talking in circles." He focused his blue-green gaze on Jenna, and she felt a bolt of power start at her head and travel to her feet. His eyes widened, and he muttered, "Fascinating."

Jenna waited a beat, but neither Krae nor Kiernan offered anything further. "Are either of you going to talk to me?" She heard a piercing note in her voice that wasn't very attractive, but she was excited and scared at the same time.

"Your father wasn't a witch." Kiernan wasn't asking a question but stating a fact.

"That's right," Jenna said, feeling like she was strung together with rusty piano wire. "He was a Druid."

"Do you know anything about his bloodlines?" Krae asked and then piled another question atop the first. "Did you ever meet him?"

Jenna shook her head. "He didn't hang around long after I was born, so I never knew him at all."

Kiernan rubbed his hands together. A smile softened the stern lines of his face. "This will be easier than I'd hoped."

"Maybe," Krae cut in. "Mixing different magics requires a deft hand."

"For the love of Pete, would the two of you talk to me?" Jenna cried. "*Me.* I'm standing right here."

"We are," Kiernan said. "You have Sidhe blood, actually a fair amount, along with Druid and witch genetics."

Sidhe blood.

Jenna's knees felt suddenly weak. "But that's scarcely possible, beyond the minimal amount great-grandmother got when we were suckered into Irichna containment."

"Nice try." Krae nudged her. "You have far more Sidhe in you than that would explain. More than half if I judge it correctly, which would mean there was a Sidhe somewhere in your mother's woodpile too." She raised a quizzical brow in Kiernan's direction, and he shrugged uncomfortably.

"That's us," he murmured. "We do get around."

"Then why is my magic so weak?" Jenna looked from one to the other, confused.

"Because you're trying to do the same thing Colleen and Roz do, and it's the wrong mix of spells and elements," Kiernan explained. "We have our own ways of doing things. You'll have to experiment to find a balance point that maximizes your abilities."

"We can get you started," Krae said, "but today is just a beginning."

Excitement heated her face, and Jenna grinned, delighted by the possibilities. "What are we waiting for? Let's get going."

"Look at you," Krae chortled. "Your face is lit up like you just discovered magic for the first time."

"Are you kidding?" Jenna demanded. "To maybe go from weak, paltry magic to power that's actually worth something is overwhelming. I can't believe it's true, but I sure as hell want to find out."

～

KIERNAN TOSSED a sweat rag at Jenna. They'd been at it for hours, but she was doing extremely well. "Wipe your face and try that one again."

"Okay." She sucked in a deep breath. Her forehead wrinkled in concentration, and she winked out of the cavern.

He turned to Krae. "What do you think?"

"She's amazing." The changeling smiled warmly. "I love it when our kind first realize what they can do, but this is even better because she's like a child, filled with wonder by the power inside her."

"What astounds me is she never had a clue." Kiernan shook his head. "How could she not have known?"

Krae shrugged. "Simple enough. She and the other two came into their magic about the same time. They trained together using tried-and-true methods for witches—and those methods worked for Roz and Colleen. When they didn't succeed for Jenna, the three simply assumed her magic was weak and started filling in for her deficits. Over the years, it became second nature. No one ever pushed her beyond their perception of her shortcomings. Jenna believed what she saw mirrored in her sister witches, and there you have it."

Kiernan raked a hand through his short hair, impressed by Jenna's magical potential. She'd become stronger and stronger as the day wore on, tackling each new task with unflagging enthusiasm. "It appears the other two never stopped meddling."

"That would be my guess," Krae replied. "Except they didn't see it that way. In their defense, they saw themselves as helping their friend. Jenna will be back soon. How about a break? If I'm any judge of time, we've been down here all day, and it's well past suppertime."

A protest rose to his lips, but he swallowed it. The changeling was right. Jenna required time for today's lessons to consolidate— and probably food and rest. As he thought about it, he was surprised Ronin hadn't summoned him back before now to join the evening's strategy discussion.

Krae waved a hand in front of him. "Earth to Sidhe-man. What do you think?"

He eyed the gnome-like creature who stood less than half his height and nodded agreement. "We've accomplished all we can today, and far more than I expected, so we can pack it in once she gets back."

The changeling narrowed her eyes. "I'll give you points, Sidhe-man. At first you wanted her down here to keep her away from the other one, but once you figured things out, you were nearly as excited as me about the possibilities her mixed magic presents."

Kiernan groaned inwardly. Tristan. He'd all but forgotten about him. For today, Jenna had been his and his alone. Once they teleported upstairs into the manor house, Tristan would be waiting for her.

And I'll do the honorable thing and fade into the background.

Krae was looking oddly at him, and he supposed the ancient creature could probably see straight through into his mind. "You're the seer. The game's not over till it's over," she said pointedly.

"Deep. You know I can't scry my own future. What exactly is that supposed to mean?"

"Hush." She jerked her chin upward. "Jenna's coming back."

Kiernan strode to Jenna's side once the air pulsating around her calmed. "How'd it go?"

She was panting slightly, her hazel eyes aglow with delight. "Amazing. Stupendous. I got very close to 1924, the year I was aiming for, but I followed directions and didn't stay long." She clasped her hands together. "This means I can track my father down and ask him about his side of the family."

"You could have done that anyway without time-traveling," Kiernan pointed out.

"Uh-uh. I didn't mention it before, but he's dead. I found out a couple of years ago from a witch who'd known Mom." Jenna paused a beat. "Or maybe he's just in the *Dreaming*. If he had enough Sidhe in him, he might be there. Right? Is that a place I could visit?"

Krae stepped forward. "He might be in the *Dreaming*, and you could probably manage a visit. But we've done enough for today."

"Aw, really?" The disappointment etched into Jenna's features was genuine. "I'm not so tired I need to quit."

"We are." The changeling smiled, moved to Jenna's side, and held out her arms for a hug.

Jenna crouched down and drew her close. "The words feel inadequate, but thank you. All my birthdays and Christmas just got rolled into one."

"You're welcome." Krae let go and Jenna straightened.

"Think I'll teleport into my room and clean up a bit," Jenna announced with more than a hint of pride in her voice. The air around her took on a shimmery aspect, and she vanished.

"I'll see you topside," Kiernan told the changeling and made his way back to the study he'd turned into a bedroom on the top floor of Ronin's manor house. Once there, he twirled in a circle, not really seeing his surroundings. What flickered before his eyes was Jenna, her cheeks flushed by victory and her eyes alight with the thrill of discovery. He balled his hands into fists and squeezed until his nails scored flesh. Maybe he could teleport home. He lived a short distance away, but it would still be a good excuse for not joining the group tonight.

It's a bit on the weak side, but I could tell Ronin I forgot... At least that way, I won't have to watch Jenna smiling at Tristan—and him smiling back. Or even worse, him following her to her room.

Jealousy bit deep, tearing a jagged rent in his heart. For the briefest moment, he considered calling Tristan out. Duels over women had gone out with the Middle Ages, but they settled things definitively. Unfortunately, that was when women were far more subservient. Somehow, he couldn't see Jenna taking up with the victor like a prize well won. No, she'd want to pick her partner, and she'd obviously chosen Tristan, at least to hear his side of things.

Because he couldn't come up with a better plan, Kiernan summoned magic to leave. It bubbled around him when Ronin's voice blared loud and clear. *"I understand you're back. We're meeting in the downstairs room where we gathered last night. Grab a plate from the kitchen, and be there in ten minutes."*

"Goddammit."

Kiernan followed the English curse with a string of Gaelic ones. He hadn't been quick enough, and now there was no way out. He ground out one telepathic word, *"Coming,"* and hoped his mind voice didn't sound as put out as he felt. It might be cheating, but he switched the focus of the magic he'd already mobilized and shaped it into a calming spell. Normally, he looked down his nose at others who used things he considered a crutch for the weak-minded. Calming spells were akin to the drugs humans swallowed by the barrelful, but tonight he welcomed the fuzzy, soothing warmth that oozed through him. When he felt certain he could face the group without giving anything away, Kiernan yanked his door open and marched down the hall to the stairs.

The trip downstairs passed in a blur until the excited hum of female voices reached his ears, growing louder as he drew near. He pushed the door to the back study open, and the noise turned into a positive cacophony. Jenna sat between Roz and Colleen on one of the couches. The three were flushed with excitement and chattering a mile a minute. Kiernan tried not to look, but Jenna was so beautiful it was hard not to. Clearly higher than a kite on adrenaline and success, she regaled her sister witches with a blow-by-blow account of everything she'd done today.

The changelings weren't anywhere to be seen, and he wondered if Ronin had left them out intentionally. Niall would follow Colleen into battle because he loved her and was bound to her. Krae marched to her own drummer and presumably Llyr—

and the other changelings—followed Krae's orders. The more he thought about it, the more Kiernan appreciated the wisdom of not adding three more opinions, especially considering that changelings had good cause to dislike the Sidhe.

Duncan and Ronin stood in a group of about a dozen Sidhe with their heads together in a far corner of the room. Hoping he could get this over with quickly—after all, how many ways could they slice and dice a strategy to deal with Irichna?—Kiernan detoured toward the liquor cabinet, planning to pour himself a healthy jot of mead. By the time he got there, he just grabbed a bottle. It would save him returning to refill his glass.

Ronin raised his head and shot a pointed look Kiernan's way. "Anytime today," he said.

Kiernan rolled his eyes and stomped over. "I thought you said I was welcome to get dinner. You'll notice I didn't bother with any."

"Sorry," Ronin said gruffly. "It's just we're so far from one mind about what to do next that I'm exasperated—and discouraged."

Tristan held out a hand to Kiernan. "Brother," he said formally in Gaelic, with half a bow. "It is good to see you."

The other Sidhe repeated their traditional greeting, and Kiernan replied in kind.

It was Ronin's turn to roll his eyes and blow out an exasperated breath. "Fine, fine. We're all jolly fellows well met, but what in the goddess's name are we going to do? So far I've heard at least six divergent suggestions."

"We'll do what we always do when we can't agree," Tristan said, his voice mild. "Continue to meet until a clear path opens before us."

"But we don't have the luxury of dragging this out for fifty years," Ronin sputtered.

"It won't take that long," Tristan said. Dark smudged places stood out beneath his silvery eyes. His tawny hair needed washing, and he looked beat.

"When's the last time you slept?" Kiernan asked.

Tristan waved a dismissive hand. "Days, maybe a week. It's been rough out there. We need blood from the witches to create more demon assassins. At least it will give us more options."

Irichna that were captured had to be escorted to the Ninth Circle of Hell. There were ways to kill them by tapping into an eldritch power source, but that magic was a bitch to control. Only the three witches—and the Celtic gods—were currently capable of ferrying Irichna to Hell. The witches were willing to share demon assassin ability, but no one had gotten around to drawing their blood just yet. Once that happened, a magical version of gene splicing would transfer their ability to a select group of Sidhe.

Not certain he was prepared for the answer, Kiernan asked, "What have you been doing to get rid of the demons in the meantime?"

"This is why you should have been here for the front part of the conversation," Ronin cut in.

Tristan exhaled wearily. "Give it a rest, Ronin." He turned his attention to Kiernan. "We've called on the Celtic gods for help. At least so far, they've been deucedly decent, but that could change in a heartbeat."

It certainly could, but Kiernan didn't say that. He glanced around the group of battle-weary Sidhe. Aside from himself, Duncan, and Ronin, the rest of them looked trashed.

"If this meets with your approval," he glanced pointedly at Ronin, "I say we get a few hours' rest and continue this conversation in the morning."

"May as well," Ronin grumbled. "We're not exactly getting anywhere this way."

"Thanks." One of the Sidhe punched Kiernan's arm on his way toward the door.

"Thanks, indeed." Tristan pushed past and trotted over to the witches. "Hello, Jenna. You're a sight for sore eyes."

With a trilling giggle that drove into Kiernan's skull like a pikestaff, she said, "Actually all of you looks pretty sore. Have a seat." She patted a place next to her and shoved Colleen aside to make room.

Feeling as if he'd just swallowed broken glass, Kiernan lurched out of the room still clutching the mead bottle close. He considered food, decided he'd probably puke if he tried to eat, and made his way back to his room.

"I can get through this," he said aloud to reinforce the words.

Now if he could just believe them… How was it he'd made it through several thousand years without a woman touching his heart? His soul? Why this one? And why now?

What blasted good does it do me to be a seer when the secret places in my own heart remain closed to me?

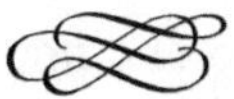

CHAPTER 5

Jenna watched Kiernan stalk out of the room from the corners of her eyes. She'd wanted to thank him for today but hadn't gotten a chance. If she was any good at reading body language, he was royally pissed off about something. She pressed her lips together. Probably he was snarked-out about having to babysit her. Something deep in her chest twinged unpleasantly. She held a great deal of respect for Kiernan after their work together today. He had an intuitive grasp of magic that she'd kill for, and he'd known just what she needed to do to coax her ability out of stasis and make it shine.

Fighting an empty feeling inside, she gazed at the spot in the room where he'd stood. If she followed her heart, she'd go after him.

"Tell me about your day," Tristan urged. "I've been catching bits and pieces from across the room." He swayed a bit on the balls of his feet but didn't accept her invitation from a few moments ago to sit.

Reluctantly, Jenna turned her attention to the Sidhe she'd hoped was interested in her. He appeared plenty attentive now, but she was having a hard time caring. "Are you sure?" she asked, searching for a way to buy herself time to think. "You look pretty tired."

"Just being near you makes me feel better." He met her gaze meaningfully. "If you'd prefer, we can grab plates from the kitchen and find a spot for just the two of us."

No wonder he hadn't sat down; he had other ideas. Jenna felt mired by ambivalence, but he looked so hopeful she couldn't stand to hurt his feelings, so she nodded. "That would be fine. I haven't had anything to eat today."

Roz nudged her and whispered, "You go, girl." Colleen shot a surreptitious glance her way and winked lewdly. Jenna pushed to her feet, pretending she didn't see Tristan's extended hand. What was the matter with her? She'd dreamt of Tristan—at least up until last night. He was the reason she hadn't picked the closest Sidhe at Colleen's crowded wedding and jumped his bones. Or at least tried to before Irichna crashed the party and all bets were off.

Maybe I'm just tired...

But she knew better. Kiernan's overwhelming male presence had blinded her to Tristan's softer looks and gentler ways. His sensitivity was one of the things she'd appreciated about the Sidhe from the moment she met him, but it was a struggle to do anything beyond hoping she hadn't inadvertently done something to annoy Kiernan.

Christ on a fucking crutch. What's wrong with me? If I'm this fickle, I deserve to be by myself. She clucked under her breath in disgust.

"...seem distracted," Tristan murmured as he led the way out of the downstairs study. She hadn't heard the rest.

"Sorry. It's been a big day. We've been at it since five this morning."

Tristan held the door open for her and waited while she walked past. "You're lucky." He smiled encouragingly. "Kiernan is one of our best teachers. Ronin told us what he was up to and why he was late joining us."

"Um, which way is the kitchen? This house is so large, I get turned about." Jenna smiled back. At least what she'd said was true, and it got her out of raving about Kiernan.

This wasn't the time or place to gush over everything he'd done for her today. It had been unbelievable how he'd known exactly what she needed to do to make a particular spell or incantation work for her. Between him and Krae, she'd turned into a far different—and more powerful—witch. Except she wasn't exactly a witch, and Jenna was still wrapping her mind around that revelation. When she thought back to all the years she'd struggled with all but the simplest of spells, she felt like an absolute fool for not recognizing the truth that was right under her nose.

"Turn here and then take the first hallway to the left," Tristan said, breaking into her musings.

To steer the conversation toward safer ground, she said, "Fill me in on the Irichna. How many showed up, and where was the brunt of the fighting?"

Tristan's footsteps sounded behind her, muffled somewhat by a thick Oriental carpet runner. "It's hard to get a head count when they keep shape shifting." He inhaled audibly. "Let's just say I don't think we made a dent despite fighting for weeks. No matter how many we disabled, more showed up. I wanted to communicate with you but never had a chance to get anywhere near a computer or a cell phone. I did try to reach you telepathically, but I'm guessing you never heard me."

"No, I didn't." She walked into the kitchen. Pots simmered on an enormous stainless steel stove. Fresh bread sat atop a board on a polished gray granite countertop with a bowl of fruit alongside. She fished two plates out of a cupboard and went hunting for silverware.

Tristan caught her up from behind and spun her to face him. "You're angry with me for not calling like I said I would. I am sorry." He smoothed a strand of hair off her cheek and tucked it behind one ear. "I spent hours thinking about you, reliving the time we spent together, and looking forward to getting to know you better." His silver gaze bored into her. "Much better." He grinned, showing very straight teeth nested in a perfect jaw. "Goddess's tits, I told everyone else how taken I was with you, I just didn't get around to telling you. Until now, that is."

How could she respond to that? He was saying all the right things. Words she would have cut her right arm off to hear before last night. She forced herself to meet his gaze and found it wasn't all that hard. Battle-stained and weary, his face held a simple elegance, even with his sculpted cheekbones dotted with many days' stubble. His lean, broad-shouldered form did equal justice to dress clothes and the battle leathers that currently swathed him, leaving very little to the imagination.

"It's not what you think," she stammered, her face growing warm.

"Then what is it?" he pressed. "You don't seem like yourself."

She considered pointing out that he didn't know her very well since they'd only spent a few hours together, but he seemed so sincere and so genuinely concerned, she didn't have the heart to say something that sounded argumentative. Jenna squared her shoulders. "Look. We're both tired, and this probably isn't a good time for any sort of deep discussion. How about if we dish up some of that food, take it to one of the tables in the dining room, and just enjoy one another's company?"

"I'd like nothing better." He levered the plates from her hand. "Tell me what you'd like, and I'll serve you."

Jenna grinned in spite of herself. "What? You think I'm a mind reader? I have no idea what's in those pots." She trotted forward and lifted lids, peering inside. "Maybe a dollop of everything. It all smells wonderful."

Tristan half bowed, a courtly, old-world gesture that touched her heart. "Your wish is my command. Choose where you want to sit, and I'll meet you there. Maybe you could select a bottle of wine for us to share."

"I prefer whiskey. What can I get for you?"

"I'll have whatever you do." He set the plates down and ladled food onto them. "I want to know everything about you, Jenna Neil." Perhaps responding to a look that washed over her face, he added hastily. "I promise I won't pick your brain clean tonight, but I want to make certain we spend all the time together we can before Irichna force us out of this haven and back into war."

She murmured something incomprehensible that she hoped sounded encouraging and returned to the back study with its liquor cabinet. The room had emptied, and she took a few deep breaths while she hunted for all the excellent reasons to let Tristan court her. They'd been front and center before, so they weren't difficult to find. He was funny and bright and amazingly good-looking, just like all the Daoine Sidhe. More to the point, he was smitten with her. That was worth far more than her mooning over Kiernan, who'd obviously been exasperated by wasting his valuable time on her—even though he'd volunteered and had done his damnedest to see she got the benefit of his skill.

"He did that because he's honorable," she murmured as she selected an unopened bottle of aged Irish whiskey. And then a thought struck her, and she stopped in her tracks. Honorable meant you didn't horn in on a friend's woman. Even if Kiernan might be interested in her, clearly Tristan had told the others about his intentions—even if he hadn't told her.

"That settles it," she said, still talking to the empty study. "As far as the Sidhe are concerned, Tristan's staked his claim to me." Half a grin twisted her mouth, and she started for the door, whiskey bottle dangling from one hand. There were worse fates. Maybe a roll in the hay with Tristan would be just the ticket for driving Kiernan out of her mind.

A still-small voice deep in her soul lodged a protest, but she told it to shut up.

Jenna made her way back to the informal dining area just off the kitchen. Tristan had laid their plates on a table. He'd also placed two lit candles nearby and come up with linen napkins. She caught her lower lip between her teeth. He was trying so hard, it was impossible not to be flattered. Jenna handed him the whiskey bottle.

"Is this spot all right?" he asked. "I know I invited you to pick it, but then I got a bit carried away setting things up for us."

"No worries. It's wonderful." She turned to hunt down some glasses.

He dropped a hand onto her shoulder. "Where are you going?"

"We need glasses for the whiskey, unless you want to pass the bottle back and forth."

He squeezed her shoulder, and the warmth from his hand was shockingly intimate. It brought back memories of how she'd felt cradled in his arms. "You just sit," he murmured. "I'll take care of it." He guided her to the place he'd set for her and joined her a few moments later with two cut crystal goblets in hand.

"Thanks." It wasn't hard to smile warmly. She picked up a fork and dug in. Once she started eating, she realized she was famished and barely set her fork down until her plate was empty. On the other side of the table, Tristan did the same thing, so she guessed field rations hadn't been all that plentiful or especially appetizing.

Tristan Edwards watched Jenna while they ate, but he wasn't obvious about it. She was so focused on her dinner, she probably didn't notice his many glances her way. He wanted to help himself to her thoughts, but just because he could didn't mean it was a proper course of action. Though he didn't know the demon assassin witch well, he'd been drawn to her from the moment they'd met at Heathrow Airport a few weeks back. He'd wanted to attend Colleen and Duncan's wedding in Seattle, primarily because it would have given him more time with Jenna, but Ronin had deployed him to fight Irichna instead.

He dreamed of Jenna more nights than not, usually waking with an aching hard-on. Even though they'd only exchanged a few kisses, he'd expected her to fall into his arms the next time they met, but she seemed nervous and uncomfortable around him. Nothing like she'd been during the few days they'd spent getting to know one another.

Taking care to maintain a neutral expression, he wondered what had happened. It was almost as if she'd met someone else and was keeping her mouth shut about it. He replayed what he knew about events since she'd left England and didn't see how she'd have had time to develop a new love interest. Colleen and Duncan's wedding occurred less than a fortnight after he'd met Jenna, and Irichna attacks had piled one atop the next, fast and furious ever since. Roz and Ronin, who'd married soon after, had barely gotten a wedding night.

So if not another man, then what? Had she rethought her earlier attraction to him? He leaned back in his chair and shut his eyes for a moment. The food was helping, but he really did need a few hours' sleep. When he tried to concentrate, his mind pedaled in tired circles.

"Are you all right?" Jenna leaned toward him and placed a hand over one of his, the concern in her voice genuine.

He met her gaze, entranced by her high cheekbones and almond-shaped hazel eyes. "Yes, just worn out. Normally, Sidhe don't need much sleep, but I've been burning the candle at all ends for a bit too long."

She smiled, and the corners of her eyes crinkled. "We've done everything but eat the pattern off the plates. What do you say we go to bed?" Color splotched across her cheeks. "That didn't come out quite right. I didn't exactly mean together."

Her words were vague, so Tristan tested the waters. "I would like to clean up. Maybe then we could just hold one another and fall asleep." He hesitated. "I'm not trying to be pushy, but I don't think we have much time before things go to hell, and I don't have the first idea what continuous Irichna battles will mean for our kind. That's more Kiernan's bailiwick than mine."

She had an exquisitely expressive face, and a panoply of emotion crossed it. He could have snuck into her mind to discover the source of her inner turmoil but forced himself to wait for her answer. Finally, when he'd all but given up, she nodded almost imperceptibly. "That would be nice. My room is the third bedroom on the left on the second floor."

His heart gave a crazy little leap, but she seemed so tentative, he covered her hand with his own. "You don't have to."

"I know. One thing, though. Don't ask me any questions or press me for much beyond kisses. Tonight I just want to sleep."

"Done."

It wasn't quite what he'd hoped for, but if it was the best he could get, he'd take it. Maybe she'd change her mind before morning. He pushed his chair back. "See you in a little while."

Tristan felt her gaze follow him as he left the dining room. He would've sold his soul to an Irichna to know what she was thinking. Succumbing to temptation, he pushed a tendril of magic toward her because he ached for information but ran up against a wall. Grateful he wasn't facing her so she couldn't read the shock that must have registered on his face, he made his way through Ronin's rambling mansion. His mind was a jumble. Whatever had happened to Jenna today was clearly cataclysmic. The sweet witch he'd fallen for a few weeks back had turned into something quite different.

For her to be powerful enough to block his magic was little shy of astonishing.

He showered quickly, wrapped a robe around himself, and made his way to her room where he tapped softly before opening the door. He'd expected her to be snuggled into bed—hopefully without too many clothes—but she sat in a chair fully dressed and gestured for him to take the opposite one. Uncharacteristic anxiety twisted his stomach into a knot. Was this where she dumped him before anything had even gotten started between them?

Jenna pressed her lush lips together. "I had a few moments to think. I know I said not to ask me any questions, but we do need to talk."

"All right." Tristan eased into the other chair and tucked his robe around himself. "I'd be glad to listen."

A crooked smile formed on her face. "This may not come out very elegantly because I'm tired too, but when I met you the first time, I knew who I was. That's not true anymore."

He narrowed his eyes. If this was a brush off, it had an unusual beginning. "Say more."

She nodded. "Today Kiernan and Krae handed me the keys to a very special kingdom." The crooked smile broadened. "Or maybe it's a queendom. In any event, it's pretty fantastic. In less than twenty-four hours I've gone from a witch who could barely spell her way out of a paper bag to someone with Sidhe, Druid, and witch blood. To be honest, it's overwhelming, and I have to find myself again before I can be any sort of partner." She paused long enough to suck in a breath before going on. "I'd love to invite you into my bed, but it wouldn't be fair to either of us until I figure out how all the magic running through me is going to shape my life."

Tristan didn't modulate his amazement, so it must have shown on his face. Jenna was part Sidhe. Why hadn't he known? *Because I didn't look.* No wonder he found her so irresistible. He leaned forward. "I'd like to help you with that."

"I'm not sure it's even possible." She drew her brows together. "The world I knew—and counted on—has been turned upside down. In some ways, I feel like Alice in Wonderland after she fell down the rabbit hole, and nothing was like it seemed." A nervous giggle escaped. "Ach, I'm babbling."

"No, you're not. Tell me what transpired today. Not all of it, but enough so I understand a little better."

She settled herself more comfortably in her chair, crossed her legs, and laced her long, tapering fingers together. "Well, it began when Krae told me to forget about the way I've always tried to teleport. I have to admit I was skeptical, but I followed her directions—and it worked. She wasn't surprised, but I certainly was. Anyway, she'd figured out witch magic wasn't primary for me, and then Kiernan did some sort of magical scan, and the two of them told me I'm better than half Sidhe, which is why very little of my magical efforts worked the same way they did for Roz and Colleen."

"No, of course they wouldn't have. If you'd spent any amount of time around the Sidhe, we would have picked up on what type of magic wielder you were." Tristan considered his next words. "It must have been...difficult for you through the years. Always feeling your magic didn't quite measure up to par."

She rolled her eyes. "You don't know the half of it. I was always worried sick I'd do something wrong, and it would be the death of either Colleen or Roz. It would've been hard to live with myself if that had happened. In terms of your race being able to figure me out—" she shrugged uncomfortably "—after what you did to us, we weren't exactly seeking an audience."

"No, I don't suppose you would have been." He tilted his head until he caught her gaze. "None of us can predict the future with any surety. Even those of us with strong precognitive ability are hard pressed to see what's in store for individuals with any level of accuracy."

Jenna frowned slightly. "There's a point somewhere in there, but I'm not exactly seeing it."

"Just that my offer to give you whatever you need is open-ended. I can teach you about your Sidhe roots and help entrain your magic. It's not like you're a youngster, magically that is. It won't take as long as you fear for your newfound skills to feel comfortable."

"Dear God, I hope not! I've got to fast-track everything, so I'm not a liability next time the demons attack."

"You won't be."

"How can you know that?"

He reached forward and laid a hand on her knee. "I just do. I hope you don't think I'm being rude, but my eyes feel like they're lined with sandpaper. What do you want to do about the rest of tonight?"

She got to her feet and just looked at him, an unreadable expression on her face. Tristan stood, closed the short distance between them, and folded her into his arms. He ran a hand under her hair and kneaded the back of her head. Her body, which had stiffened when he touched her, relaxed against him, and she leaned into his touch.

"That feels so good," she murmured.

"Magic is heady, almost like its own aphrodisiac," he said. "The first time you truly grasp the roots of your power, it's like touching a high voltage wire, exhilarating and adrenaline-charged." He moved his hand down her neck, rubbing as he went. Her breasts pressed into his chest, their nipples hardening. His cock stiffened where it was trapped between their bodies, and Tristan's breath hitched. He wanted this woman beyond wisdom and reason, had dreamed of exploring her soft curves and sinking his length into her. To have her in his arms again was a temptation that made his knees weak and turned his brain to mush.

He cupped her face with his free hand, tilted it up, and closed his mouth over hers. He kept the kiss light and tentative to give her a choice, but she wrapped her arms around him and opened her mouth to his tongue. Heat roared through him. He tried to contain it, but desire turned into a live thing clawing at him, saturating every nerve with need.

Jenna clung to him, kissing him with a ferocity born of everything she'd lived through that day. He could have stood there forever, drinking her in, but when he dropped a hand to her ass and snugged her against his erection, she pulled back, her lips swollen from their kiss.

"I shouldn't have done that," she said with a husky catch in her voice and stepped back from him. "The old Jenna would keep right on rolling. You're a beautiful man, and my body is screaming for you, but I meant what I said earlier. I have some things to sort through, and I have to be alone to do that."

His heart raced and his groin thrummed with need, but he inclined his head and repeated what he'd said earlier. "I'll give you whatever you need, Jenna. You're worth waiting for."

"Thanks," she said, her voice soft. "Sleep well."

"You as well." Tristan backed out of the room because he couldn't bear to take his eyes off her. He made his way to his own room with a welter of feelings bombarding him. Maybe he shouldn't have kissed her, but she was so irresistible he hadn't been able to stop himself.

At least her body wants me, even if her mind isn't certain.

The thought was cold comfort. He strode through his door, kicked it shut, and threw himself onto the bed facedown. His hard-on throbbed with hunger. Every time he inhaled, Jenna's scent and the musk of her arousal just made things worse. But when he flipped onto his back and started stroking himself, that wasn't what he wanted. He could make himself come, but what was the point? He yearned for the heat of her body around him, not his own hand.

Tristan forced himself to take deep, steady breaths. He truly was beyond exhaustion, and before very many minutes elapsed, he passed into an uneasy sleep.

CHAPTER 6

*J*enna paced from one side of her room to the other. Her body still quivered from Tristan's embrace, and her mind was a boiling muddle of indecision. How could she have gone from old maid status to feeling torn between two very different men virtually overnight? Of course, Kiernan might not want anything to do with her, but still... The wisest course would be for her to give a hundred percent to her magic for however long she had before the shit hit the fan. What she'd told Tristan about not knowing who she was anymore was painfully true. Until she could figure that out, she had no right linking her life to anyone's.

She rubbed her temples to modulate a headache pounding behind one eye and then summoned a bit of healing magic. Her bed looked like a better bet than burning up the rug all night, so she dropped onto it and twitched the duvet over herself, squirming to free the part she was lying on. She switched off the lamp with a thought. Darkness washed over her, and she closed her eyes, seeking peace through rest, but her mind wouldn't shut down. After cataloguing all the reasons she should count herself lucky Tristan cared about her, she started in on what an enormous unknown Kiernan was, but just thinking about his impossibly broad shoulders made her breath hitch.

Even though she wasn't asleep, a silvery path unfolded behind her eyelids, and she snapped her eyes open to see if it was real. Jenna stared at the shimmery trail snaking into darkness.

Dreamers' Paths, but why here and why now?

Was it a summons from the dream guardian? She squeezed her eyes shut, hoping it was a hallucination, but the path was still there when she opened them. She shook her head. Could her life get any more complicated? The Dreamers' Paths were a boon to magic wielders, providing both an escape and a way to focus and hone power, but the ancient spirit who controlled them could be nasty and intolerant. Only witches with strong precognitive powers ventured into the dream guardian's realm. Jenna had lost an aunt to its mesmerizing power, and she'd always avoided it, except for one time when she hadn't had a choice.

But I'm not exactly a witch anymore, now am I?

She grimaced. It didn't sit right to not identify as a witch, so she altered her internal self-description to *witch-plus-more* and left things at that.

An unpleasant pricking sensation swept from her head to her toes, rather like her earlier sexual arousal had taken a wrong turn. Jenna lurched to her feet, recognizing the summoning for what it was. The dream guardian would keep upping the ante, and she'd rather not have him pissed off before she even got there. A frisson of discomfort rippled down her back. What if this was an Irichna trick? She shook herself as a dog might and gathered magic. Before, she wouldn't necessarily have had enough power to answer the ghostly summons, but this was a brand new ball game.

She caught a glimpse of her face in the full-length mirror attached to one wall and did a double take, barely recognizing the grim-faced woman who stared back at her with burning hazel eyes. The prickling feeling increased, and she released magic in a rush to gather information. She didn't exactly find the dream guardian, but neither did she identify Irichna.

Good enough, I guess.

She hustled onto the silvery path and girded herself. She'd never traveled the Dreamers' Paths without the dream guardian to soften the way, but Roz and Colleen had. Both told her they'd been bombarded with their worst nightmares. Jenna focused her gaze straight ahead, expecting boogeymen to jump her from both sides where the path fell away into black nothingness, but it never happened. She came out at a clearing she remembered from her only other visit to the dream guardian's stronghold. Ancient trees surrounded an altar illuminated by moonlight.

Her heart thudded dully against her chest, but she got hold of her frayed nerves and lectured herself sternly. *Nothing bad has happened so far. Let's see what he wants.*

She didn't have long to wait. A rustling preceded the guardian, and he strode to where she stood off to one side of the white stone altar covered with runic writing. He was taller than she was by half a head, his elegant form swathed in brown robes sashed with moonbeams. His silvery hair was bound by a circlet of moonbeams that sat on his brow, and his clear blue eyes swam with an ever-changing collage of images.

Jenna inclined her head. "You rang?"

He drew his silver brows together. "Excuse me?"

She cringed at her lack of preparedness for dealing with someone so close to being a god on a one-to-one basis. "Sorry, I shouldn't have been so informal. You summoned me. Please tell me why."

"Ah, but it was you who summoned me, young miss."

"Um, if I did, I wasn't aware of it."

"No, you might not have been, since you don't use my paths on your own."

She waited, confused, hoping he'd say more. After a pause so long she was certain he'd forgotten about her, he said, "I have known about you since your birth, and I've been waiting, but you never showed any interest in exploring your magic beyond a cursory level. Finally, I sought help from one of Earth's children because I was afraid those infernal demons would be the death of you before you discovered who you were."

"Earth's children? Do you mean the changelings?" At his nod, Jenna marshaled her courage. Krae's puzzling words from earlier —the thing she wouldn't talk about—found sudden meaning. The dream guardian had solicited Krae's help, and she'd shown up on Jenna's plane. "Who am I, exactly, that it was important for me to get off my duff and stop dithering about with witch hexes and charms?"

He cocked his head to one side, and she lost herself in the changing imagery floating in his eyes. "That is a question you'll have to figure out for yourself. All I will say is your presence will play a critical element in the Irichna wars."

Jenna narrowed her eyes. "You foretell futures, don't you?"

"Sometimes. I hold the gift of prophecy, but I rarely share my visions. People misinterpret them or expend ridiculous amounts of energy trying to escape their destinies, except it never works."

"I don't suppose you could tell me anything about—"

The dream guardian held up a hand. "Stop right there because the answer is no. You were on the right track earlier, though, before I opened a way for you to find me."

"On the right track earlier," she repeated, considering what he meant. "Could you narrow that down a bit?"

He shook his head. "Your time here is coming to an end, but don't be shy about returning. You'll find it a haven to augment your powers."

Jenna opened her mouth to ask one last question, but the glade dispersed around her, and she landed with a *thunk* back in her bedroom at Ronin's. The bed was close enough to crawl onto. She tucked a pillow beneath her head and pulled the duvet up to her chin. What the hell had just happened? She replayed her conversation with the guardian almost word for word. The part she kept coming back to was that he'd *known about her*. It was comforting and disconcerting at the same time, and she didn't know what to make of it. If it wasn't the middle of the night, she'd have scared up Roz and Colleen to discuss it with them. They were probably cuddled in with their new husbands, though, and she didn't want to disturb them.

She snorted, but it came out more like a grunt as she recalled she could be bedded down with Tristan if she hadn't been so damned honorable. Maybe if she'd opened her body to the Sidhe, the whole drama with the guardian wouldn't have happened.

But that doesn't mean what he told me isn't true...

To divert herself, she forced her overheated brain to review all the magic she'd learned earlier in the day. The very best had been time travel since witch magic couldn't touch the bands that separated one era from the next. By the time she was done recapping the various incantations and mixtures of elements, the sky outside her window was lightening with the coming dawn.

If there was a plan for the day that included her, Jenna didn't know about it. Figuring she'd never sleep at this point, she stalked into the adjoining bathroom and started the tub filling. At least she felt more settled, the interlude with the guardian having faded from center stage.

"Magic first, men later," she muttered as she stepped into the steaming water.

She was just rinsing shampoo from her hair when frantic pounding battered against her bedroom door. Before she could lever herself out of the water, Krae whooshed into the bathroom like a small whirlwind. She seemed to have one speed: wide open. "Get the rest of that soap off you and get dressed," the changeling instructed briskly.

Jenna tilted her head back under the water and called it even. She opened the drain and grabbed a towel. "What's going on?"

"I don't want to talk about it until we're somewhere shielded."

"Can I tell Roz or Colleen where I'm going?"

Krae rolled her green eyes. "The three musketeers. No. I've been in communication with Kiernan telepathically. Between him and Ronin—who he's on his way to talk with—they'll alert your sidekicks."

Stepping over the high rim of the tub, Jenna towel-dried her hair. She quirked a brow at the changeling. "Anything in particular I should be dressing for?"

"Whatever do you mean?"

Jenna shrugged and proceeded to finish drying herself. "Oh you know. Cold weather, gunshots, magic blasts, visits to the borderworlds. I like to be prepared."

"Very funny."

"That's me, the original funny girl." Jenna pushed past the changeling and stopped on the other side of the door into the bedroom. "You didn't answer me."

"Warm, practical clothes."

"Does that mean no high heels?"

"That's exactly what it means. Stop talking and hurry things up."

KIERNAN STOOD in an alcove in the hallway just outside Ronin's door. It slid open, and the Sidhe leader walked quietly down the corridor, gesturing for Kiernan to follow him. Apparently Roz was still asleep, and Ronin didn't want to disturb her.

He led the way into a small sitting room and warded it as soon as Kiernan was inside and the door was closed. When Ronin turned to face him, Kiernan saw new lines etched around his eyes.

Ronin didn't waste words. "What was so critical it couldn't have waited until at least six a.m.?"

"Irichna are massing, right along with their minions."

Ronin blew out an exhausted sounding breath. "And you know

this how?"

Kiernan unclamped his jaw so he could answer. "It's embarrassing, but Krae and Llyr told me. When I was skeptical, they showed me."

"So we're finally moving into the thick of things." Ronin sank heavily onto a padded leather chair and motioned for Kiernan to take the one opposite, but he shook his head. His muscles felt like tightly wound springs, and the last thing he wanted to do was sit.

"It appears that way. Krae is taking Jenna to meet with a group of changelings. She told me something about Jenna's combination of magics being crucial to our side. Krae said she'd do her damnedest to prepare the witch, but she sounded frantic about not having more time."

"Where does that leave Roz and Colleen?" Ronin drew his brows together into a worried line that cut across his forehead. "The witches have to be together to maximize their magic." He paused for a beat. "I'm not totally sure that's true, but the three of them certainly believe it."

"I don't know." Kiernan debated his next words but finally spit them out. "Something about all this doesn't feel right. The changelings know far too much. Since when do they identify more critical information than we do?"

Ronin pursed his lips into a tense expression. "Since we alienated them by stripping much of their power. Thank the goddess we fixed that problem, but they still have demon blood—and ample reason to hate us."

"You're not making me feel any better. I got to this particular party rather late, but at least the one changeling seems quite bonded to Duncan's wife." Kiernan blew out a ragged breath. "We need a game plan."

"You think?" Ronin asked sardonically. "More like a few of them. It doesn't help that it's been a couple of centuries since we made a full commitment to a war."

"Did we ever get any of the witches' blood?"

Ronin nodded. "Late last night Duncan and I got enough from Roz and Colleen to recruit about fifteen Sidhe back into the demon assassin business. Duncan said he'd take care of parceling it out before he went to bed."

"Humph. Do we have any idea—?"

"—how long it will take to work? Nope. Probably not more than a day or two, though. Or it might be as much as a week."

"I'm not sure we have that long." Kiernan changed his mind and folded his long frame into the chair across from Ronin.

"We may not have that long before the demons strike," Ronin said, "but a war could last for weeks. Maybe months or years."

"Not according to Krae—or my visions." Kiernan frowned, not wanting to go there. "Fuck. I wish to hell I was certain the changelings were on our side."

"Me too, since they've shanghaied Jenna. Why so suspicious? You spent an entire day working with Krae and the witch. Did the changeling do anything devious?"

"Of course not." Kiernan's nostrils flared. "I'd have ended the session right then and there. We were on Sidhe turf. It would have been simple enough to expel her."

"All right." Ronin sat straighter. "For now, let's assume positive intent. If there was anything amiss, the dream guardian would probably have picked up on it when we stopped there on our way back from the demons' borderworld."

"Eh. Maybe you're right. As I recall, Krae was pretty cozy with the guardian. My visions haven't implicated the changelings in any negative way, but one of my biggest problems is figuring out whom to trust. When it was just Sidhe working with one another, at least we knew who was dependable."

"Not always." Ronin shot a pointed look his way. "There's been plenty of treachery in-house. Remember—"

"Let's not get sidetracked with a history lesson."

A corner of Ronin's mouth twitched downward. "Ever the practical one. All right, back to problem solving. The way I see it, our biggest challenge is keeping the witches alive. And I'm not just saying that because one of them is my wife."

Kiernan rotated his shoulder blades trying to work the tension out of them. "Say more."

"I had a brief opportunity to scry the future."

"So did I. You first." Leaning forward, Kiernan laced his fingers together. Ronin was talented, and his visions tended to be as accurate as Kiernan's own, at least some of the time.

A muscle twitched in the Sidhe leader's jaw. "It's not as definitive as one might hope. I saw two divergent futures. The one with the witches was much brighter than the one without."

Kiernan exhaled sharply. He'd seen several iterations of what they were heading into, and he would've described things far differently. In truth, he'd kept his information close to the cuff for fear of riling everyone unnecessarily. When so many possibilities presented themselves, it was impossible to put much credence in any of them.

He glanced up to find Ronin's gaze on him. "What?"

"I might ask you the same thing. What aren't you saying?"

Kiernan slouched against his chair. "I wish I had more to give you. The problem is every time I try to home in on what's going to happen, I see something different. There's at least one traitor in our midst. He may be our undoing, but the future is less clear to me than it's ever been."

"Anything else critical you've kept to yourself?"

"Probably." Kiernan smiled grimly. "If things become less murky, you'll be the first to know."

"Gee, thanks." Ronin closed his mouth with an audible *clack*. "What bothers me is if I hadn't asked, you wouldn't even have told me as much as you did."

"I told you less than nothing. It's not helpful to know we have a turncoat with no ready way to identify them. It will only make you suspicious where you'd be better served focusing on the big picture."

"When I want advice, I'll ask for it."

"You just did when you requested information about my visions. Carping at me for sharing them isn't productive. We need to gather everyone." Kiernan started to get up, but Ronin waved him back into his seat.

"Stay put. I need to present—at most—two courses of action to vote on. I do *not* want a repeat of last night where everyone argued their point of view. You're the last one who spoke to Krae. Call her telepathically and find out what she's up to since we can't make any type of plan without knowing."

Kiernan nodded and moved his tented fingers beneath his chin. *"Krae!"*

Her answer was immediate. *"What took you so long, Sidhe man?"*

He chose to ignore her barb. *"I'm guessing you left. When will you return the witch?"*

"In a few hours. I need to indoctrinate her in how to work with changelings and our magic, now that her powers are so much greater."

"Define a few hours. Better yet, give me a time."

"Noon."

"Plan to stay once you return, and bring your decision makers with you. We're holding a war council."

Tinkling laughter cut through him like shards of glass. *"You do not order me about, but time is short and hurt feelings will only get in our way."*

"Does that mean you'll be here?" Kiernan pushed for clarification.

"Yes."

Kiernan started to say more, but an echoing silence told him the changeling had broken their connection. "Will that do?" he asked.

"Excellent." Ronin scrubbed the heels of his hands down his face. "Now let's come up with a couple of tactics that just might keep the witches alive and us out of the *Dreaming* for the rest of our immortal existences."

CHAPTER 7

*J*enna blinked a few times to clear her vision after a quick teleport into an enormous circular room. A lack of windows suggested it was underground, but there was no way to tell. The walls curved slightly and were layered with intricately woven tapestries. Light came from torches stuck into sconces at intervals. When she looked at her feet, sand extended in all directions with subtle rake marks as if someone tended it.

Makes sense. If they draw their power from earth, they'd want to be in contact with it...

Changelings surged toward her from all directions, a veritable sea of the three-foot tall, gnome-like creatures. Krae barked a word in a language Jenna didn't recognize, and the flood halted. Several changelings detached themselves from the group and walked forward briskly with their characteristic bowlegged gait.

"Where are we?" Jenna asked, peering closely at the crowd. "Is Niall here?"

Krae snorted. "Quite the question girl. We're in one of our protected places. Niall remained behind with Colleen. That way he can let me know if anything untoward happens back at Ronin's."

"You said you'd explain once we were in a safe place," Jenna said, overwhelmed by the sheer number of changelings. She'd figured Niall wasn't the only one in the world, but she'd spent the last forty years with him and hadn't laid eyes on any others until recently. No wonder it never occurred to her he had so many kinfolk.

"Indeed I did." Krae's gaze flashed green fire. "You are a crucible that can intensify our power tenfold."

Jenna drew back, her eyes widening as she swallowed surprise. "Huh? Oh, I heard you all right, but it's hard to believe. Is that just for changelings, or does my humble presence have a similar effect on all magic wielders?"

"We're not certain." Krae shook flame-colored hair over her shoulders.

Llyr detached himself from the dozen or so changelings ringed close to her. His dark eyes glowed, and his dark hair had been braided close to his head. He bowed slightly. "Thank you for heeding Krae's summons."

Jenna snorted. "There have been several tonight, and it didn't appear I had much of a choice any of the times."

"There is always choice." Krae's voice held a solemn note. "Making the correct decision has never been more critical."

"Why do you think I'm a catalyst?" Jenna inhaled and held it, not certain she wanted to know the answer.

"It wasn't the word I used," Krae said, "but it will do. Because you were foretold."

Breath whooshed from Jenna's lungs. The guardian had said much the same thing. She'd partially written off his inference, but it was harder to do now that she'd heard the same thing twice. She squared her shoulders until her spine was painfully straight. "You've got to tell me more than that. If I have some sort of prophetic role to play, I need to understand it."

"There's not time," Krae protested. "I promised Kiernan I'd have you back by noon, and we must practice—"

"I'm not doing anything until I know more. I don't need the *War and Peace* version. Just hit the high points." Anxiety shrilled her voice, but Jenna didn't care.

"It's only fair." Llyr planted himself dead center in front of her and crossed his arms over his chest. "When the Sidhe stuck your forbearers with demon containment and stuck us underground without enough magic to light a candle, Cenél Eoghan burned the last of his waning power searching the future."

"Who was that?" Jenna asked. "Isn't that Niall's last name?"

"It's a variant of many of our surnames, and Cenél was one of our best known seers." Llyr shook a finger at her. "No more questions." When Jenna nodded her understanding, he continued. "Cenél told us time would pass—likely hundreds of years—and then one of the demon assassin witches would rise with power far outstripping her peers. That witch would hold the ability to concentrate changeling magic and be instrumental in hobbling the Irichna once and for all."

Jenna waited, but Llyr was clearly done talking. "There has to be more," she protested.

"He told you enough for you to figure out you're the witch in the prophecy," Krae snapped. "There are only three of you left, and it certainly isn't the other two. Let's get on with it."

"Get on with what? What exactly do you have in mind?" Jenna turned in a full circle. Changelings surrounded her as far as she could see. "How many of you are there?"

"This is far from all of us," Krae said. "What I *have in mind* requires trust on your part." She moved so Jenna had to look at her. "Can you trust me, witchy-girl?"

Jenna shoved her tongue against her teeth. "I'm not sure. What will we be doing?"

"I saved you on the airplane," the changeling reminded her. "You have no reason not to have faith in me."

"That may be true, but everything is so…different, it's hard to trust anything—including myself." Jenna wove her fingers together and rested her chin on them. "My whole world turned upside down in the last twenty-four hours. I'm still a witch, but I'm a bunch of other things too, and I don't understand any of the new elements well enough to make decisions based on them."

"Whining is a luxury." Llyr tilted his head back and directed his dark gaze at her.

His words were so off the wall—and so right on the money—half a snorting laugh escaped her. "You've got my number. I'm queen of the whiners."

"Stop!" Krae made a chopping motion with one hand. "If the situation weren't so desperate, we could spar with one another. Hell, we could sit down to tea and share life histories." She exhaled noisily. "If the goddess blesses us, at least a few of us will be able to do that afterward."

"Okay." Jenna hunkered so she was at eye level with the changelings. "Tell me how this works."

"We will feed power through you gradually, only adding more as you can tolerate it," Krae said.

"That sounds ominous. Is there a downside?"

"All magic has a downside, witchy-girl. If you don't stay on top of things, this could kill you."

"Gawk!" Jenna straightened and fought down a sick sensation in her gut. "Maybe it's not such a good idea, then. I've never been very good at controlling magic, and—"

"Oberon's balls. I had you pegged as naïve but not as a coward." Llyr rolled his eyes. "She only told you that to reinforce the seriousness of our situation. Of course we'll take care not to harm you."

"I'll do my best," Krae cut in, "but there are no guarantees. The sooner we get started, the sooner you can face your fears and move past them."

"You sound like Roz," Jenna muttered.

"Bully for her and her infamous temper." The changeling showed broad, squared-off teeth in a parody of a smile. "If I remind you of her, perhaps you'll pay closer attention. Stand tall and gather the three parts of your magic until they surround you in layers. Sidhe magic closest to your body, then Druid, then witch. Once you've done that, let me know."

Even though Krae had said earlier that there were always choices, somehow Jenna didn't think saying something like, *this whole thing makes me as nervous as the last lemming. Forget jumping over the cliff, I'm out of here* would fly well. Besides, if anything could move them to the other side of the Irichna problem, she was all for it. They'd been the bane of her existence from the moment she'd crafted her first spell and inadvertently set fire to a chair.

Krae smiled encouragingly, and Jenna suspected she'd been eavesdropping on her thoughts. After a couple of steadying breaths, she summoned magic and layered it as Krae instructed. Power lapped around her, ebbing and flowing like a tide.

Once Jenna had the three magics structured as Krae wanted, she nodded at the changeling who said, "No matter what, keep those layers intact. You'll feel our magic, gentle at first, but it will build. If things go well, this will be a life-changing experience—for all of us. Ready."

It hadn't been a question, and Jenna held herself open. Fighting what was coming would make things worse. Power sensed ambivalence and punished it, almost as if the goddess at the root of all living things was affronted that anyone would eschew her magic. Pins and needles began in the soles of Jenna's feet. She planted them firmly to secure her stance. Heat seeped into her feet and moved up her legs. It wasn't soothing. Far from it. The sensation was electric, almost as if something alive with sharp edges had entered her body.

Duncan had likened an ancient source of Sidhe power to harnessing lightning. She'd watched him manage it a few times.

And now I get to find out firsthand what it's like.

Glowing, prickling warmth morphed into heat, verging on the edge of painful, but Jenna held her ground. Beyond the discomfort, there was something numinous about the energy surging through her, filling her with the oldest power of all.

Earth magics were primary. Today brought that home as nothing else ever had.

Witches relied on earth charms to start incantations but always limited the amount and mixed other elements into their spells. It was the same strategy she'd tried over and over again, with disappointing results.

No wonder. My magic is different, except I didn't realize that until yesterday.

Time flowed around and through her as sensation built and built again. Each time, she thought she couldn't hold any more magic but found she was wrong.

"Look at yourself," Krae cried, excitement thrumming beneath her words.

Jenna's eyes had been closed to help her concentrate. When she opened them, shock ricocheted through her. Her entire body glowed with a soft, golden light. It streamed from her as if she were a beacon. She searched for words, but her tongue felt thick and awkward.

Finally, she managed, "Is this right?"

"Couldn't be righter," Krae and Llyr said almost in unison.

Laughter bubbled from a well deep in Jenna, and the thousands of changelings surrounding her began to chant. She picked up the unfamiliar words, repeated them, and felt her power intensify a hundredfold, then a thousand.

She spread her arms wide. "I'm Superwoman."

"Except you're real, and she wasn't." Krae grinned. "We did what we needed. You're much stronger than you know."

"What happens next?" Jenna batted at the light streaming off her. Maybe she wasn't really Superwoman, but she sure felt like her. Like she could conquer worlds without breaking a sweat.

Watch it, a sober inner voice cautioned. *Hubris will get me into trouble. I may have a pisspot of power, but my ability to make it do anything has yet to be proven.*

Krae narrowed her eyes to slits. "Wise thoughts, witchy-girl. Hang onto them once the battle begins."

"I'll do my best. What happens next?" Jenna repeated her question.

"We withdraw our power, now that we're confident you can funnel it, and then we return to Ronin's for a war council."

KIERNAN PACED from one side of the large meeting room on the first floor of Ronin's manor house to the other. Ronin was outlining their options, but the twenty Sidhe ranged about the room were talking among themselves rather than listening. Working together had never been a strength. One of the byproducts of immortality was everyone was certain they knew best.

Collaboration be damned.

He wondered where Titania and Oberon were. Surely they were listening from some nearby vantage point, but they wouldn't interfere unless something particularly interested them—or they became annoyed by the endless discussion.

Roz and Colleen sat straight in chairs near the front of the room. Unlike the others, their attention was focused on Ronin. The first of today's arguments had been over whether the witches could even be part of a Sidhe strategy session, but they'd refused to leave, and no one wanted to raise power against Ronin's and Duncan's wives.

Duncan got to his feet. "I wouldn't interrupt, but—"

"What?" Ronin skewered him with his blue gaze. If looks could kill, Duncan would be on his way to the *Dreaming,* a place Sidhe who were tired of immortality retreated to when they couldn't face another day of seeing the same faces and doing the same things.

"Are we going to include the Unseelie Court?"

A hiss rose from every corner of the room, gathering in intensity. Duncan squared his shoulders, and a determined look blossomed on his face.

"Is that your recommendation?" Ronin kept his voice carefully neutral.

"Yes." Duncan tilted his chin defiantly. "It should be yours too, given they fought side by side with us on the borderworld. And proved instrumental in us winning the day."

Breath whistled from between Kiernan's clenched jaws. Once the dark and light halves of Faerie had been one, but all that changed millennia ago, replaced by a deep and abiding enmity. While he'd known that an Unseelie couple had helped Duncan and Ronin and the witches, he hadn't considered the implications of stepping beyond eons of distrust.

After a brief internal battle, Kiernan strode to Duncan's side and faced Ronin. "This is everyone's war. If the demons win, we'll be forced to retreat to a borderworld, right along with the Unseelie. No one can even remember why we shunned them, so I agree with Duncan."

Ronin's wife sprang to her feet, her long dark hair eddying in waves around her, and turned to face the room. "I promised Ronin I'd keep my mouth shut," Roz said in a loud, carrying voice, "but that's not my style. Humans can't run away to the borderworlds like you can. They aren't immortal, either." She crossed her arms over her chest and planted her booted feet shoulder-width apart. "I've spent my entire adult life fighting demons so humans could remain on Earth."

Colleen bolted upright, joined Roz, and said, "Decisions we make today impact everyone. I won't let you forget the humans, either. From what I've seen, the Unseelie are damned helpful. Besides, the dream guardian was quite clear about light and dark fae mending their broken bridges. Whatever went wrong between you was a long time ago. I say you bury the hatchet and—"

A Sidhe warrior with his black hair braided in Celtic warrior style surged to his feet and pointed a finger at Colleen and Roz. "You have no right here," he growled. "This is why we don't marry outside our bloodlines."

The air near Ronin developed a shimmery quality, and Oberon stepped through, followed by Titania. Kiernan pressed his lips together to smother a grin. Apparently the king and queen of Faerie had heard quite enough. And were even closer than he'd figured they were.

"My lieges." Ronin half bowed, but no one else did.

Oberon's discerning amber gaze swept the room before settling on Ronin. "At least you acknowledge me." He smoothed his black robes into place and tightened his red silk sash. Golden hair hung loose to the middle of his back, and a slender crown circled his head.

Silence thickened, but the witches remained on their feet. Kiernan gave them credit for boldness. He decided to set a good example and inclined his head toward Oberon. "It is good to see you again, my liege. You were absent for many years."

"At least you noticed." Oberon's eyes glittered menacingly. "Notice also that I am back and intend to remain here."

Titania stepped forward and linked arms with Oberon. Her ice-blue eyes were serious, and her long, silvery hair was held back by jeweled clips. A gossamer gown of mostly jewels swirled about her long, lean form. "We have discussed the Unseelie—" she paused for effect, but she didn't need to since all the side conversations had died to nothing "—and we agree with Duncan, Kiernan, and the witches. It is long past time to come back together as a people."

The dark-haired warrior sputtered something incomprehensible. The air about him developed a multi-colored aspect, and he vanished. Titania stared at the space he'd been standing in. "If any of the rest of you feel as Locar does, this is as good a time as any for you to leave. Of course, you'll be branded a traitor and cut off from other Sidhe—forever. Likely Locar knows that."

Ronin stepped into the breach. "You heard our queen. If any of you cannot fight side by side with our Unseelie kin, leave now. What Duncan's wife said about the dream guardian's edict was accurate. His exact words were, 'I am encouraged the two halves of Faerie have found common ground. You will do whatever you must to ensure the animosity between you stops now.'"

No one moved, which surprised Kiernan. Given free rein, many Sidhe would side with Locar, but apparently no one in this room. "What about the dark fae?" he asked. "No doubt they'll have their own set of difficulties accepting us."

Ronin shrugged. "That's their problem. I have enough of our own to keep me busy."

"If we're going to include them, allow me to link to Sperrin and Moire, Unseelie who've helped us in the past," Duncan said and motioned to his wife to sit, but she shook her head.

Tristan spoke from a corner where he'd taken up residence. "I'd be glad to smooth those waters any way I can. I never understood why our people hated one another so."

"Fine." Ronin pointed at Tristan and Duncan. "Go wherever you have to and bring some Unseelie military tacticians back here."

"We'll request their presence," Duncan murmured. "No point in doing anything to make them feel even less kindly disposed toward us than they already are."

"Ever the diplomat. If they won't come here, we'll go to them." Ronin made shooing motions with both hands. "Get moving. There's not much point in going over everything twice. We'll reconvene once we have a full contingent."

"I hear and obey." Duncan walked briskly to Tristan's side. The air around them thickened, and the pair vanished.

"If I had any idea how little respect I'd get when you stuck me with this job," Ronin grumbled at Oberon, "I wouldn't have been so quick to accept."

Oberon ignored him and rubbed his hands together. "Brilliant. Means there's time for a meal."

"As I recall, the chef here is excellent," Titania chimed in. She latched a hand around Oberon's arm. "Shall we?"

"After you, my dear." Oberon escorted her out of the room.

Kiernan glanced at an antique grandfather clock. It was closing on noon, which was when Krae had promised to have Jenna back and bring her own set of decision-makers along. Maybe for once, things would proceed smoothly.

"The changelings should be here soon," he noted just to make certain Ronin remembered.

"Actually, we're already here," Krae's voice sounded from behind him. Kiernan twirled in time to see her take form. A dozen other changelings followed. Krae grinned broadly. "It's instructive listening from the sidelines."

"You should have made your presence known," Ronin gritted from behind what sounded like clenched teeth. "It's rude to eavesdrop."

Krae shrugged. "Since when are we bound by your social constraints?"

"Never mind about that. Where's Jenna?" Roz demanded, her brows drawn together like a thundercloud.

"Right here, sweetie." Jenna tumbled into the room, obviously having teleported, and leapt to her feet.

"Good thing," Roz muttered. "If they'd harmed so much as your little finger—"

Jenna held up both hands. "They didn't. I'm fine. More than fine, actually."

Kiernan had already figured that out. His breath caught in his throat, and desire exploded throughout his body. Jenna looked like a goddess. She glowed with an inner light that stole his breath. Before he could stop himself, he trotted to her side and murmured, "You must be starving. Let me find you some food. Duncan and Tristan have gone off to invite an Unseelie contingent to our war council, and it will be at least an hour or two before we reconvene."

"I thought you Sidhe didn't care much for them." Jenna frowned, clearly seeking understanding.

"Oberon and Titania showed up."

"Got it. I recall them warming somewhat to the concept of reintegrating dark fae into Faerie before Roz and Ronin's wedding. Or maybe it was during."

Ronin screwed his mouth into a wry grin. "If you were to ask the Unseelie, they'd tell you they represent the true Faerie, and we're the interlopers. How about something to eat?"

"That would be wonderful," she said. "I know it's early yet, but maybe a glass of whiskey would go well too. I didn't get any sleep last night."

Didn't get any sleep.

Did that mean she'd spent the night with Tristan? Jealousy sent a white-hot knife through Kiernan's soul, but it also reminded him the other Sidhe had first claim to this woman.

"You told me noon," Krae said in a reproachful tone that pulled him back into the moment.

"Did you need more time?" Kiernan latched gazes and sparred with her unsettling green eyes.

The changeling's expressive face dissolved into a grin. "As it happens, Sidhe-man, no. We're good."

He exhaled and turned to Jenna. Her eyes sparkled with wonder, much as they had the previous day when he'd unlocked her magic for her. "Ready?"

She nodded. "More than ready. Lead out."

CHAPTER 8

Kiernan waged an internal battle as they made their way to the kitchens. He wanted Jenna with an intensity verging on fanaticism. Every nerve, every cell, yearned to draw her close, crush her against him, and never let go. But he couldn't because of Tristan, who'd actually had time to get to know the witch and clearly adored her.

I have no idea how she feels about him. Or me, for that fact.

He tugged the raw edges of his emotions together. They faced enormous problems: a war that could annihilate life on Earth and make it impossible for anyone but Hell's minions to live there. If he could just hang onto that thought, maybe he could avoid making a total ass out of himself. He cleared his throat and held the swinging kitchen door open for Jenna. "Tell me what the changelings wanted with you."

"Let's get our food first. Between here and there, I'll try to come up with a coherent order to talk about what happened. To be honest, it's so unbelievable, I'm having trouble pigeonholing it myself." She gestured toward the stove. "Is there always food ready to serve?"

"Pretty much."

She dished a few things onto a plate. "Who cooks?"

"I'm not sure. Most of us use a combination of magic and humans who are sworn to loyalty and know how to be mostly invisible. Ronin employs a chef and sous-chef, but I've never seen either of them."

"Where do you suppose Titania and Oberon are?" Jenna sliced butter and placed it next to the bread on her plate.

He shrugged. "They were at the meeting before you got there. It's anyone's guess where they are now, but I suspect they helped themselves to food and then retired to one of the upstairs rooms where they wouldn't be disturbed."

"Not overly social, huh?" Jenna carried her plate through to a small dining area, set it down, and started out the door.

"You could say that." Kiernan followed her and slapped his plate down on the table she'd chosen. "Can I help you find anything?"

"I'm headed for the liquor." She laughed with a self-conscious edge. "I know where it is. Can I bring some back for you?"

"Mead." He stared after her retreating form and added, "You seem to know your way around pretty well."

She turned just before the doorway and smiled. "Not really, but this is the same as last night when I had a late dinner with Tristan."

Because she left right after she'd spoken, hopefully she didn't see the expression that had to be stamped on his face. Kiernan grimaced and summoned another calming spell. He would not let her know how eaten-up with jealousy he was, and he also refused to question her about her time with his friend and fellow Sidhe warrior.

He forced himself to sit and fold a napkin across his lap. By the time Jenna returned, he'd taken a couple of bites, chewed, and swallowed. The food could have been sawdust, and he was grateful he hadn't loaded his plate. Getting through what was on it wouldn't be easy.

"Here we go," she trilled and set down two bottles and two glasses. She twisted the cork out of the whiskey bottle, poured a jot into her glass, and quirked a brow. "I'd like to propose a toast to victory, but I need someone to drink with."

"Sorry. Of course." He picked up the mead bottle, his fingers clumsy with opening it, and poured amber liquid into his glass. "Cheers." He raised his glass her way.

She settled into her seat, her glass still in one hand. "This calls for far more than *cheers*." She clinked her glass against his. "Here's to victory against the demons, now and forever. We'll never kill all of them, but we can reduce them to something manageable."

"Victory. Now and forever," he echoed and drank.

Jenna drained half her glass, looked longingly at it, but then picked up a fork. "Food first," she murmured.

Kiernan grinned. "Have spirits been a bit of a downfall?"

"At times." She swallowed a couple of bites from her plate. "Mostly when I'm tired. Booze is such a good pick-me-up, I could settle in with it and skip eating, but that isn't what my body needs."

He gave her time to eat before he asked, "Are you going to tell me what happened?"

She looked up from a mostly empty plate and snorted. "Oh my God, I inhaled that. Shame on me for skipping breakfast, but I didn't have any choice."

"You're avoiding my question."

"I suppose I am." She poured more whiskey into her empty glass. "The short version is I'm like some sort of psychic lightning rod. The changelings pour power into me, and it intensifies their magic—and my own."

Kiernan narrowed his eyes. "I've heard of such things. We have power sources we leverage in similar ways. Were you frightened?"

"Terrified, but I couldn't tell that enormous group of changelings I was leaving after they disclosed some seer's prophecy about me. It was obvious they believed it to the marrow of their bones. The look in their eyes…" Her voice trailed off.

"Did they force you?" Kiernan balled his hands into fists where they lay in his lap.

"Not at all." She glanced at her plate and seemed to be gathering her thoughts. When she finally looked at him again, she said, "I'll tell you the same thing I told the changelings. I spent my whole life thinking I was Jenna the incompetent witch—"

"And how long is that?" he cut in.

A corner of her mouth quivered into half a grin. "It's not polite to ask a woman her age. Witches live for hundreds of years, but we're far from immortal. Anyway, my sense of who I am has turned catawampus. It will take time for me to redevelop my equilibrium."

She looked so vulnerable and so beautiful, he reached across the table and covered her hand with his own. Consequences be damned! "It's a lot to take in," he agreed.

"You're not kidding." She didn't pull her hand from beneath his. "I was just trying to come to terms with the work you and I and Krae did when this whole new wrinkle showed up."

He smiled. "I'd say it's a lot more than a *wrinkle*, more like a total game-changer."

Jenna rolled her eyes. "For some reason, it seems odd to me whenever one of you uses modern phraseology."

"Why?" He swirled his fingertips across the back of her hand. Touching her had an electric effect on him. "If we still spoke Old English, or even Middle English, we'd never blend in anywhere."

"I suppose that's so, but to me you're storybook characters fresh out of legend."

"I suppose you're waiting for me to don armor, grab up my sword—that of course has a name—and whistle for my horse."

She giggled. "Something like that."

"Tell me more about what it felt like to channel changeling magic."

She drew her brows together and captured her lower lip between her teeth. "I'm not sure I can answer that. Once I got past my initial terror, it was the most affirming experience I've ever had. This will sound crazy, but I felt linked to the universe, like I could do anything."

Kiernan opened his mouth to lecture her about not taking chances, especially with a new power source she had limited experience with, but he snapped it shut. Events were barreling forward at breakneck speed. More than anything, Jenna needed to believe in herself.

A soft smile intensified her beauty, and she asked, "What? You looked as if you were about to say something."

"I was, but I changed my mind." He got to his feet. "Would you like to walk a little? We'll be sitting for a long time after the Unseelie arrive—unless someone has a temper tantrum."

"Surely no one would raise magic against Sperrin and Moire." Jenna cast a worried look his way.

"I'm not sure which of the dark fae will come, but regardless of who shows up, I wouldn't bet on my kin all making nice." Kiernan blew out a breath. "We can be a bloodthirsty lot and stiff-necked and unforgiving to boot." He held out a hand. "I don't want to get lost in what-ifs that have yet to occur. How about that walk?"

"I'd love to." She took his extended hand and stood. Color bloomed on her cheeks after she touched him, and hope flamed in his heart. Driven by need so profound it overshadowed everything, he closed the distance between them and crushed his mouth over hers.

WHEN KIERNAN LAID his hand over hers, Jenna's heart danced in a crazy little spinning beat. She dropped her gaze and hoped to hell her cheeks didn't turn into red geraniums like they always did when she was thrilled by something. She'd managed to hide her elation at him being there after she returned to Ronin's. And when he'd suggested a meal, she nearly had a coronary. Adopting a calculated nonchalance had taken more than a jot of magic, studiously applied. She tried to tell herself he was just being kind, but in the deepest recesses of her soul, she hoped against hope it was more than that.

And now he was kissing her. Really kissing her like she meant everything to him. His arms went around her, and he cradled her against him as his mouth did wild things to hers. She opened herself to his kiss, and he sank his tongue inside, tasting spicy from the mead he'd drunk. Jenna threaded her arms around him. She'd planned to keep her hands above his waist, but they had a mind of their own. Before she knew it, she had his high, firm butt cheeks in a death grip and pulled his body hard against hers. The length of his erection tantalized her where it was sandwiched between their bodies, and her breath quickened. The temptation to simply push her pants down and bend over one of the tables was overpowering.

"Ahem!"

Jenna started at the voice and jerked away from Kiernan, who looked equally startled. When she turned to see who'd interrupted them, Colleen and Roz burst out laughing. Moments later, Jenna joined them.

When she could talk again, she choked out, "I should kill you two," between chortles.

"Really?" Roz sounded the soul of innocence.

Colleen turned to Roz and crossed her arms under her breasts. "Why on earth would she want to harm us? Her sisters in crime and all that rot."

"We want to know what happened with the changelings," Roz said.

"Yeah, we asked Krae, and she was surprisingly close-mouthed," Colleen added.

"How about if I catch up with you later?" Jenna grinned. "Kiernan and I were about to take a walk."

"It really looked like you were, um, *walking*," Roz observed in a deadpan way that only she could have pulled off.

"We were getting around to it," Jenna informed her roguishly.

Kiernan bowed with a flourish. "If you ladies will excuse us."

"None of us are ladies." Colleen winked "We'll take a raincheck, but we expect our pound of flesh soon, Jenna."

"Take five." Jenna laughed. "I could stand to lose thirty."

"Come on." Roz hooked an arm through Colleen's. "I'm starving."

Jenna blew a kiss after their retreating backs and walked toward a door that looked as if it led into an arboretum.

"It must be wonderful to have friends like that," Kiernan observed from a few feet behind her.

Jenna turned, surprised. "But Sidhe live forever. Surely, you—"

He shook his head. "Uh-uh. We develop a tolerance for one another, but we rarely banter back and forth like the three of you were just doing. Come this way." He beckoned. "There are always greenhouse flowers, even in the dead of winter."

Jenna trotted after him. "But I've heard Duncan and Ronin joking with Colleen and Roz. Hell, they've teased me."

"That's because you welcome it. Sidhe are a deucedly solemn lot. We take ourselves far too seriously." He pushed open a glass door, and the scents of green, growing things filled her nostrils. She inhaled deeply, breathing in the clean smell of herbs and flowers, and walked inside.

"It's lovely in here." Jenna turned a full circle, gazing at a riot of color. "Thanks for bringing me. I'm not sure I agree about Sidhe being dour. Look at Oberon. He's a hoot. I remember him cracking jokes at Roz and Ronin's wedding."

"Maybe things will shift now that he's back. Titania became downright bitter these past few hundred years."

Jenna snorted. "I don't blame her. It's a long time to warm an empty bed." Her hand flew to her mouth. "Oops! Probably shouldn't have been quite so graphic. Me and my big mouth."

"I quite like your mouth." He traced its outline with an outstretched finger.

Before she got lost in his overpowering maleness again, Jenna took a step back. "Maybe it was a good thing we were interrupted back there."

"Why's that?" He cradled the side of her face. "If you don't want to be touched, you'll need to put more distance than this between us."

"Please." She pulled his hand away from her. "This isn't easy for me. I'm attracted to you. It would be really easy to drag you into a corner and…and…" Heat rose from her chest and swooshed over the top of her head, and she knew she was blushing furiously.

"And what?" His blue-green eyes ignited into twin fires.

She tried to look away, and her gaze landed on the tented front of his trousers. Her throat went dry, and her pussy flooded. She wanted that cock, wanted to see it and touch it and taste it.

"Mmm-hmm. I feel the same way about your woman's parts," he rasped, his voice thick with need.

"Awk! You were in my head." She did put a few feet between them this time. "Don't do that."

"Why not? It's instructive."

"You heard Ronin get after Krae earlier. It's also rude and inconsiderate." Jenna lassoed her overheated libido and packaged it up. "What I didn't quite get through saying earlier is I have to figure out who I am. I'm not the same woman I was when I got on that airplane for London. Until I manage that, I will not let my body get the better of me. And I will not make any promises I can't keep."

"Who says I want promises?" His eyes darkened to midnight. "If you were immortal, you'd discover they're overrated. No one can keep their word forever."

Jenna swallowed hard. "I don't know what you want... Well, maybe I do, but that's beside the point. I just told you what I need, and that's space until I sort out how to deal with the magic I just discovered I have." She straightened her spine and tilted her chin. "You were extremely helpful the other day when we worked with Krae. I'd be grateful for more help harnessing my power. I'm smart enough to realize I have a different problem now, magic that's potent enough to get away from me. Before I never had enough. Now I have too much."

He half bowed. "As you will, Miss Jenna. There's no such thing as too much magic, though."

She'd expected him to launch an argument about why she should reconsider his kisses and sexual attention. That he didn't go there gave her pause. Maybe he came on to every new woman, giving her the once over, but if they were too difficult to bed, he went in search of easier pickings. She raked a hand through her hair. "I'm not sure what kind of time we'll have left to practice."

"Neither am I, but we'll make the most of whatever opportunities arise. Feel free to wander among the blossoms. You'll find them soothing."

She started to thank him, but he vanished. No shimmery air, no rush of magic. One moment he was there, and the next he wasn't. Jenna walked to the spot where he'd stood and inhaled hungrily. The air smelled like him, and she kicked herself for being a fool. She'd turned down two perfectly good offers for sex in a very short time. It was some kind of record, at least for her. Since she didn't often find willing men, she grabbed them up before they could change their minds.

"What the fuck is wrong with me?" she muttered, taking a few steps in one direction but circling back to where Kiernan had been. "If the world's really going to end, why not go for the gusto?"

You know why not, her inner voice answered. *It's because I don't want to hurt Tristan.*

Jenna hung her head, feeling ashamed despite not having actually done anything beyond one heated kiss. If Tristan found out, and he very well might, he'd be stunned—and crushed. She'd felt that way enough, the last thing she wanted to do was spurn a man who cared for her.

Crap! What a fucking mess this has turned into.

"Indeed." Krae morphed into being a few feet away.

Jenna rolled her eyes. "Do not tell me you overheard that."

"Every word."

Jenna lunged for the changeling. "I should throttle you."

"But you won't," Krae said and sidestepped her neatly.

"Humph. I suppose you have advice for me too."

Krae crossed her arms over her chest. "As it so happens, I do. But you already know what it is. Now is the time to figure out your magic and give the Irichna everything you've got. If—and that's a pretty big word right now—you're still alive at the other side of things, then you can sort out your love life."

Jenna narrowed her eyes. "Do you know which of them I might end up with?"

"Of course." The changeling shot a knowing leer her way. "What was that phrase that was just in your head? Something like *go for the gusto?* I'd say it's relevant here."

Krae's expression told Jenna that she wouldn't say anything further, but she made a come-along gesture with two fingers anyway. "Aw, come on, sweetie. Fellow woman and all that."

"Nope. This is one puzzle you'll have to work out on your own."

"I don't suppose they could share me." Jenna arched an inquisitive brow.

"What do you think?"

"I honestly don't know. My first guess is they'd tear one another limb from limb before they'd let that happen. But they may pair up in other than twosomes. Sidhe mores weren't part of the syllabus when I studied ancient history."

"Smart witch." Krae grinned. "There are threesomes—and even moresomes—in Sidhe-land. They're surprisingly modern."

"Except it isn't particularly modern," Jenna pointed out. "The Greeks and Romans were omni-sexual."

"Thanks for the history lesson." Krae snorted. "I actually remember when the big push toward one man-one woman began. It was when Europe was emerging from the Middle Ages."

Jenna eyed the changeling. "So, do your kin, um, do the multiple partner thing?"

"Quite the indelicate question." Krae leaned close and lowered her voice to a conspiratorial whisper. "Of course we do. We have boys who like boys, girls who like girls, and groups that form. It's one of the reasons the Church banished us to the hills and barrows shortly after their power consolidated."

"There you are!" Niall shambled down one of the greenhouse rows. Jenna had no idea where he'd come from and assumed he'd been listening from a convenient hiding place until the conversation bored him. "The Unseelie are here, and we're about to begin."

"How long ago did Colleen send you to find us?" Jenna asked.

The changeling shrugged. "Never was much good at time, but we do need to get moving."

"So how long were you listening?" she persisted.

"Please." Niall sounded pained. "Would I—"

"Yes," she cut in. "Goddess preserve me from changelings. You all fancy yourselves miniature James Bonds." Jenna tossed her head. In a burst of frivolity, she plucked a shaded pink rose from its bush, stuck it behind one ear—ignoring its thorns—and stalked out of the greenhouse.

CHAPTER 9

"Carmen I presume?" Ronin inquired dryly after Jenna swept into the meeting room. It was large and airy with leather easy chairs arranged across the back and in the corners, and chairs and tables placed in rows, classroom style, taking up the center of the room. Floor-to-ceiling, leaded glass windows looked out onto verdant, rain-soaked lawns scattered with ornamental shrubs and trees. Priceless paintings and sculptures graced the walls and tables, and the floor was covered with thick, Aubusson rugs.

Jenna mimed a sweeping bow. "The operatic effect would be more dramatic if I had skirts, but you get the idea."

"Wouldna she need a red rose to play Carmen?" A tall, graceful woman in a skintight black jumpsuit walked forward. Her shoulder-length black hair framed tilted green eyes. "Nice to see you again, dear," she told Jenna.

"You too, Moire." Jenna hugged her, glad to see the Unseelie again. "Is Sperrin here?"

"Of course. And a few more of us. Six in all."

Sperrin detached himself from a group of people she didn't

know. He was garbed in his usual black robes, sashed in teal this time, and his smoke-gray gaze sought hers. "Ye're looking well." He shook his unbound dark hair over his shoulders. "I heard what happened on your flight over here."

A corner of her mouth twisted into half a grimace. "Guess it's a good thing I can teleport now. No more airlines for me."

He raised a brow. "The traveling ether does tend to be safer, but not always."

Jenna nodded and looked away, remembering how a friend of hers who headed up the Witches' Northwest Coven had been trapped there, along with three of her witches.

Nowhere is truly safe anymore...

"Jenna!" Tristan loped toward her from a corner of the room and took her arm. "I've saved you a seat near me."

Nonplussed by his sudden appearance, Jenna searched the room and found Roz and Colleen toward the back, deep in conversation with Niall and a few other changelings. "Thanks," she flashed Tristan an uncomfortable smile, "but I think it would be better if I was close to them." She pointed toward her sister witches. "If there are decisions to be made, we need to be near enough to talk."

"Of course." Tristan squeezed her arm, the warmth from his hand compelling. "I wasn't thinking. Perhaps we can manage a meal once the meeting ends." He rolled his silver eyes. "Hopefully, it won't last till the wee hours. I don't know about you—" he bent close to her ear and lowered his voice "—but I didn't get much sleep last night." He pressed his lips against her ear and kissed her lightly before walking back the way he'd come.

Her skin tingled from his touch, and the fine hairs on the back of her neck prickled as if she were being watched. Without looking, she knew Kiernan had observed the exchange. Jenna clamped her jaws together and hastened toward Roz and Colleen. "Hey!" she said breezily once she got close.

"Hey yourself." Roz turned her penetrating dark gaze on Jenna.

"Hey, indeed." Colleen joined the staring party. "Well?" she cocked her head to one side.

"Yeah." Roz grinned. "We want to hear everything. The X-rated version."

Jenna's face heated. "Not here with all these people," she hissed.

"It's not like you'd have to name names or anything." Colleen slanted a lewd look her way.

Jenna switched to telepathic speech. *"Can it, both of you. I'd love to talk. In fact, I need to, but not until we're alone, and I can ward what we say."*

"Sounds serious." Roz dropped her bantering tone.

"Whatever you need, hon." Colleen hugged her.

"Attention, everyone. Now!" Oberon cried with his unmistakable bass voice. Conversation died, and Jenna folded her body into a surprisingly comfortable straight back chair, flanked by Roz and Colleen.

She gazed about the room, most of which was in front of her. Oberon and Titania faced the assembled group. Jenna counted about twenty-five Sidhe, six Unseelie—though she was only positive about Sperrin and Moire, she assumed the group around them were also dark fae—and a dozen changelings. The few folk seated in the last row of chairs behind her were presumably Sidhe, since Tristan had faded in that direction. She couldn't see Kiernan, which meant he had to be behind her too, not a comfortable thought. If she stretched a thin band of magic, she was almost certain she could feel his energy, feral and demanding, pulsing against her back.

She tightened her mouth into a firm line to drive thoughts of anything but today's proceedings from her head, but images of the two Sidhe dogged her. Tristan was kind and sweet and cared for her. Kiernan wasn't any of the above. Despite his good looks, he was dark and dangerous, and just thinking about him made her belly flutter and her crotch wet.

What the fuck is the matter with me? Until yesterday, I wanted Tristan like that. Now I want them both. Am I really such a fickle bitch?

She bit down on her lower lip. If she was, she had no right spending time with either man. None at all—until she got her priorities straight. She focused on Oberon, who'd already started talking, and hoped she hadn't missed anything important.

"...and so today marks a critical juncture. It's the day we swallow our misplaced pride and welcome our brethren back by our side."

"Yes!" Titania's clear voice rang out. "We are one people from this moment forward, just as we once were, and we welcome royalty, and all others, from the Unseelie Court."

"We're as close as ye'll get to royalty." Sperrin rose to his feet along with Moire, and they walked to the front of the room.

Though Oberon tried to mask it, a surprised expression formed. "What? You never raised kings and queens of your own?"

Moire turned to face him. "We saw what mayhem the two of you created and decided we couldna run the risk."

The corners of Oberon's mouth twitched. "Touché, my dear."

Sperrin straightened, his gray eyes solemn. "Levity aside, know that we bow to no one, not even the King and Queen of Faerie. We discovered we got along fine without titled royalty."

Oberon did laugh then, long and loud. When he had himself under control, he snorted. "Join the crowd, son. No one else pays us the slightest attention, either."

The tense set of Sperrin's spine softened, and Moire grinned. "Brilliant." She clasped her hands together in front of her. "Shall we proceed?"

"Excellent idea." Titania smiled, and for once she looked warm rather than forbidding. She nodded toward Ronin. "Your turn."

Ronin rolled his eyes. "Ah yes, leader of the Sidhe and all that."

He crooked a finger at Sperrin. "I have a capital idea. Shall we share this burden?"

"I'd be honored." Sperrin found his way to Ronin's side. "'Tis not as if it's been smooth sailing among our people. Many of them doona trust you."

"It's the same on this side," Ronin said. "We're excommunicating those who don't wish to fight alongside their erstwhile kin."

Sperrin furled his brows. "Draconian."

"Yes," Ronin narrowed his eyes, "but effective. On to the topic at hand. We've been damned lucky the Irichna have left us alone long enough to conduct this meeting."

"Agreed." Sperrin frowned. "It is suspect. Any idea what they have up their sleeves?"

Krae bounded to her feet. "They were massing to attack, but something may have happened, and I think they're running scared."

"You wouldn't have said that if you'd been in the field with us," Tristan noted dryly. "They didn't look scared to me."

Jenna exchanged glances with Roz and Colleen and got to her feet. "May I have permission to speak?"

Ronin snorted. "So polite. No one else asks. Certainly, dive in."

"We—" Jenna gestured at Roz and Colleen "—have found it's a waste of time to try to second guess Irichna. Instead, we develop a couple of game plans and deploy the one that fits best when the demons show up. Despite all the years we've fought them, we've never been able to predict their strategy with any level of accuracy."

"Well spoken," Moire said and shot a meaningful glance at her mate.

Sperrin cleared his throat. "Here's what we came up with, but first, how many of you, er maybe that would be us now, have been injected with the witches' blood to resume demon-stalking ability?"

"Fifteen." Duncan spoke from his seat in the front row. "It's going better than I'd hoped. They should be capable of ferrying demons to the Ninth Circle in another twelve to fifteen hours."

"How can you be sure?" Ronin asked. Duncan coughed but didn't answer. "Talk," Ronin urged, his tone sharp. "I suspected you were up to something."

Jenna snuck a peek at Colleen and saw her color. She sat back down, nudged the other witch, and whispered, "Do you know what's going on?" Colleen nodded but placed a finger over her mouth.

"All right." Duncan blew out an audible breath. "We have an Irichna held captive in one of the lower dungeons, swathed in layers of spells to mask its presence. The group who were in the field brought it back here."

"Gives you something to practice on, eh?" Sperrin looked pleased.

"Why didn't you say anything?" Ronin asked as his gaze swept the group. "Several of you had to be in on this."

"Duncan thought it best if we kept it to ourselves," Tristan said, "and I happened to agree. We didn't want anyone wandering down to the dungeon and doing away with our patsy."

"It's really hard to lead any of you when you keep secrets from me," Ronin said in a pained voice before turning to Sperrin. "I believe the ball was in your court. You'd requested information and were going to share strategies."

The dark fae bowed with a courtly flourish. "Doona feel bad. I have the same problem back home. No one tells me anything until their backs are against the proverbial wall. Our plan is both simple and quite bold. We think it best to teleport to the demons' primary borderworld. It will be easy to find since we were just there."

"We can set up an assembly line of sorts," Moire cut in. "We'll kill some by combining the dark and light magics of Faerie, others by corralling them and ferrying them to the Ninth Circle of Hell.

If we bring enough people, we should be able to pick that world clean in short order."

"But that's not all of them," Roz protested. "The dream guardian said so. Besides, didn't he block the paths out of their world so they couldn't leave?"

"He may have caged Irichna on their world, but nowhere did he forbid us to use the traveling ether to go there," Moire said.

"I'm not understanding exactly how that works." Jenna chewed on her lower lip. "Are you certain we'll be able to leave their world once we're done there?"

"Aye, quite sure," Sperrin replied. "Our energy is very different from demon emanations. Ye've no cause for concern that the dream guardian might mistake one of us for a demon attempting to flee."

"What about other Irichna?" Colleen asked, mirroring Roz's earlier concern. "The ones who aren't trapped on the borderworld."

"Not much we can do about them. But a direct hit to those on their primary borderworld will knock a significant hole in their powerbase," Sperrin said.

"Maybe one they'll never recover from," Titania mused.

"I like it." Oberon took a small step forward. "It beats being on the defensive all the time."

Jenna swallowed a snort; she'd said much the same thing after a major Irichna attack, amid the wreckage of Colleen's wedding at Witches' Northwest Coven headquarters. Then she'd been arguing it was smart for them to retreat to their home in Fairbanks to force the demons' hand. She shook her head. Irichna had attacked as predicted, but they'd been much smarter and better organized than before. It had nearly been the death of her, Roz, and Colleen when they'd been shanghaied and taken to the borderworld Sperrin just referred to.

"Penny for your thoughts," Tristan said into her ear. She started. She'd been so deep in thought, she hadn't heard him come up behind her. "I'm sorry, sweetheart. I didn't mean to startle you."

"It's okay." She half turned toward him. "We shouldn't be talking, the meeting's not over yet."

~

KIERNAN SANK LOWER in his easy chair in the very back of the room. It was a good vantage point and meant he didn't have to waste power watching his back. Even without a shred of magic deployed, he sensed Tristan's deep caring for Jenna—and her confusion. Part of what she said about needing to come to grips with the new version of herself held a great deal of truth, but he knew he was part of her problem too.

The attraction between them was so strong, it took most of his considerable self-discipline to not batter down her bedroom door and take her. When he took a few steps back and locked in the rational part of his mind, leaving his cock out of the equation, his weakness for her surprised him. His sexuality had always been fluid, and he'd enjoyed hundreds of women, maybe thousands, without becoming particularly attached to any of them. If one turned him down, there were always others willing to warm his bed.

On the whole, he preferred human females to Sidhe, and his favorite times had been when he and another Sidhe shared a woman—or two. There was so much more opportunity for creativity with more people involved. Maybe it was a corollary of living so long, but one-on-one sex had lost its allure hundreds of years before.

Until now, that is. He wanted Jenna as fiercely as he'd ever wanted any woman, and he vowed to have her somehow.

He laced his fingers together, only half-paying attention to the meeting. He'd do whatever the group decided, so he didn't need the blow-by-blow discussion of exactly how they'd proceed. He'd never been much of a military tactician, but it went with the territory. His primary gift was as a seer, which leant him an otherworldly quality so pronounced even the other Sidhe sometimes commented on it.

He gazed at Jenna's blonde hair hacked off at uneven levels and spilling down her broad shoulders. Desire knifed through him, and he clasped his hands together so hard the knuckles whitened. Despite wanting her so intensely it overwhelmed common sense, he really should leave her alone. She'd need all her concentration to focus her fledgling gifts. Feeling hamstrung between him and Tristan might divert her enough to spell disaster.

He'd never paired up with a Sidhe female because they were stuffy, full of themselves, and boring when you got right down to it. And he'd never seriously considered a human female mate—until now. Except Jenna wasn't exactly human. Regardless, it appeared Titania and Oberon had relaxed their stance against Sidhe-human pairings. Look at Duncan and Ronin, all cozily ensconced with witches of their own. A thought intruded that slapped his heart into double-time rhythm. Jenna was a modern woman. No reason she'd have to choose between him and Tristan. Hell's fire, she might enjoy two men worshipping her body. The thought, and imagery associated with it, brought his cock to full attention.

Kiernan reined in his overactive imagination. None of this addressed Tristan and his prior claim to the witch in question. Almost as if Tristan had read his thoughts, he left Jenna's side and took the chair next to Kiernan. He didn't say anything, just nodded pleasantly and turned his attention back to something Ronin and Sperrin were saying. They'd moved to drawing something out on a whiteboard. Little *X*s and *O*s that made Kiernan's head hurt. He nudged Tristan and whispered, "Do you understand all that formation mumbo-jumbo?"

"Most of it." The other Sidhe grinned. "Not your style, huh?"

"Nah. I'll just tag along and lend firepower."

"We'll take it." Tristan's low voice held a grim note. "I'm not at all certain Sperrin's idea will work. If it were me, I'd remain here and let them attack. At least we'd have the home court advantage then."

"You might be onto something. Jenna told me the minion that kidnapped them sapped her power. If it's that easy to drain us, we should be worried."

"Think I'll get a little closer to the front and float that point." Tristan patted Kiernan's shoulder, got to his feet, and strode forward.

Kiernan watched the swing of his hips as he walked. They'd been young men together about a thousand years ago, and as young men frequently did, they'd had a tryst or two where they shared women. The day had come when Tristan turned him down, and Kiernan understood the other Sidhe was hoping to establish a family of his own, but a traditional one. They'd never talked about it—because people didn't discuss such things back then—but Kiernan wondered what would have come out of a conversation where he suggested they form a permanent ménage with one or more women. If he'd been daring and taken the lead, would Tristan have been forthright enough to own up to similar leanings? Insofar as he knew, Tristan had never married, unless he had a human stashed somewhere and hadn't told anyone about her, which didn't seem likely.

As Kiernan recalled how they'd traded women back and forth, his hard-on amped up another notch. He blew out a breath and funneled magic toward his nether regions. He'd have to stand up sometime, and it wouldn't do to sport an obvious erection. Particularly in light of the seriousness of the conversation running through the assemblage.

Of course, he could always fade out of the room and take care of himself. Probably no one would even notice if he were gone for a few moments.

The longer he thought about it, the better his idea seemed.

And the magic that was supposed to calm him was having the opposite effect. With a spell well in hand, he teleported from his chair to a small storage room on the opposite side of the wall behind him. His cock throbbed with need, and he yanked the lacings of his old-fashioned breeches open to free himself.

It took an embarrassingly short time before semen pumped through his shaft and into a handkerchief he'd wrapped around himself. Gasping for breath, he pulled himself together and cleared his mind of the scene that had driven him to such an intense climax. He'd been with Jenna and Tristan, both watching them and joining in. She'd been laughing, having the time of her life, her skin rosy with passion as he and Tristan brought her to several orgasms with their mouths and fingers and cocks.

He shoved his still hard penis back into his pants, redid the fastenings, and balled his hands into fists. Part of him wanted to break every rule and scry his own future, but that would anger Danu beyond measure. She might be so furious, she'd refuse to help them against the Irichna. He chucked the soiled handkerchief into a nearby rubbish bin.

"I've got to get myself under control," he muttered and faded back into the meeting room, careful to use a minimal amount of power. No one so much as blinked. At least his absence hadn't been noticed.

Good. I have to keep things under wraps. The witches need our help. Jenna needs a clear head. By the goddess, I'll do whatever I have to do to see she has one.

Brave words, but would he be able to follow through on them? *I'd damn well better, or I deserve a turn in that dungeon right alongside the Irichna.*

His next thought rose unbidden. He and Tristan needed to talk. The other Sidhe was obviously falling in love with Jenna, and Kiernan wasn't far behind. Maybe the conversation he should have had with his friend many years ago wasn't as overdue as he feared.

I'm jumping the gun here. I have no idea how she'd feel about two of us.

Hell, I don't know how she feels about me—or him.

Kiernan smiled gamely. Never shy of confrontation, he figured he'd have the answers to all of his questions before the next sunrise.

CHAPTER 10

*J*enna stifled a yawn. The lack of any sleep at all the previous night was catching up to her, but at least the meeting was over, and they had a mostly-viable plan built on Sperrin's suggestion.

"My God but they're long-winded," Roz muttered. "Thank bloody Christ we're done here. A woman could grow old and starve to death."

Ronin made his way to them and held out a hand to Roz. "Ready for dinner, darling? I'm sorry that took so long."

"I was ready two hours ago." Roz got to her feet.

"Hold up there." Jenna stood too and smiled apologetically at Ronin. "I need a few minutes with Roz and Colleen."

"That's right," Colleen murmured. "I'd almost forgotten."

"How about if the three of us take a little walk?" Roz glanced out the window. "It's dark, but I think it finally stopped raining."

"That'd be great," Jenna said. "I'd love some fresh air. Let me grab a jacket, and I'll meet you guys next to the front door."

After a quick detour upstairs to discard the house slippers she'd donned after returning from working with the changelings, Jenna laced up her boots. She trotted back down the stairs and found Roz and Colleen waiting for her. They hadn't had to change shoes.

"I peeked outside. It's a lovely evening," Roz declared. "Not even that cold—especially compared with Alaska. Just a bit squishy underfoot."

"The whole U.K. could be described that way since it never stops raining. And you're spot on about nothing feeling particularly cold after Alaska." Colleen laughed and pulled the door open. "Shall we?"

The lush smell of damp greenery assailed Jenna, thicker and more pervasive than in the greenhouse. "Thanks. I know I'm taking you away from your husbands."

"What are friends for?" Roz nudged her. "Tell us about that hunk you were kissing when we stumbled across you in the dining room."

"I want to know too." Colleen's voice kindled with interest. "Even for a Sidhe, he upped the ante on raw sensuality. If I wasn't head over heels in love, I might give you a run for your money."

"He's scarcely mine." Jenna picked up the pace, and they walked around a series of bronze statues. "The problem is, I'm attracted to both of them. Kiernan and Tristan. Not just attracted. Hell, they're all I can think about."

"Ooooh." Roz let out a low whistle. "I guess I'm not understanding how that's a problem."

Inquisitive to her core, Colleen bent toward Jenna and asked, "Have you had sex with either one?"

"Let's just get down to brass tacks." A laugh bubbled from Jenna's throat. "It's one of the things I love about both of you."

"You didn't answer her," Roz noted.

"No," Colleen agreed, "she didn't, but that was a fairly elegant dodge."

Jenna ground to a halt and spun so she faced her friends. "No. All I've done is kiss them, but they both make me so hot I can barely breathe."

"Why'd you stop with kissing?" Roz asked, sounding genuinely curious.

"Because I have no fucking idea who I am right now." Jenna's voice took on a frantic note, and she muttered, "Sorry. Too much has happened in too short a time."

Colleen moved forward and hugged her. "You never really had a chance to tell us everything about all your new magic, either. Or what happened today with the changelings."

Roz jostled Colleen aside and hugged Jenna too. "Beyond that, we have to carve out some time to practice working together."

"I know," Jenna said and stepped back from Roz's embrace. "It's something like problem forty-three on my list."

"We can talk about that one inside," Colleen said. "Back to your guy issues, why not spend more time with each of them?"

"Yeah, no one says you have to pick a life partner in the next few days," Roz cut in.

"It feels…dishonest." Jenna spoke slowly. "I like both of them, so I should find a way to get everything out on the table. You know, let each of them know I'm drawn to them—and to someone else too." She inhaled thoughtfully. "I've been cheated on plenty, and it makes me feel like crap. I don't know. Maybe I'm making a mistake, but if I'm up-front and one of them tells me to go pound sand—" she tossed her hands skyward "—at least the problem will go away."

"Um, hon, it's possible both of them will pitch a fit," Colleen said.

"I agree," Roz chimed in. "If it were me, I'd keep my mouth shut until I'd at least had a taste of both of them. Maybe things will feel clearer."

"I don't think so." Jenna raked a hand through her hair, turned, and started walking again. "I'm so attracted to each man, I practically came just kissing them. That's not going to go away. Once we get our clothes off, the fire will only burn hotter."

"Do you think Sidhe might be into ménage?" Roz asked.

"Who knows?" Jenna shrugged. "Even if *they* are, these two particular Sidhe may not be. Hell, I don't know if I am. It feels complicated. I've never even figured out how to have a relationship with one guy. I'd be in deeply uncharted waters with two."

"Look at the possibilities." Roz was obviously on a roll. "One could be touching you while the other is fucking you."

Something about her tone caught Jenna's attention. "Have you ever...?" Her words trailed off since she couldn't frame her question tactfully.

"Uh-huh. It was incredible, at least while we were in bed. Getting along the rest of the time was impossible."

"That's what I'm afraid of," Jenna muttered. "How do you share and not be jealous?"

"Well, they're not exactly like us," Colleen ventured. "The longer I spend with Duncan, the better I understand that. They take much more of a long-range view, for one thing."

"Makes sense," Jenna said, "because they live forever."

"Let's turn around," Roz said. "I really am hungry." She latched a hand under Jenna's arm, and the trio started walking back. Light spilling through the manor house windows illuminated their way. "What do you want?"

Well, what do I want?

Jenna thought about Tristan's tawny good looks and silvery gaze and about Kiernan's dangerous alpha demeanor, with his black hair and ancient glacier eyes. "No matter which I choose, I'll feel like I'm missing something. Tristan only looks gentle on the surface. He's a warrior, and I watched him develop some great additions to the battle plan today."

"And Kiernan?" Colleen asked.

"He looks imposing and tough, but he has a dreamy, impractical side. I think it goes along with seer magic being primary and having spent so much time in trance states."

"Interesting," Colleen said.

"Indeed," Roz cut in. "They're different enough, it just might work."

"What do you mean?" Jenna asked.

Roz drew in a sharp breath. "If both of them were warriors, they'd probably fight over you because that's what warriors do."

"Ronin and Duncan are warriors," Jenna said. "Kiernan considers himself one, but I don't get that particular flash of energy off him. Not that he isn't courageous, but he was bored out of his skull by today's strategy discussion. I, um, listened in on a conversation he had with Tristan."

"Ronin struggles with the whole warrior thing," Roz said thoughtfully. "Oh, he's plenty brave, but he's only the Sidhe leader because he's able to keep chaos from devolving into total insanity."

"Duncan's ambivalent about his warrior aspect," Colleen spoke up, "but he'd never deny that part of himself."

"I guess I need to talk with Kiernan and Tristan," Jenna said, "before things go any further. I don't feel right about seeing both of them and not saying anything."

"It's going to take a delicate touch," Colleen cautioned.

"Maybe you should wait until after this next skirmish with the Irichna," Roz said. "We need you front and center with your magic right now. Speaking of that, how about we get together to practice at five tomorrow morning?"

Jenna groaned. "Awk. I didn't get any sleep last night."

"Well if you trundle up to bed as soon as we get inside, you'll be nice and fresh in the morning."

"Without any dinner?" Jenna turned stricken eyes toward her friend.

Roz shrugged. "Make up a plate and take it upstairs with you." She dusted her hands together.

"Yeah, that will only work so long as I don't run into either of the men on my way back and forth from the kitchen," Jenna grumbled.

"I'm game for an early morning practice," Colleen said and mounted the broad front steps leading into Ronin's home. She turned to face her friends. "Duncan will pitch a fit. He loves mornings for...other things."

"So?" Jenna grinned. "Get up at four."

"You can report in tomorrow morning." Roz winked lewdly. "Nothing like a bit of salacious description to spur a morning practice session to glory."

"You two are impossible." Colleen blew them a kiss and sprinted down the hallway, presumably to get something to eat.

"What'd you decide about dinner?" Roz asked.

"I'm skipping it." Jenna patted her hips. "I could miss a few meals, and I really am more sleepy than hungry."

"Sweet dreams, sugar." Roz gave her a quick hug. "Best of luck with your decision."

"Thanks." Jenna watched her friend wander the same way Colleen had gone and then started up the stairs. Out of all the advice she'd expected from her friends, the *pick both of them* option hadn't even occurred to her.

Can I even do that?

Though she worried it might make sleep elusive, Jenna mulled the question over as she made her way to her room. She needed a firm answer before she talked with either man.

Maybe Roz is right, and I should shelve the whole thing until after the battle.

Even if she is, I can at least think this thing through far enough to see if it's worth bringing up with Kiernan and Tristan. If I can't see myself with both of them, I may as well pack up my toys and go home.

"Tristan!" Kiernan called after his friend as they left the meeting room. "Got a minute?"

"Sure, but maybe not too many. I'm beat." When he turned to

face Kiernan, his eyes held a pinched look, and apprehension floated in their depths.

"Still worried, huh?"

Tristan looked from side to side, as if he didn't want to be overheard. A muscle twitched in his jaw, and he said, "Let's teleport into the underground chamber where we practice. It's the safest place I know to talk."

Kiernan summoned magic. From the looks of things, maybe this wasn't a good time to bring Jenna up. At least not before Tristan spoke his mind. They shimmered into being beneath Ronin's manor house. Tristan shambled to a chair and fell into it.

"What's wrong?" Kiernan pulled out a chair and positioned it so he sat opposite Tristan.

"What's right?" the other Sidhe countered. "We'll be fighting side by side with Unseelie. We don't trust them. They don't trust us. Oh yes, and did I mention we'll be doing this on the Irichnas' borderworld? If things go to hell there, and they could very quickly, the demons will mow through us like so much crabgrass."

"Why didn't you say more at the meeting?"

Tristan rolled his eyes. "What, and break up the Kumbaya, let's come together at the river, moment everyone else seemed to be having?"

"Sarcasm feels good, but it's not helpful."

"Probably not. I tried to talk sense into Ronin during one of the brief breaks we took, but he was full of conciliatory phrases. At the end, when I got more pointed, he told me détente with the Unseelie was a done deal because of the dream guardian, if nothing else." Tristan balled one hand into a fist and brought it down on a nearby table. "I understood that part. What I didn't get was why we're going to go running off to Irichna-land."

"You'd rather have our, um, maiden voyage with our kinsmen closer to home?"

"Exactly." Tristan blew out a pained breath. "Not much I can do about it but go along and be a good soldier, except I have a lot of bad feelings about this." His gaze snapped to Kiernan, and he narrowed his eyes to slits. "Have you scryed—"

"Yes, but nothing is clear."

"If you saw disaster, maybe you could make them see reason." Tristan spread his hands in front of him.

"Even if I wanted to look again, a spell like that—one that might actually clarify things—takes several days. There's not time."

"Fuck." Tristan scrubbed the heels of his hands down his face. "What did you want to talk about? Surely not battle strategy."

"No. That's about the last thing I'd ever want to discuss." Kiernan grinned wryly. "This probably isn't a good time. You're tired and upset and worried."

"Jenna's not doing very well, either." Tristan shook his head. "On top of everything else, I'm concerned about her. She's had a lot dumped in her lap since that minion targeted her on the airplane."

Kiernan scrunched his face into a frown, debating. Tristan had brought Jenna into the conversation, but was he in an open enough mental state to talk about sharing her? When he looked up, the other Sidhe was eyeing him with an odd look on his face.

"Whatever it is," Tristan growled, "spit it out. I'm too tired to work my way past your mental warding, but I'm quite skilled at reading expressions."

"I'd hoped for a more neutral backdrop, one where both of us are rational and rested—"

"Apparently this isn't a time for either of us to get what we want. Tell me what's in your head and do it soon, or I'm teleporting out of here. I haven't the energy to spar with you."

Kiernan sucked in a steadying breath. "All right. I want to talk about Jenna."

"What about her?" Tristan clamped his jaws together. "You want her too, I suppose?" He pounded the table again with his fist. "Christ, Kiernan, playboy of the western world, all you want to do is fuck her and break her heart. I can give her the life she's always dreamed of."

"That's not exactly what I had in mind." Kiernan kept his voice mild and smoothed the air between them with threads of a calming spell.

"What is?" Tristan got to his feet and stomped in front of Kiernan. "Fuck your goddamned spells. I don't want soothing—not from you."

"Hard as this may be for you to believe, I care about Jenna too. Probably more than is good for me. What I was going to suggest was we find a way to share her."

Tristan fell back a step. The expression on his face couldn't have been more shocked if someone had told him his long-lost mother had returned from the *Dreaming*. "H-have you discussed this with her?" He cleared his throat.

"No. I wanted to talk with you first." Kiernan got to his feet so they were looking right at one another. "I understand you laid claim to her first. No matter how I feel, if you make it clear I'd be an unwelcome addition to any plans you have with her, I'll go away."

"That doesn't sound like you. What do you have up your sleeve?" Tristan's tired eyes widened. "Have you bedded her?"

"No. Have you?"

"No." Tristan's mouth twisted into a wry grin. "Not for lack of trying. I could have pushed it last night, and she wouldn't have fought me, but I didn't want her that way."

"Understood. I feel the same way."

"Let me get this clear. You're proposing something like we used to have when we shared women, except you want it to be a permanent arrangement?" Once Kiernan nodded, Tristan continued, "What makes you think you'll stick with it? That you won't get bored, like you have with all your other women, and leave."

Kiernan tapped his breast. "Because she resonates in here for me. No one else ever has."

"If you're truly feeling that way, you wouldn't offer to step aside." Tristan shook his head. "Sorry, but that doesn't quite make sense to me."

"Me, either. I've never felt this way before."

"What if she's not interested in both of us?" Tristan furled a brow.

"Well then, I guess she'll have to choose." He rotated his shoulder blades to release the tension between them. "It's possible she might not want either of us."

"Too many variables." Tristan smiled tiredly.

Kiernan waited since he was certain Tristan wasn't done talking. Thank the goddess the other Sidhe seemed to have gotten past his anger.

"I need to sleep on this." Tristan pressed his lips together and thumped Kiernan's chest with his index finger. "Promise me you won't talk with Jenna about any of this until we've had a chance to discuss it further."

"Sure. That won't be a hard one to keep. I'd like to extract the same promise from you, though." Once Tristan nodded, Kiernan added, "I have a feeling we'll more than have our hands full in the next few days before we march out of here."

"We're not marching. We're teleporting to a borderworld. I wouldn't be nearly so frantic if we were marching, or even remaining anywhere on Earth." Tristan shook his head again. "Don't mind me. I'm beyond exhausted. What I really want is for us to wait for the goddess-damned demons to attack us." The air around him took on a numinous aspect, and he vanished.

Kiernan stared after him and wondered if tipping his hand had been a mistake. "It's too late to worry about that now," he muttered and summoned a spell to take him to his room.

CHAPTER 11

*J*enna tossed and turned. She even cast a soothing spell, but sleep was elusive. Behind her closed lids, Kiernan morphed into Tristan and then back to himself. Both men kissed her, folded her between their bodies and what felt like amazing cocks. Each whispered love words into her ear and reassured her they'd be together always—the three of them.

It can't be that easy. It just can't. Someone will get pissy or jealous or bitter. Worse, Titania or Oberon would surely put the kibosh on something outside the norm, since I'm not one of them...

Her red, aching eyes snapped open with the realization she *was* one of them, maybe not full-blooded, but enough to at least have a seat at the table. And if she got down to brass tacks, she had no idea what their cultural norms looked like. Krae had intimated the Sidhe formed trios and quads, right along with the changelings.

She flopped onto one side and closed her eyes. They felt gritty, like they were lined with ground glass. "I'm tired," she said into her pillow. "And confused and horny. I need rest, not all this crap that's keeping me awake." She thought about trooping downstairs for a bottle of whiskey, but drinking herself into oblivion was a bad call. What if Irichna showed up?

"*Blech.*" She pounded a pillow with her fist and chucked the other one across the room. It thumped against a wall and fell to the floor.

Her body ached, breasts heavy with need, and her clit throbbed relentlessly. More than anything, she wanted strong arms to hold her, and a brawny, sweaty male—or two—breathing desire into her. That would jar her mind out of its petty cycle of *what-ifs.*

She sucked in air and made a snuffling noise, almost like a pig hunting for mushrooms. The unexpected image yanked her back to her childhood when there were still lots of demon assassin witches, and taking care of Irichna was someone else's responsibility. One of her many aunts had traded in exotic herbs, plants, and other spell ingredients, and she relied on a small herd of pigs to nose out special medicinal and hallucinogenic plants. Jenna had apprenticed in her shop, and it was one of the main reasons she, Roz, and Colleen ran a similar establishment in Alaska.

"Ach, Christ! Pigs, mushrooms, and men. I'm losing it." She sat up in bed and stretched over her coverlet-clad legs until her hands rested on her ankles.

"I like the men part," Tristan's voice said with an underlying chuckle. "Not so sure how I feel about pigs and mushrooms in the same sentence."

Jenna bolted upright and searched the gloom of her bedroom. The voice sounded like Tristan, but what if it was an Irichna? "Where the fuck are you?" Her mage light flared into being, but she couldn't see anyone.

"Getting there. My magic's weak." A corner of her room brightened, and he stepped through with a sheepish grin. "Apparently there's not enough juice left to peek into your head and teleport at the same time."

She added a few lumens to her mage light and gave it a kinetic push nearer to him. Jenna blew out a distressed breath. He really did look trashed. She scrambled out from beneath the covers, grateful she had a pair of sweats on. "What happened to you?" She started toward him. "You look like crap. Much worse than you did this afternoon."

"Which version do you want?"

"The short one." She'd never been able to stand to see anyone in pain and held out her arms. He walked into them and folded his around her.

He was silent for a few heartbeats, but when he started talking, he didn't answer her question. "When you and the other witches went off by yourselves earlier, what did you talk about?"

Jenna was grateful her head was tucked in next to his so he couldn't see the frantic expression she was certain washed over her features. "Uh, lots of things."

"I'm not trying to pry. Let me be more specific. Did you talk about our plan to travel to the Irichnas' borderworld?"

She blew out a breath, not realizing she'd been holding it. Thank fucking God he didn't want to know what they'd really talked about. "No. We probably should have, but we did agree to get together at five tomorrow morning—or maybe it's this morning by now—to practice blending my new magic with theirs. I can bring it up then and let you know."

"Jenna." He pushed back enough to look at her. "Do you want to return to that hellhole?"

"Of course not, but if it buys us victory, what I want doesn't matter." Something about his expression gave her pause. "Even if Roz, Colleen, and I didn't dissect Sperrin's plan, it looks like you have."

"I don't like it." He chewed on his lower lip, and a muscle twitched beneath one eye. "Too many things can go wrong." His expression relaxed into an awkward grin. "That's not why I'm here, though."

"Let me guess." She held his gaze, which might be a mistake

because it would be easy to lose herself in those unusual silvery eyes. "You helped yourself to my thoughts and showed up to save me from myself." Jenna held her breath. Had he seen her graphic imagery of being wedged between two aroused males?

Lust kindled in his eyes, making them glow like burnished gunmetal. Instead of answering, he angled his head and covered her mouth with his. She was so stimulated from her earlier imaginings, she dove into the kiss headfirst and tightened her hands on his back, reveling in his firm, muscled body. Unlike his last kiss, this one started at one hundred ten percent and never let up. He sank his tongue into her mouth and nibbled on her lips. His hands roamed down her back and settled on her ass, pulling her hard against him. She sparred with his tongue, inhaling his spicy, exotic scent. At first she couldn't place it, and then she recognized juniper and the tang of hawthorn berries.

His erection jutted into her stomach. Jettisoning common sense, she reached between them and cradled him in her hand. He growled deep in his throat and pressed his mouth harder against hers. His cock bucked in her hand, the heat from it sending a trill of pure lust up her arm and straight to her crotch.

He dragged his mouth away and said, "If you derail this moment, I'll..."

"You'll what?" she said breathlessly, her eyes flashing a challenge.

"Take you anyway." He grinned ruefully. "Not really, but Jenna, neither one of us may be alive soon. Waiting is not a good idea."

"But you're immortal."

"If I'm hurt badly enough, I can get stuck in the *Dreaming* to wait out my immortality. It's not so different from being dead."

His cock jumped against her hand again. Desire clawed at her. She tried to glom onto all the reasons to not let the man in her arms make love to her and couldn't think of even one.

"There's my witch." His silver eyes gleamed with triumph, and he ran a string of kisses down her neck.

"You were in my head again."

"So? Better get used to it. The goddess gave us magic for a reason."

Jenna giggled. "Probably not to spy on our loved ones."

Tristan's head popped up, and his bantering aspect vanished. "Say that again."

"Say what? That maybe it's not right to spy on our loved ones?"

His hands tightened on her ass and pulled her hard against him. "Bring it on home, darling. If I'm one of your loved ones, that means…" His gaze bored into her.

Her face heated from more than lust. "I, uh, aw crap." She looked away. "I care about you. I thought about you a lot after I was here before, and I was disappointed you weren't at Colleen's wedding."

"If I had been, would you have invited me to your bed?"

"Wow! You Sidhe don't believe in walking around a point, you just throw yourself off a cliff and hope for the best."

He rolled his eyes and grinned. It brightened his face and made him look both ancient and very young at the same time. "Don't forget, you're actually one of us. I didn't ask for a lecture. How do you feel about me, Jenna? I know you like my body, but how do you feel about me?"

How can I answer that without talking about Kiernan?

Don't make this harder than it is. He didn't ask about Kiernan, he asked about himself.

"I care about you." She tossed her head back, but didn't let go of his cock. "I've been burned a bunch of times. It makes me careful with my heart."

Tristan stroked her cheek. "How could any man not want you? You're the most beautiful, most courageous woman I've ever met. You have eyes like twin stars, and a mouth made for kissing." He rubbed his chest against her erect nipples. "I've whiled away more than a few hours imagining what your breasts look like. You remind me of a Rubens painting, except far more vibrant."

Her throat thickened, and her belly clenched with need. She wriggled from his grasp, took hold of her sweatshirt top, and tugged it over her head. A muted gasp from him pleased her beyond measure.

He unsashed the robe he'd wrapped about himself and pushed it off his shoulders. It was her turn to gasp. "My God! You're amazing." She gaped at strapping shoulders, a flat stomach, and slender hips. Arms and legs flared with muscles of their own, and a scattering of tawny hair decorated his nipples, which were tight little buds. His cock sprang from a mat of golden curls. No wonder it felt so good in her hands. It was long and thick and lovely.

His eyes twinkled. "I'm glad you like what you see." Tristan closed the distance between them and shoved the elastic band of her sweatpants down her hips. She'd always been shy about being naked when men could see her, conscious of her well-padded stomach and thighs, but she didn't try to hide herself from him. More importantly, he didn't look away. His gaze drank her in, and his cock swelled even more.

"Beautiful. You're so beautiful." He placed his hands on her shoulders and pushed her toward the bed. "Better than my best imaginings."

She opened her mouth to tell him no, that she was too round to be beautiful, but he covered her mouth with his and tumbled her onto the bed. The feel of his body next to hers, skin-to-skin, was electric. She'd thought she was aroused before, but it was nothing compared with the white-hot need knifing through her. All the things she wanted to do, like taste his amazing cock, flew right out of her mind. She needed him inside her, had to have him. It was that simple.

He stopped sucking and biting her lips and ran his mouth down to the hollow in her neck. From there, he laved her breasts with kisses and suckled her nipples into achingly hard points. A climax ripped through her just from that, and she writhed beneath his touch.

"Tell me." He breathed heat against her breasts. "What do you want?"

"You. I want you. Now. Inside."

"Are you sure?"

"Yes, damn it. We can do the fancy stuff later." It was hard to get words out because her throat was clotted with desire.

Tristan knelt over her, his gaze never leaving hers. She spread her legs and looped them over his shoulders, opening herself for him. He touched her tight blonde curls almost reverently and dipped fingers inside her swollen labia. When she wriggled beneath his touch, he wrapped a hand around his shaft and guided himself inside, stopping after only an inch or so was in her pussy.

She gyrated beneath him. "Please. All of you."

Using the hand still holding himself, he moved his penis in small circles, tantalizing her, and sank inside a tiny bit farther. Jenna grabbed his hips and pulled hard, but he held his stance easily. Another climax boiled deep in her belly. He must have sensed it because he stroked her clit with his free hand, rubbing her nub between his fingers until release took her, and she cried out. Somewhere in the midst of her orgasm, he sank full length into her, stretching her, plumbing her soul.

She rocked against him, saying his name over and over.

"Yes, darling," he crooned. "Yes. You're perfect. Amazing." He withdrew slowly and pressed back inside. A slow heat ignited her core, and she came again and then once more, the end of one orgasm melting into the beginning of the next.

Because she'd never stopped gazing at him, lost in the wonder of his beauty and his lithe, graceful body suspended above her, she saw something shift in his eyes. Banked embers blazed, and he moved his cock faster. She tightened herself around him, wanting to pleasure him as intensely as he had her. His cock juddered hard inside her, flooding her with liquid heat. Happiness, an elusive emotion, washed through her, and she drew him against her body and held on tight.

Time passed while their breathing slowed, and she felt herself drift toward sleep. Finally.

"Yes, love," he murmured against her hair. "Rest, and I will too."

"You're staying here?"

He pushed up on an elbow and supported his head on his hand. "Unless you'd rather I didn't. Lovers sleep together, they don't just have sex and run like hell."

Guilt over her feelings for Kiernan pricked her, and she murmured, "There's something we have to talk about, but not tonight."

He stroked hair back from her face and lay next to her, holding her close. "Whatever it is will be fine. Don't waste a second worrying about it. I love you, Jenna. I fell hard the second you got into my Rolls when I was playing chauffer for Duncan." He nuzzled her neck. "At first I told myself it was just because I'd been alone for a long time, but the more hours we spent together, the surer I was you were the woman for me. You're most of what I thought about these last three weeks chasing Irichna from one side of the U.K. to the other."

She took a breath, wanting to say something, but he shushed her. "The most important thing in the world to me is your happiness. Nothing else matters."

"Don't you think we need more time to make such critical decisions?"

He shook his head. "That concept is a relatively new development. How long does it take before a person makes a commitment? Is a month too short a time? How about five years? Is that too long?"

"It's different for each couple—" she began.

"Exactly. I'm old. Maybe not old in the sense you understand it, but I've lived a long time. Long enough to know what I want and need."

"We still need to talk. It's... Um, there's..."

He kissed her gently. "We can talk in the morning. You're sleepy. Rest, love. I'll keep watch over you."

Drowsiness stole over her, making her limbs heavy and her head buzz pleasantly. "But you're tired too," she protested. "So tired, your magic's not up to snuff."

"I'll rest in my own way." He settled her head against his chest. "It warms my spirit that you care enough to be concerned."

She tried to say more, but darkness closed about her. The last thing she remembered was Tristan murmuring to her in Gaelic.

TRISTAN'S entire being vibrated with joy. Maybe he'd cheated a little. He'd known she was aroused when he entered her bedchamber, but she hadn't pushed him away. No, she'd reached for him with a hunger—and a desperation—akin to his own. He felt himself smile. What an amazing woman and a warm and giving lover. His cock stiffened where it lay against her body, ready for more of the same. He hadn't broken his promise to Kiernan, either. He hadn't discussed the possibility of the three of them with Jenna.

She clearly wanted to talk about it with him. He saw the confusion—and guilt—in her mind. Her honorable side made him love her all the more. Tristan settled her gently in his arms, careful not to waken her. Kiernan might be furious, but then again, he just might understand. One of them had to start things, had to move Jenna off her "I need to figure out who I am" stance.

She can work out what she needs to. I'll help her, and so will Kiernan.

He thought about the other Sidhe's statement that he'd retreat if Tristan really didn't want to build a ménage household, and realization flooded him.

It's not about me. This is about Jenna and what she wants. If it's the two of us, like in her sexual fantasy before I interrupted her, I can support that.

Hell, I will support it.

He'd always respected Kiernan. Unlike some of the other Sidhe, who were spineless or lazy or so narcissistic it was impossible to be around them, Kiernan had principles. He and Tristan had been boys and young men together and had worked hard to perfect their magic. Where some of the Sidhe gave up when spells didn't take quite right, the two of them stuck with it until they were satisfied.

Tristan closed his eyes, lulled by Jenna's even breathing. He added a bit of a spell to ensure she stayed asleep and mulled the situation over a bit more. Kiernan was a good man, but then he couldn't imagine Jenna being enticed by someone who wasn't. She said she'd chosen poorly in the past and that men had dumped her, but he had a hard time believing it.

"It doesn't matter, darling," he whispered in Gaelic. "What's past is past. We'll carve a brand new future together." She stirred in his arms, and he let himself sink into a restful place. Not asleep, but a waking trance where he could make certain no one disturbed his love.

CHAPTER 12

*J*enna rubbed sleep from her eyes and stumbled down the staircase a few minutes before five. Part of her hoped Roz and Colleen would stand her up, so she could go back to bed and the warmth of Tristan's body. Guilt about Kiernan nagged her. She had to have *that* conversation—the one about Kiernan—before anything further happened between her and Tristan. At the very least, she needed to 'fess up about her intense attraction to the other Sidhe. Tristan had said, *whatever it is will be fine. Don't waste a second worrying about it,* but he might not have taken such a sanguine approach if he knew what was in her mind.

She stopped at the bottom of the stairs and clutched the handrail hard enough for it to dig into her hand. Maybe Tristan had known. After all, he'd pretty much taken up residence in her head.

"Hey, sunshine," Colleen's cheery voice rang out.

"Bah, humbug," Roz countered. "I need coffee."

Jenna hurried to join her friends who were sprawled on an overstuffed sofa in the front parlor. Like every room in Ronin's house, it was tastefully furnished with antiques. "Where do you want to practice?" Jenna asked, not bothering to sit. If she collapsed onto the inviting looking cushions, she might not get back up.

"We were just kicking that around before you got here," Roz said. "Ronin mentioned some sort of underground practice arena that's so well shielded no one would ever bother us." She looked up at Jenna. "He said you'd know how to find it."

"I do. It's where I worked with Kiernan and Krae."

"Speaking of Kiernan," Colleen pushed to her feet, "did you give that situation any thought?"

"Let's get coffee and teleport to the arena," Jenna said, not wanting to talk about anything personal where some nosy Sidhe might overhear.

Roz groaned and stood. She plucked a thermos bottle off a nearby table. "We can fill this and share."

Colleen eyed it. "Looks pretty small."

"Fine. Find your own." Roz stalked out of the room and turned toward the kitchen.

"Ms. Grumpy," Colleen noted and followed after her.

"You know how she is before she has at least three cups on board," Jenna said and trailed after the other two.

"Do I ever," Colleen muttered, turning to focus her words on Jenna.

"I'll bet we can find at least one more sealed container to take with us." Jenna's words turned out to be prophetic since some thoughtful soul—maybe Duncan or Ronin—had placed old-fashioned thermos bottles already filled with coffee next to the sink. Each of them took one and added sugar and cream to her own particular taste.

"Ready?" Colleen asked.

"Ready as I'll ever be," Roz took a hefty swig of coffee and spun the lid on her thermos.

Jenna mind-linked to the others. It was much easier using her new magic, and in moments, the spare stone walls of the arena shimmered into being around them.

"Holy crap!" Roz turned in a full circle. "We need something like this under the house in Fairbanks."

Colleen snorted. "Are you kidding? This much excavation would make the houses on either side of us collapse. Probably ours too."

Jenna chugged coffee from her thermos and set it on a table. "Do you honestly believe we'll ever see the Fairbanks house again?"

The other two turned to stare at her. "I haven't let myself think much about it," Colleen said slowly, "but the odds aren't great, are they?"

Jenna considered how much to say, but there'd never been any secrets between them, so she leapt in with both feet. "Tristan came to me last night." At the expressions on Roz and Colleen's faces, she held up a hand. "Salacious details later. What's more important is he asked if we'd talked about Sperrin's plan. I told him we hadn't. Anyway, he's plenty worried about it."

"I'm not surprised." Roz settled her tall frame onto a stool and sipped more coffee. "There's the Unseelie problem, not that they're a problem *per se*, but the Sidhe don't trust them, and the feeling is mutual. Even Ronin is sucking up a lot to follow the dream guardian's instructions about mending the rift in Faerie. And then there's the 'into the lion's den' problem where we hurtle back to the borderworld full steam ahead." She shivered. "Good God, I'd hoped to never see that place again."

"Duncan and I talked about it some," Colleen admitted. "He thinks if there's not a bunch of friction between them and the dark fae—and they're not calling them that anymore—things will work out."

"Seems like a pretty big if. You saw that one guy, Locar, exit stage left," Roz said and added, "For what it's worth, Ronin believes things will be all right, but I know he's anxious. It doesn't help that we'll have to work fast once we get to the borderworld since our magic won't hold up all that long there."

Jenna set her thermos down with a *thunk*. "Let's get this practice session going. I'll feel better once I know we can still anticipate each other's moves."

"Lead out." Colleen set her coffee down too. "What do you want to try first?"

"How about shape-shifting?" At Colleen's nod, Jenna stepped out of her shoes and stripped off her clothing. The others followed suit. Jenna closed her eyes, emptied her mind, and summoned the first shape that came to her: a lion. She barely had to reach for its form when she felt her skin and bones melt into the change. She'd never shifted so quickly, nor so easily.

"*Smarty pants,*" Colleen said into her mind. "*Impressive, though.*"

"*Next form,*" Jenna instructed, and changed into a dragon-esque reptile.

Over the next half hour, they took on a dozen forms. Jenna discovered she could boost her friends' transformations with excess magic.

Finally, Roz said, "*Enough. We've got this one down. Let's do something else.*"

Jenna's feet formed, and she pushed her toes against the stone floor. She felt energized in a way she never had after a series of shifts. In the past, that magic always drained her.

Roz shook her long hair over her shoulders and bunched it between her hands, twisting it into a knot. "Pretty remarkable." She eyed Jenna. "You weren't kidding about the more magic part."

"Color me astonished." Colleen grinned at Jenna. "What I want to know is where I can tap into your magic."

"When you find out," Roz mumbled, "let me know. I'll be right behind you."

Jenna shook her head. "What a switch. It will take time to get used to it, but look at the bright side. I've got power to spare, so I can be a help—finally—rather than always being the weak link in the chain."

"What's next?" Colleen asked. "Should we get dressed?"

"Nah, we might end up shifting again. Follow me." Jenna trotted to the far end of the circular room and tapped a few buttons. A three-dimensional screen flickered to life.

"Holy fuck!" Roz sputtered. "It's like something out of *Star Wars.*"

"I can call up holograms of opponents," Jenna said, happy to share the Sidhes' technology with her fellow witches. "Who would you like to fight?"

After a lengthy pause, Colleen screwed her mouth into a frown. "I don't want to fight them, but we should make this as realistic as possible."

"You didn't exactly say Irichna," Jenna said, "and to be candid, I don't want to do that. This simulation is real enough, I'd be terrified actual demons would work their way in somehow."

Roz blew out a ragged breath. "How about goblins or succubi? Maybe a troll. Something simple."

"You got it." Palpable relief swept through her, and Jenna manipulated the control panel. The room filled with swarthy, stinking goblins and a few of the undead.

"I'll take that one." Colleen pointed, and power blazed from her hands. The goblin exploded in an eerily realistic red haze, but another popped up to take its place. "What the fuck?" Colleen shouted in Jenna's direction.

"It's practice," she yelled back, "so the enemy replenishes itself."

"Makes it even more realistic," Roz growled and pointed at a particularly loathsome goblin. "That one is mine."

KIERNAN WOKE FROM AN UNEASY SLEEP. It was still dark, but that didn't mean much since it didn't get light until mid-morning this time of year. He sent his magical senses outward, sensing, probing, and jolted upright cursing in Gaelic. Jenna wasn't in her room, but Tristan was in her bed. With his hands bunched into fists, Kiernan sprang from the couch he'd slept on and bolted from the room. To hell with teleporting. He wanted to be fully corporeal when he confronted the turncoat bastard who'd slept with Jenna.

"We had an agreement. A fucking agreement," Kiernan bellowed as he kicked the door to Jenna's room open, to the accompaniment of splintering wood.

Tristan lounged lazily in her bed, an unreadable expression on his face.

"Get up," Kiernan shouted, dancing from side to side on the balls of his feet with his fists up and ready.

"Why?" Tristan eyed him. "What are you going to do? Pound me into dog meat?"

Kiernan blew air like a farrier's bellow. "You know I can't raise magic against you, so yes hand-to-hand combat will have to suffice."

"I didn't break my promise—" Tristan began, his tone placating.

"The fuck you didn't. You slept with her."

"Yes." Tristan pushed himself to a sitting position and tucked a pillow behind his back. "But I did not discuss the three of us— even though she wanted to." His gaze never left Kiernan's face and a soothing spell eddied between them.

"You dare raise magic against me?" Kiernan stalked closer.

"It's not aggressive, and you know it. Shut the goddamned door, or what's left of it," Tristan said. When Kiernan ignored him, a blast of magic whistled past his head, and the badly splintered wood slammed shut of its own accord.

White-hot fury blinded Kiernan, and he lunged for Tristan but ran up against an invisible barrier. Beyond reason, he pummeled the ward with his fists until they bled. To give his hands a break, he kicked the ward and then tried to dismantle it with magic of his own.

"Fine," he spat, breathing as if he'd just run a marathon. "You're a hell-spawned coward on top of everything else."

"There's no point in both of us getting trashed over this. When you're ready to listen instead of reacting, let me know."

"Why you sanctimonious son of a bitch!"

"Christ! Kiernan, stop it. I'm not your enemy. She never said she didn't want you. I've been lying here thinking of ways to make the three of us work. At least I was before you barreled in here loaded for bear. Now I'm not so sure."

Kiernan buried his fist in the warding again, but drew it back. Blood dripped onto the carpet. "What did you say?"

Tristan sat up straighter. "Oberon's balls but you're thick-headed. Go wash the blood off your hands. Soak your head while you're at it, and then we'll talk."

"I don't think so. There's nothing to talk about. You got to her first in spite of everything we said downstairs."

Tristan pursed his mouth into a hard line. "I may have bedded her first, but one of us had to break the ice. She was convinced she had to stay away from both of us to let her magic ripen."

Kiernan shook his head. At least the red haze over his vision was dissipating. "I... Aw, to hell with it. I'll just leave."

The warded air around Tristan sparkled into nothingness, and he landed on his feet next to the bed. "You're not thinking. Here." He snapped his fingers and a bottle of mead appeared, suspended midair.

Kiernan closed his fist around it before Tristan could, broke the seal, and drank deep. He wiped the back of one hand across his mouth and tasted blood. "Shit!"

"I'll take that." Tristan made a grab for the bottle. "Do something. You're bleeding all over everything."

Kiernan gazed at splotches on the carpet that were shrinking back to pristine wool fibers as the magic that kept the house clean did its work. He sent healing magic to his sore knuckles and feet and stomped toward the bathroom where he rinsed himself off. A glance in the mirror startled him. His eyes sported red rims, and lines carved deep into his face. He blotted his injuries with a towel and made his way back into the bedroom.

Tristan had wrapped himself in a robe, and he sat in a chair. He pointed to another one facing him and offered the mead bottle.

Kiernan took the liquor and fell into the chair. "I don't know what's worse," he muttered, "losing the only woman I've been interested in in centuries or making an ass out of myself."

The corners of Tristan's mouth twitched into half a smile. "Whew! For a little while there, I was afraid you'd simply teleport out of here, and I'd have to waste time and magic running you to ground."

"Why bother? You already have what you want."

"You still don't get it." Tristan snatched the bottle back. "This isn't about what I want. It's about what Jenna needs, and that's both of us."

"How the hell would you know that? Give." He took the mead and swallowed hungrily, hoping for some level of oblivion from his pounding head and aching hands.

"Because I was in her mind." Tristan blew out a breath. "Your gift is scrying the future. Mine is reading emotions. I'm an empath, or have you forgotten?"

Kiernan flexed a hand and winced. "What did you see?"

"Before I intruded on the sanctity of her bedchamber, she was having a scorching hot fantasy about the two of us."

"I find that difficult to believe." Kiernan took another drink, feeling the honey wine warm him, or maybe it was Tristan's words.

He spread his hands. "I have no reason to lie to you. You'd read the falsehood in alterations in my aura."

"Now I feel like even more of an idiot." Kiernan pinched the bridge of his nose between his thumb and forefinger before looking at Tristan and handing the bottle back.

"Get over it." Tristan spoke with his usual asperity. "I tried to tell you this after you steamrolled in here, but you were so lost in fury, you didn't hear me. She wanted to talk about you last night, but I forestalled her. For one thing—" he leveled his silver gaze at Kiernan "—I'd promised you we wouldn't have that conversation. But more importantly, she was exhausted and needed sleep."

Kiernan sagged against the chair. "We all need to sit down together."

"Agreed."

"I'll go get her. She and the other witches are in the arena." He started to get up, but Tristan shook his head.

"Let's at least try to make this a romantic moment." He took a slug of mead.

"What? Do I need to gin up a violinist and cut a few flowers from the greenhouse?" Kiernan rolled his eyes.

A laugh bubbled from Tristan. "A start. Those would be a start, but before that, both of us might want to clean up, and I'd like to pick one of the fancier bedchambers here and spruce it up a bit."

"I'll help."

"Excellent."

Kiernan snorted. "Maybe I'll learn a thing or two. The lassies have always been so eager for my body, all I've had to do is provide them with this." He patted his lower lap.

Tristan made a wry face. "I haven't exactly had that particular problem. Listen up, though. Let's ensure the witches have as much time as they need to feel comfortable working together, given Jenna's new power."

"Which means we'll wait until they show up topside before we escort Jenna to the bower we've created for her." Kiernan nodded.

"Exactly," Tristan replied. "It's self-serving on my part, but we'll need everyone's skills as finely honed as possible when we turn into lemmings and follow Sperrin to perdition."

Kiernan snapped his head up. "If you're dead set against storming the borderworld, why didn't you say something yesterday?"

"Because Ronin and Oberon told me to suck up my misgivings."

"That's not how we've operated in the past." Kiernan drew his brows together in consternation. "We've always offered everyone a voice and haven't moved forward until we all agreed."

"Yes," Tristan said dryly, "and look where it's gotten us."

"I see your point. We devolve into endless discussion and do nothing. That's not an option this time." Grateful his mind had cleared and he was thinking again, Kiernan added, "Another reason to leave the witches be is it will calm Jenna's concerns about her new magic. She'll probably be ecstatic about everything she can do to help Roz and Colleen. I showed her how to use the holographic imagery machine, so they can engage in some fairly realistic warfare. Back to your other concerns, though, have you talked with Sperrin?"

"No."

"Why not?"

"Yesterday I was so spun out, I'd have had a hard time being civil."

Kiernan grinned. "It's not yesterday anymore. I remember him from before the rift. He's solid and he'll listen. It doesn't mean he'll agree, but he's one of the best commanders I've ever known."

"Funny, but Oberon said the same thing. He reminded me that while we sprang from common roots, the other side of Faerie's magic is a complement to our own. He was also abundantly clear we'd be fools to ignore such strong potential added to our ranks." Breath whistled through Tristan's teeth. "I'm going to take a shower. How about if you do the same, and I'll meet you in that empty suite at the end of the third floor."

"I'll be there." Kiernan set his jaw firmly. Apologies didn't come easy for him. "I'm sorry my temper exploded back there."

"No worries." Tristan got up and held out a hand. "I'd have done the same thing. She's an amazing woman. Let's do everything we can to love and cherish her."

Kiernan clasped the proffered hand and stood. "Too bad she won't let us protect her along with it."

"Isn't it? Ronin and Duncan were grousing about the same thing yesterday. See you soon, mate."

The air around Tristan shimmered, and he vanished. Kiernan teleported back to his own room and started the shower running. The broken place in his heart that had shattered when he'd realized Tristan had been with Jenna didn't ache quite so much. They had lots of ground to cover, but at least Tristan hadn't shut him out, and from what he said, neither had Jenna.

Steam rose, surrounding him, and he welcomed the water sluicing sweat and tension from his body. He'd just turned the taps off and reached for a towel when Ronin's voice blasted him.

"Kiernan. Downstairs now!"

"Ach, that can't be good," he muttered. Kiernan dressed in record time, considered teleporting, but didn't know what he'd find and decided a quick lope through the manor house would be nearly as fast.

CHAPTER 13

Kiernan summoned warding and hurried into the downstairs room where Ronin's energy pulsed like an alarm—or a warning beacon. He raised his hands to call power, ready for anything, but all he saw were Ronin, Duncan, Oberon, Tristan, and about twenty other Sidhe. He dropped his hands to his sides and asked, "What happened?"

Ronin's intense blue gaze swept the room. "Enough of us are here for me to begin. I don't want to have to repeat myself endlessly. Locar gathered about thirty like-minded Sidhe. They ensnared the Unseelie in a magical net and transported them…elsewhere."

Kiernan rocked backward. Despite the traitor he'd seen in his visions, he was still stunned. "Fuck! You've got to be kidding. With all the problems we have with Irichna, Locar and his associates want a civil war on top of everything? What idiots."

"Oh, it gets worse. Much worse." Oberon's acidic tone could have etched glass. "They have Titania too."

"How is that even possible?" Tristan asked, his usually gentle voice strained.

"She was dining with Moire, Sperrin, and our other Unseelie

guests when Locar's raid occurred. I'm fairly certain they also netted a scullery maid or two in their sweep," Oberon said. "It's a damned shame because the traveling ether kills mortals who lack magic."

"We have no idea where they are?" Kiernan asked. He had a hard time believing so many with strong magic could disappear without a trace.

"None. It's almost as if Locar teamed with Druids or other mages—or Goddess forbid, demons—to subvert Sidhe magic enough that I'm not able to track it." Oberon paced in a tight circle. His brows were drawn into a single line low across his forehead, and he looked as if he wanted to kill something. "If I can't figure this out soon, I'll be forced to call in the Celts."

"I almost hate to ask, but have we alerted the Unseelie Court?" Tristan asked.

"Yes." Ronin spat the word as if it cost him.

"And?" Tristan made come along motions with two fingers.

"What do you suppose? They're furious, but I suspect they can tell you that themselves. I expect a contingent to converge on us momentarily." Ronin whirled to face Tristan. "You will not voice any negativity. Do you understand me?"

"Of course. It's a little late in the game for my concerns about fighting side by side. Why would they trust us after this? Or want anything further to do with us, for that fact?"

"They will both trust us and work with us—" Oberon leveled his gaze at Tristan "—because we will pull out every trick at our disposal to locate their people. And your queen."

Ronin shifted his attention to Kiernan. "You will not utter so much as a single word about seeing a traitor in your visions. If you do, they'll blame us even more for not taking adequate steps to protect their kinfolk."

"Understood." Kiernan nodded tersely. He considered launching into an explanation about many things that originated from his trance states not necessarily coming to pass, but bit back the words. Now wasn't the time to describe the fine points of seerdom.

A placating spell rolled off Tristan in waves. The other Sidhe forced Ronin to focus on him by asking, "Next question. How will we narrow where to search? We don't have time to spend years cracking every corner of Earth open, plus all the borderworlds."

"We haven't come up with anything viable," Ronin admitted, his expression grim. "Moreover, Oberon only wants to beg for aid from the Celtic gods as a last resort because they'll never let us live this down." He shook his head. "If we perform this badly as a race, maybe we don't deserve to exist."

"I'm hoping the Unseelie will have an idea or two," Oberon admitted. "Beyond that, Titania and those with her are far from helpless. They're surely working on an escape plan."

"If you took me to where they were when they disappeared, I could scry the past," Kiernan said, thinking of what he'd need to make something like that work. "I may not succeed because they took great pains to hide their tracks, but it's worth a try."

"I considered that," Ronin said. "Because I couldn't come up with any alternatives, I actually tried it, but the only thing I raised was clouds of muck."

Kiernan inhaled sharply. "Goddess's breath. I hope you didn't destroy anything. Clues to such events are incredibly sensitive—"

Oberon stepped between them. "No bickering. This is bad enough without recriminations. I'll take Kiernan to where the group was eating. When the Unseelie show up, the rest of you can hold them at bay till we get back." The king snapped his fingers and left the room at a lope. Kiernan hurried to catch up. He knew better than to try to talk. Besides, there wasn't much to say.

They came to a halt in a cozy nook off the kitchen that looked out onto the arboretum. The remains of a meal sat on a round, oak table. Apparently, the group had been sharing food and conversation. At Oberon's nod, Kiernan tested the room and settled on a power spot. Standing right on top of it, he cleared his mind and summoned his gift. Scrying the past was deadly accurate, but it was a real power hog. He hoped he hadn't blown so much magic during his earlier fury that his spell would be too weak to be effective.

No negativity.

He breathed deep and then did it again, seeking a clear, calm center where his magic bubbled, waiting. At first nothing came, but he understood how to be patient. Images finally formed behind his closed lids, and he saw the six Unseelie and Titania gathered around the table. They were eating and laughing and genuinely enjoying one another. He considered a type of fast forward, but was afraid he might miss a critical juncture and clues as to what had happened, so he kept his breathing steady and waited. Thank the goddess Oberon wasn't interfering. He had to be frantic about Titania, but he had enough sense to allow Kiernan space to practice his craft.

Time passed. It was impossible to tell how much in his trance state. Titania broke off mid-sentence, unusual for her since she was famous for having the last word—on everything. Her spine straightened, and she stared at something apparently only she could see.

"Show yourself," she hissed. "I feel Sidhe energy."

Sperrin came to his feet, his smoke-gray gaze sweeping the room. Moire stood next to him. Tension radiated off the pair. "What is it?" another Unseelie asked. "I feel nothing out of the ordinary."

Titania pushed her chair back so hard it fell, clattering to the floor. She raised her hands and blue-white power crackled from them. "You can't feel it—" she bit off each word "—because it's Sidhe magic, and they're masking themselves. I don't like this. I'm calling Oberon."

The minute she said that, the edges of Kiernan's vision blackened. Thick smoke descended, and he couldn't see, but he could still hear Locar say, "Tsk, tsk. Bad call. I wouldn't do that if I were you, *my queen*." His gravelly voice dripped sarcasm.

"What are your intentions?" Titania's tone held steel beneath it. "I order you to tell me."

"You lost the ability to command me when your husband excommunicated me. Slaves owe allegiance to no one."

"If this is about us," Sperrin said, obviously struggling to remain calm, "we can come to a mutual understanding. We wish you no harm."

"Hah! Keep your mouth shut, Unseelie scum," another Sidhe chimed in. "Or I'll shut it permanently."

"Try it," Moire said, her voice deadly quiet. "It will be the last thing ye ever do."

"Oberon's balls, but we're wasting time," a Sidhe cried. "Let's send this sorry lot to the demons' borderworld and have done with things once and for all."

Elation swelled in Kiernan, but he waited, unwilling to sever his magic too soon. If someone would corroborate their destination, he'd be done, and they could get moving.

"Shut up!" Locar shouted. "You weren't supposed to say anything."

"There's enough demon magic mixed in, no one will ever be able to follow their tracks," the other Sidhe said. "Don't be an ass, Locar."

"The Irichnas' borderworld," Titania said, sounding positively jovial. "Why thank you. We were headed that direction anyway."

"By the time they figure out where you are, you'll all be locked in the *Dreaming* forever," Locar snapped. "Enough talk."

The smoke thickened so much, Kiernan coughed, despite it being illusion. He withdrew his magic and turned to face Oberon. "Did you catch any of that?"

"I did. In some ways, this kills two birds with one stone, but we have to hurry." He swept past Kiernan, headed for where they'd left the others.

"I hope the Unseelie share your need for haste," Kiernan muttered and trotted after his king.

∼

JENNA PULLED her clothes back on and glanced at Roz and Colleen. "There aren't any clocks down here, but it feels like the afternoon's nearly shot because my stomach is giving me hell."

"Know what you mean," Colleen said. "That was a whole lot of magic to blow through on a couple cups of coffee."

"Okay." Roz smoothed her black turtleneck over her flat stomach. "I'm ready. Shall we?"

"Let's aim for the kitchen," Jenna suggested. "It will save time."

"Go for it," Colleen said. "Convenient there's always food made. I'd like to borrow whoever keeps those pots full."

"You and me both," Jenna said. "Alrighty, girls, here we go." She summoned power, and the kitchen formed around them. Mouthwatering smells made her stomach growl, and she strode to the cupboard and pulled out three plates. Everyone helped themselves, and they made their way through the swinging doors on the far side of the kitchen that led into the dining area.

Colleen plopped a pitcher on the table along with her plate. "Water," she said firmly. "We all need to hydrate before we even think about booze."

"Yes, Mom!" Jenna grinned and dug into the steaming casserole on her plate. It tasted wonderful, with bits of chicken mixed with potatoes and a delectable cheese sauce.

The only sounds for a while were the scrape of cutlery on china. After the worst of her hunger was sated, Jenna glanced up. "Pretty quiet, wouldn't you say?"

"I hadn't thought about it," Roz said, "but now that you mention it, things feel...odd."

The food Jenna had just eaten curdled in her belly. She lurched to her feet. The euphoria from channeling more magic than she'd ever dreamed of faded, and weariness set in. "I'm going to figure out what's going on."

"You never did tell us much about last night," Roz said, her sharp-eyed gaze boring into Jenna.

"No, and I'm not going to now, either." She headed for the door leading into the main part of the house.

"Do you need us, sweetie?" Colleen asked. "I'm about done here myself."

Well, do I?

Jenna glanced over a shoulder. "Maybe so. It's farfetched, but I hope the men didn't get into some kind of shit arguing over me."

Roz and Colleen stood. "What I feel is more global than that," Roz said. "Not that Kiernan and Tristan might not have had a dust-up, but there's something seriously wrong with the vibes here that extends way beyond that."

With her heart hammering in trepidation, Jenna focused her magic and walked briskly toward where she felt other magic wielders. The door to the meeting room was closed, and she turned to the other witches. "Should we knock?" she whispered.

"I don't think so," Roz countered in a normal voice. "My husband is in there."

"So's mine," Colleen said, twisted the door handle, and pushed the heavy wooden door open.

Jenna stared through the open doorway. A group of Unseelie she didn't recognize except for the distinctive patina of their magic stood off to one side, red-faced and looking furious. Ronin, Duncan, Oberon, Kiernan, Tristan, and about twenty-five other Sidhe faced off against them.

"Come on." Roz marched past her and made her way to Ronin's side. "What happened?"

Colleen hastened to Duncan, and Jenna followed more slowly. It wasn't as if she had a nurturing husband to lean against. Though she felt both Tristan's and Kiernan's eyes on her, she kept her gaze plastered on the floor.

"Ye welcome witches into your midst, but raise war against us?" an Unseelie with long, gray hair demanded. He had a noble bearing and was swathed in a pure white robe sashed in black.

Jenna flashed back to her conversation with Tristan. "Please tell us what happened," she said. "Where are Sperrin and Moire?"

"Kidnapped. By. Sidhe," the Unseelie said, enunciating clearly and pausing between each word for emphasis.

"Yes, pity the Sidhe queen got shanghaied right along with them." Another Unseelie, a woman, stepped forward. Golden hair cascaded down her back, and her green eyes sparked dangerously. She wore a form-fitting teal jumpsuit, not unlike Moire's garb except for the color.

"Titania's gone too?" Roz focused on Ronin.

"Unless there's another Queen of Faerie I missed." The Unseelie female smirked.

"And you are?" Roz raised both brows into question marks.

"Och, can ye ever forgive my lack of manners?" The blonde's words were etched with sarcasm. "My name is Erika."

"Do we know where Titania and your kin are?" Colleen asked. Worry pinched the skin around her eyes.

"I think so," Kiernan said. "I used my gift to piece together what happened. Locar and a group of renegade Sidhe captured the Unseelie and Titania, and spirited them to the demons' borderworld."

"Yes," Ronin said sourly. "Some of the demons may not be able to leave their world, but nothing says they can't co-opt others to do their dirty work for them."

"I don't get it." Jenna squared her shoulders. "Why didn't someone come downstairs and get us? We have to rescue them. It's not as if we weren't going there anyway." She pushed herself even straighter, taking advantage of her height to get her point across. "Damned convenient if you ask me because it means we don't have to split our forces."

Kiernan caught her gaze. Pride and agreement shone from his

blue-green eyes. He nodded slightly. "The reason we haven't left yet—" he began.

"—is because our Unseelie kin are understandably furious with this turn of events," Oberon finished for him.

"Fine." Jenna balanced her hands in the air in front of her, palms up. "In the meantime, Irichna may be killing Sperrin, Moire, the other Unseelie, and Titania. Their magic will fade the longer they remain in that world. We have to move—"

"Who are ye to speak so boldly?" the Unseelie male's voice cracked like a whip.

"My name is Jenna Neil. This is Roxanne Lantry-Redstone." She pointed. "And that's Colleen Kelly-Regis. We're the witches who got stuck corralling Irichna after the Sidhe decided they didn't want to do it anymore a couple hundred years back." Jenna took a step toward him. "Who are you?"

"Aedan. Sperrin's brother. Between us, we rule the Unseelie Court."

The pounding of footsteps sounded behind her, and Jenna realized she hadn't shut the door. Krae, Niall, and Llyr blasted past her and dove into the space between the Unseelie and the Sidhe.

"I just found out," Krae said, breathlessly. "Why in the goddess's name didn't someone come get us?"

Niall skidded to Colleen's side. "What?" he demanded. "Were you just going to leave us here?"

"Calm down." Oberon said. "We do not need more drama."

"Let's get on with it, then." Krae folded her arms over her chest. "We should have left as soon as Kiernan figured things out. Except it's a good thing you didn't because then we'd have gotten separated."

"A bigger question," Oberon said, "is how you came by your knowledge. I shielded this room."

"I have my ways. When are we leaving?" Krae practically bristled with energy.

Oberon turned to face Aedan. "An excellent question. Are you finally convinced Locar's renegades are a splinter group, and the rest of us mean you no harm?"

Aedan tilted his patrician chin a notch. "I must confer with my people." The air around the Unseelie thickened until a virtual wall formed.

Jenna blew out a breath and gazed at the assemblage. "I may be speaking out of turn. I asked this before, but with things this desperate, why didn't any of you interrupt our practice session?" She pounded a fist into her open hand. "Demons are where we live. If you're headed back to the Irichnas' borderworld, you have to take us."

Roz narrowed her eyes, zeroing in on Ronin. "Surely you weren't considering leaving us behind," she said, her voice carefully neutral.

"Like he planned to do with us," Krae chimed in. "Stupid, Sidhe. Shortsighted…" The rest of her words devolved into Gaelic muttering.

"No one was going to be left behind." Oberon sounded drained —and worried. "Hell's bells, we needed to get past—I meant to say integrate—whatever the Unseelie showed up with before we even had a plan to share with anyone."

"Thank you. That's good to know." Jenna jerked her chin toward the magical enclosure with Unseelie inside. "No matter what they come up with, we still have to leave."

"The sooner the better," Colleen said.

"None of you—" Roz's dark gaze raked the group "—know those demons quite like we do."

"We obviously won't be doing anything until Aedan and his people are done talking," Kiernan said and headed for Jenna. Tristan followed right behind.

Jenna zeroed in on the men. What the fuck could they possibly want with her? Had Tristan chatted with Kiernan about last night? Her stomach twisted into a sour knot. He may well have. The men had known one another for at least a thousand years.

Shaking off feelings of impending doom, Jenna straightened and faced the men squarely. Heat suffused her face, and she felt like a cheating slut, but she couldn't do much about it.

"We need to talk with you," Tristan said.

"Indeed we do. It's important," Kiernan captured her gaze and held it.

"What if I don't want to talk with you? There's a whole lot going on right now." She narrowed her eyes and scrambled to hold her ground.

"Relax, sweetheart. You look like a sheep about to be led to the slaughter." Tristan sent a calming spell to eddy about her. She batted at its threads, but they enveloped her anyway.

"Clearing things up will ease your mind. Trust us." Kiernan summoned magic to shield their conversation. "Private moments are hard to come by. We'd be fools not to take advantage of this one."

"Now isn't the time for anything personal." Jenna tried to stave off what was shaping up to be an uncomfortable confrontation. "The last thing I need is something to cloud my judgment. I have to be sharp, at the top of my game."

"We won't alter your alertness—except by making it better," Tristan said, ignoring her comment. "I agree with Kiernan. We need to seize the moments as they're offered, which includes this one. We care about you, Jenna."

Jenna looked from one man to the other, stunned. Was it possible they'd come to some kind of détente over her? Even if they had, how the hell would something like that even work?

She cleared her throat. "I still think this is a lousy venue for any kind of personal revelations, but the two of you aren't angry at each other?"

Kiernan's mouth twisted into a wry grin. "I admit I pretty

much lost it once I discovered lover-boy here had beaten me to the punch…"

"…but we got past it," Tristan cut in.

"What exactly does that mean?" Jenna asked, her mouth suddenly dry. The Irichna problem vanished, and the only thing filling her mind and heart was how much she adored both of the men standing beside her.

"Do you want us?" Kiernan asked, shifting to telepathic speech. *"More specifically, since you've already accepted Tristan, do you want me the same way?"*

Her face caught fire, and breath knotted in her throat. Because she didn't trust any form of speech, she just nodded. Tristan caught her up from one side, Kiernan from the other. Four arms wrapped around her, and both men nuzzled her neck with kisses.

"Can this really work?" She wasn't sure she'd projected the thought until she got an answer.

"Of course it can, darling," Tristan said from his vantage point inside her mind.

"I want you more than life itself." Kiernan's mind voice was husky with need, the words low and breathy.

Joy boiled from her belly and shot through her. Jenna wound her arms around them and wondered just how long they'd have before the Unseelie got done with their machinations. Maybe, just maybe, there'd be a small window where they could slip away…

Tristan laughed. "Lovely idea, but we won't get that lucky."

"No, you won't," Oberon's voice cut in, and Jenna realized he'd walked right next to them, penetrating the magic Kiernan had shrouded their conversation with. "I have no jurisdiction over the witch, but you two are my subjects. I don't care if you've just discovered Aphrodite returned from the other side of the veil. Untangle yourselves and stand front and center. This is much more serious than your love life."

"Sorry, my liege." Tristan inclined his head and separated himself from Jenna.

Kiernan did the same, but cast a longing look her way that made her knees go weak.

Her fantasy from the previous evening with both men making love to her cascaded through her mind. Before she did something that would shame herself, Jenna swallowed hard and refocused, but the graphic imagery was stubborn and slow to retreat.

The casting around the Unseelie shattered. Magical motes danced through the air, and Aedan strode forward, flicking them aside. "We have come to a decision," he announced.

CHAPTER 14

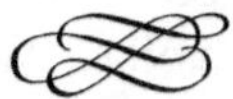

"That was fast." Ronin sported such a surprised look, it had to be genuine. Jenna scooted closer to hear what Aedan had to say. Her head was still whirling from Tristan's and Kiernan's nearness. More than anything, she wanted time alone with them to talk about her fears and concerns and hopes that they could find their way together.

I've never even been able to make things go with one guy. Why the hell do I think two will make things any easier?

Before she sank into a funk—and gave up before she even began—she forced her attention on Aedan, who'd already started talking.

"...may have been quicker than ye expected, but lives hang in the balance. We will work with you because there are no other options. Ye obviously know the location of the Irichna border-world. We'd have to figure it out. And then we'd be at odds once we got there. We face a deadly enemy. 'Tis better to do so with a united front. We can sort out our differences once our people are safe."

"Do we have a plan to activate once we arrive on the borderworld?" Erika shook hair over her shoulders and strode to Aedan's side.

Jenna glanced at Roz and Colleen. Without exchanging a word, the three of them formed a tight row. "We show up shielded and with maximum magic ready to deploy," Colleen said.

"Last time, we were dragged there, and they sabotaged our power." Jenna projected her voice. "We were able to trick one of Hell's minions into returning it, or we'd probably be worse than dead."

"Explain." Erika spat out the word.

"She's talking about the Irichnas' proclivity to borrow human women and use them for breeding stock," Ronin cut in smoothly.

Erika drew back. "I had no idea they did that." She looked from one witch to the next, and her face crinkled with distaste. "How hideous."

Colleen snorted. "Jenna and I had no idea before we got there. We always thought new Irichna came from the ranks of the dead. Roz disabused us of that notion about the time the minion was herding us to its master."

"Let's save the history replay for later," Krae said. "Unless there's something we need to prepare, I say we leave."

"Will you bring more than three changelings?" Oberon asked.

Llyr strutted forward. "Yes. Our people are...close and will come at Krae's command."

Ronin shot an odd look Oberon's way. "Did you know?"

"I suspected." Oberon made his way to Krae and bowed. "Thank you. You have reason to hate us, yet you risk yourselves to help."

"Seems ye alienated many races," Aedan observed in a sour voice.

"Isn't that the truth? Let's see, there's us, changelings, Unseelie..." Jenna clicked them off on her fingers but stopped when Oberon made a slight hacking motion with one hand.

"That isn't useful," the king muttered. "We are only too aware of our faults."

"Yes, and the chickens have all come home to roost," Duncan muttered.

"More like shit all over us," Tristan cut in.

The corners of Aedan's mouth twitched as if he were trying not to smile. "Better realizations that come late than not at all," he said.

"The demons will be expecting us," Roz noted.

"Of course they will. Your point?" Oberon asked.

"Several, actually. It means the Unseelie and Titania will be closely guarded. We won't simply sweep in, pluck them up, and leave."

"We'll have to figure out where they are and take things from there," Aedan said. "What else?"

Roz skinned her lips back from her teeth. "Last time the dream guardian saved us. We won't be so fortunate again. The Irichna will want to either enslave us—or kill us." She pointed at Jenna and Colleen. "In fact, this whole charade could be their way of luring us to where we're vulnerable. Irichna have never given a shit about collateral damage."

Roz's words held the ring of truth, and Jenna narrowed her eyes. "Don't be surprised if they offer a deal. Us for their captives. It would be a very Irichna-like thing to do. They're basically lazy bastards, and if they can get out of a major confrontation where a bunch of them get killed, they'll be all over it."

"Humph." Aedan stared at her. "We don't exactly need you. That could work."

"Oh no it wouldn't." The words spewed from Ronin like bullets. "Roz is my wife."

"And Colleen is mine," Duncan said, his tone equally deadly. If looks could kill, Aedan would have dropped in his tracks.

"Besides," Ronin broke in, "it's our fault the witches are in this mess. We will not compound our sins by committing new ones."

"Fine." Aedan waved an airy hand. "In order to get any good ideas, ye have to float a lot of them."

Jenna tried pushing into his mind. She got a little way before he shoved her out. *He could be a problem,* she sent to Roz and Colleen.

"Ya think?" Roz's sarcasm was apparent, even in her mind voice.

The air around Oberon thickened as he summoned power. "We leave now. We'll sort details out once we're there. Remember everyone—" his amber gaze was pointed as it swept the group "—we're allies. No shenanigans, no behind the scenes maneuverings. If I discover anyone here tried to sell someone else out, there'll be hell to pay."

On that dark note, Jenna gripped hands with her sister witches. The next thing she'd see would be the Irichnas' border-world, a place she'd heartily hoped to never be again. Her stomach twisted in apprehension, and she was afraid she might vomit up the meal she'd just eaten. "We stick together," she cautioned.

"Always," Colleen seconded.

"We're stronger as a unit," Roz reminded them. "Goddammit, but I really, really do not want to do this."

"Try not to think about that," Jenna murmured. "It will just make the impossible harder."

"I feel soooo much better now," Roz snarled. "If this new magic thing doesn't pan out, you can always be a therapist."

"Stop it! Things are dicey enough as it is." Colleen herded their power. "We need to step on it or get left behind."

"Now there's a thought," Jenna mumbled.

"Not a viable one." Colleen's grip cut into her hand. "Buck up, sister. Let's go get 'em."

Kiernan marshaled his power, linked it with the others, and

readied himself for battle. He'd spent plenty of time playing warrior, but the last major skirmish had been hundreds of years before. He was older now—and hopefully wiser. The thrill of clashing with an enemy no longer filled him with anticipation. Now he simply hoped everyone he cared about would make it through unscathed.

What? Have I spent so much time scrying the future I've turned into a coward? Lost my ability to live in the present?

Stop thinking, he commanded and readied himself to do whatever needed doing. He'd only faced demons a handful of times, but they were impossible to forget because they murdered with chilling efficiency.

Why would I expect anything different? They have no souls.

Aedan posed another problem. Even though he'd backed off when Ronin challenged him, Kiernan didn't care for the way the Unseelie had looked at the witches. As if they were expendable. Cannon fodder. He recognized the mindset. Hell, the Sidhe were equally guilty of looking down their noses at other races—and not caring what happened to them.

He'd seen darkness hovering at the edges of his visions for so long, it had started to feel normal. He'd warned Oberon and Titania—and then just Titania after Oberon left for hundreds of years—that they trod a slippery slope, but they treated his concerns as the deranged wanderings of a mind that spent too much time alone.

"The Unseelie will not sacrifice the witches, or anyone else, on my watch," he muttered as the black of the traveling ether shaded to gray, and he knew he'd be on the borderworld soon. The same went for the Sidhe. Their days of running roughshod over people they considered inferior was over.

He gathered magic just in time to cushion his landing, bolted upright, and gazed at a barren landscape. Nothing living stirred, at least not anywhere nearby. Cracked dirt spread in all directions, broken only by the occasional dead shrub. Around him,

Sidhe, Unseelie, witches, and changelings shimmered into being. Some hit the ground hard enough to knock the breath out of them, and Kiernan suspected they didn't teleport much.

"We all seem to have made the transit," Oberon spoke softly.

"They're here," Aedan said without preamble. He didn't have to define who he meant by *they*.

"I figured that out too," Ronin sidled so close to the Unseelie's side, Kiernan saw him wince. Damn it all to hell. Maybe Tristan's fears hadn't been baseless after all. Aedan had thrown in his lot with them because he was flat out of choices, not because he either liked or trusted them. Having Ronin shoulder to shoulder with him clearly gave him the creeps. It wasn't a good recipe for waging war with a deadly enemy. Not trusting your allies was a one-way ticket to destruction.

Kiernan unclenched his jaws before his teeth broke. Nothing to be done about it now, but he wished Ronin hadn't told Tristan to stuff his concerns.

"If you haven't done so already, ward yourselves," Jenna said, her lovely features screwed into something harsh and forbidding.

Krae beckoned her group of about forty changelings. They surrounded the witches, and Kiernan felt them spin a protective web around the witches and themselves. He smiled grimly. He'd been impressed by the hours he spent with the redheaded changeling. An old soul, her power was rooted in the bones of the Earth, and so potent, he was certain she hadn't plumbed a tenth of it during their practice session. Despite not knowing the specifics of the binding, he felt better knowing Jenna was linked to Krae and her Earth children.

His nostrils flared, catching a whiff of pure evil. Kiernan didn't hesitate. "To arms!" he shouted, borrowing an ancient battle cry. "Something's nearly here."

The air crackled with power, but they were barely ready when a fiery portal formed thirty yards away. Kiernan sent magic auguring into it, trying to blast it into nothingness, but even if the others had helped, he didn't think it would have mattered. His spell sputtered and died, inhaled by dark enchantment. Three Irichna strode through the gateway, not fazed by its flaming rim. Why should they be? Fire was their native element. Fluid shape-shifters, they'd chosen human form. All men, they could have passed for Harvard MBAs, dressed in tasteful suits, with shiny shoes and expensive looking ties. Their hair was trimmed and styled.

The dark-haired one mock bowed and said, "What an unexpected surprise. Welcome to our world. We're the greeting party."

Aedan quivered with outrage. "Where are my kinsmen?"

"Safe, at least for now," the blond spoke up. He smirked. "Maybe your visit wasn't exactly unexpected."

"Depending on the outcome of this meeting, we may release your kinfolk—and the Seelie queen," the third man, who had tawny hair, added.

Oberon stalked as close as he could and still remain within his warding. "Now see here. We do not bargain with evil."

"Oh we don't, do we?" the blond sneered and mimicked Oberon's tone. "Seems you're scarcely in a position to negotiate since we have Titania, but perhaps you've wearied of her after all these years—"

"Silence!" Oberon thundered. "You profane her when her name crosses your lips."

"I told you this was a waste of time," the dark-haired demon said, rolling his eyes skyward.

Kiernan noticed something out of the corners of his eyes. The witches and changelings were cooking something up. To give them the time they needed, he moved to Oberon's side. "My liege, perhaps we should hear them out."

"I don't think so." Oberon stared at Kiernan as if he'd turned into something with claws and scales.

"What do you think?" Kiernan switched his gaze to Aedan. If

any of them were into playing *Let's Make a Deal*, it would be the Unseelie leader.

"What he thinks doesn't matter," Oberon said coldly. "Last time I checked, you owe allegiance to me."

"I'm merely seeking a democratic center." Kiernan smiled guilelessly.

"I agree about hearing them out," Aedan said. "We could expend huge amounts of magic on both sides and end up with a stalemate."

"Our thoughts exactly." The dark-haired demon grinned, displaying very white, very even, teeth.

"At least some of them are still thinking," the tawny-headed one observed.

Oberon angled his head near Kiernan's ear. "What the hell? You've never been insubordinate before."

"We have very good ears," the blond demon chortled.

"Indeed, and we give points for insubordination and for anything else that smacks of noncompliance. It's much more fun being part of our ranks than yours," the tawny-headed demon cut in.

Kiernan filed it away as good information. Perhaps it meant they wouldn't be as well organized as he remembered. Maybe there'd been some changes in Irichna hierarchy since he'd run up against them. He rifled through his brain for a name. "Uh, Rastoko. Is he still in command?"

"You mean Rastoote." The blond waved a dismissive hand. "He was much too regimented. He's been gone for decades."

"No, for centuries," the dark-haired demon corrected him and stepped closer to Kiernan. "Is there some reason you remember him?"

"None in particular." Kiernan stole a glance at the changeling-witch coalition to try to figure out how much more time they might need. If he were any judge, they were closing on something major. He cocked his head to one side and took his time answering the demon. "Rastoote impressed me as a competent general. Troops beneath his command paid attention."

"Until a group of them turned his magic against him," Blondie broke in. "We didn't make that mistake again. None of our remaining generals were into being fragged."

Kiernan snorted. "I do a double take when one of us uses modern phrases. They sound even odder coming from you. Was fragging a big problem in demon circles, th—"

Power surged. The air sizzled with it, and the dark-haired demon cursed in a perversion of ancient Gaelic. Black-tinged fire flew from his raised hands.

Jenna stood in the center of a group of changelings like an ancient beacon holding evil at bay. She was shrouded in numinous light, and power crackled from her outstretched hands. Colleen and Roz held positions by her sides. When Kiernan looked more closely, he realized she was a conduit for ancient Earth-linked magic. The changelings mined it, poured it into her, and she targeted the demons. The other two witches magnified Jenna's newfound power.

"Quick!" Kiernan exhorted everyone. "Hold the demons right here. Do not let them leave. Give the witches and changelings time to destroy them."

"You knew," Oberon shouted.

"Yes. Make this work," Kiernan gritted through clenched teeth. "We won't have a better chance. Or another one. Our magic will dwindle the longer we're here."

Magic roared through the air as they all targeted the Irichna. Fires blazed and smoke thickened. The sharp stench of ozone and sulfur stung Kiernan's nose.

"Don't let them get away," Krae shrieked, mirroring Kiernan's frantic plea. "They'll warn the rest."

"Yes!" Jenna shouted when one folded in on himself and burst into flames. "Two to go. Come on, goddammit, give me more."

"You were born for this," Krae cried. The charged air currents swirling around Jenna, Roz, Colleen, and the changelings intensified.

"That one's ours," Roz said, and she and Colleen focused their power. The second Irichna hurtled imprecations and yelped at direct hits from their magic.

"Help me! Hurry!" Tristan streamed power at the gateway. "Blow it to kingdom come, so they don't have a ready escape route."

Duncan jostled Aedan. "Join your power to mine. Sperrin showed me how. We'll give Tristan what he needs."

The Unseelie nodded grimly. Where their power joined, it burned crimson and raced toward the fiery portal as if it recognized its target. The third demon tried to link with the second in a race to leave, but the portal shattered into bits.

"You forget, this is our world," the third demon, his fine clothes a smoking ruin, growled. He jerked a hand upward and disappeared.

The demon Roz and Colleen had targeted lay face down in the dirt. "He's playing dead," Oberon warned. "Finish him."

"Gladly." Almost lazily, Jenna pointed a finger, and the demon curled into a ball of howling agony before fire consumed him.

"What are ye?" Aedan tried to get to Jenna, but changelings ringed protectively around her and the other two witches.

"Stay back." Krae held up a hand. "She is special to us. Your intentions are murky. Until I figure them out, you will not get close enough to harm her."

"I take that as an affront," Aedan said. "We werena the ones to strip your power, ye arrogant bitch." His face set in such harsh planes, he looked ready to fragment into a million pieces.

"This stops immediately! Forget the infighting." Ronin raised his voice for emphasis. "We need to move. Now. Before the one who got away raises the alarm and they mobilize against us."

Kiernan bared his teeth in Aedan's direction and stomped next to Krae. "I stand with you to protect the witches. We must teleport closer to where Titania and the Unseelie are held prisoner."

"Count me in protecting the witches." Tristan made his way to the circle of changelings and saluted Krae. "You're amazing."

"Thank you, but you'd be better served to thank the goddess someone had sense enough to restore our magic."

"I accept that," Tristan said sadly. "We were the worst kind of fools. I'll see we do everything we can to make it up to your kin."

In the few seconds before they moved out, Kiernan gazed unabashedly at Jenna. She was the most beautiful thing he'd ever seen, with the bearing of an ancient Valkyrie keeping her own safe from harm. He blew her a kiss and mouthed, "I love you."

The corners of her mouth curved into a smile, and she blew a kiss his way. Tristan nudged him. "Isn't she incredible? I'm astonished. I knew I loved her, but I had no idea her power put ours to shame."

"I suspected after that day I spent with her and Krae." Kiernan clapped him on the back. "Let's finish this so we can go home and claim our wife properly."

CHAPTER 15

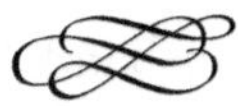

Titania leaned against a wall. The bunch of them were imprisoned in some sort of tower room. It was round and lacked a door or windows. Demons had teleported them inside and left. Naturally, something about the clammy, gray, stone walls muted her magic and presumably the Unseelies' also. Sperrin, Moire, and the other four had been huddled in a tight circle ever since they arrived, speaking telepathically. Titania could have breached their communication, but she didn't bother.

Because standing still grated, she paced, stirring up clouds of gritty dirt. Their prison obviously hadn't been cleaned in years—if ever. She sneezed and picked up the hem of her gown so it wouldn't scatter quite so much coarse material. Bits of stone that had crumbled off the walls and floor battered her ankles and lower legs, but she kept walking in a tight circle. Off to one side, deep grooves gouged the floor, evidence of a prior occupant's fury...or terror.

What a fucked-up mess this had turned into. She didn't have to dig very deep to understand she didn't trust the Unseelie any more than they trusted her. If the dream guardian was so all-fired insistent about them burying the hatchet and getting along, he should've left his sanctuary to oversee the process.

Disgust filled her. *It's not the dream guardian's problem, but mine. I have no one to blame but myself. I set a miserable example for my people with my highhanded ways.*

The Unseelie separated, and Sperrin moved toward her. "We doona blame you for this."

"Nay." Moire joined her husband. "If ye meant us ill, ye'd have come up with an excuse and left the room afore those bastards caught us."

Titania quirked a brow. "It took you the better part of half an hour to come to that conclusion." She raked a hand through her floor-length silver hair and blew out a strained breath. "This isn't any easier for me than it is for you. Imagine the conversations hitting the walls at Ronin's. I'm certain your kinfolk have shown up and are ready to spit nails. They'd probably rather kill us than work together. I hope to hell Oberon's not so distraught about losing me—and looking for a place to lay blame—that he's done something ill advised."

"Aye, we discussed the possibility of that too." Sperrin's voice held a grim note. "We dinna spend the entire time worrying over you."

"What a relief." Titania shook her head. "Sorry, that wasn't called for, and me being sarcastic won't help us."

"Do ye have any idea how we can help them rescue us? Or how we can rescue ourselves?" Moire asked.

"My magic's pretty dead in here," Titania said. "Yours?"

"The same," Sperrin replied.

"Without doors or windows, or magic to blast our way out, we're rather stuck," one of the other Unseelie spoke up. He looked a lot like Sperrin with dark hair and gray eyes. Unlike Sperrin, he was dressed in blue jeans, a beige T-shirt featuring a beach scene, and a denim jacket.

Titania balled her hand into a fist. "There must be a way out of this."

"Were we in a tower on Earth, there would be," Moire said. "We're too far from the roots of our power on this borderworld."

A mouse made a dash from one side of the room to the other and disappeared. "What in the goddess's name?" Titania followed its path. "How did it get in or out?"

"Mayhap 'tis a magical creature," Sperrin suggested.

"Or a spy for the Irichna," another Unseelie said dourly.

"Och and ye're not thinking," Moire said. "They can spy on us all they want with their own magic. They scarcely need mice for that purpose."

In the meantime, Titania used the side of her foot to scrape layers of broken rock and dirt away from where the mouse had disappeared from sight. Kneeling, she found a small, round hole, perhaps two inches across, at the floor's edge. She stuck a finger down the hole experimentally and focused magic through it. For the first time since she'd been imprisoned, her power didn't bounce back at her. It was weak, truncated, but it was there.

"Ye've found something." Sperrin joined her.

"I did. It's not much, but I'll take whatever I can get. This hole breaks whatever's dampening my power."

"Can we enlarge it?" Moire asked, hope flaring painfully beneath her question.

"Maybe." Titania withdrew her finger until just the tip was inside the hole and summoned power. It arced in a shower of sparks, but stone chips fell away, and the hole grew a little bigger.

"At this rate, 'twill take until next year, plus we have no idea what's beneath us. It may well be another room just like this one," Moire muttered.

"If I make the hole big enough to project telepathically," Titania said, still balancing power and enlarging the space, "maybe I can communicate with whoever shows up to rescue us."

"Ye're assuming they can figure out where we are," Sperrin said.

"Ronin and Kiernan are excellent at scrying the past. They'll piece it together." Titania spoke with a bravado she was far from feeling. Spending eternity on the Irichnas' borderworld—or in the *Dreaming*—wasn't high on her list. "Help me." She jerked her chin toward Sperrin. "This will go faster with two of us and our blend of different magics."

He hunkered next to her. "The rest of ye do the best ye can to shield us," he instructed.

"I don't think we'll ever make it big enough to escape," Titania said. "Best I'm hoping for is if I funnel magic through it, I'll be able to let the rescue party know where we are."

"How do ye know the Irichna won't detect your magic first, come in here, and flay the skin off us?" an Unseelie woman with short, red hair and brown eyes asked.

"I don't." Titania winced and glanced up. She was taking a lot for granted, and these weren't her subjects. Once upon a time they had been, but not anymore. "I'm dragging all of us onto even riskier ground than we already stand on. Before I go farther, are we in agreement on this?"

"I doona like it, yet I doona see any other way," the Unseelie woman said. A chorus of assent rose around her, and Titania turned back to the ever-widening opening.

"'Tis better than waiting for the demons' pleasure," Sperrin muttered darkly.

They worked in silence as time ticked by. Titania's throat was tight, and her heart pounded against her chest. She was afraid they wouldn't finish before demons interrupted them and undid their work. Finally, the hole was fist sized.

"It's enough." She sat back, panting. Sweat ran down her back and sides, and her jeweled gown stuck to her body. "Give me a minute to catch my breath, and I'll see what I can find out there."

"It might be better if we tried together," Sperrin said.

Titania shook her head. "If we blend both halves of Faerie power and project it outside this tower, the demons will surely notice. Let's save that for when they drag us out of here."

"If they never did," Moire said with a dour note, "we'd fade into the *Dreaming*."

"Aye and I've been thinking," the Unseelie male with blue jeans said, "'tis possible we were simply bait, and what the demons truly want are the witches. Once they're out of the way, there'll be nothing standing between Abbadon and his insane desire to break free from Hell and set himself up as ruler of Earth."

"I'd come to much the same conclusion," Titania said. "It's unlikely the demons know we inoculated a group of Sidhe with the witches' blood so we could reclaim our demon assassin responsibilities."

"None of this matters," Moire spoke firmly. "We must remain in the moment. Go ahead." She tilted her chin toward Titania. "See what ye find out there."

Titania set her jaw in a determined line. She'd been in tight spots before. The important thing was to keep thinking, keep trying, and keep her spirits up. Once she gave in to despair, the game would be up.

"All right. Here goes."

She focused a narrow beam of power carrying a telepathic message through the hole. To minimize risk of discovery, she kept it short. A simple *I am here* repeated a dozen times, silence, and then a new burst of communication. Any Sidhe would recognize her sending. After three cycles, she rocked back onto her heels and waited.

"Maybe I should try," Sperrin said and broke off pacing in a tight circle to stand over her.

"No." She held up a hand, fingers splayed. "Give it more time. It's barely been five minutes."

Titania draped herself over the opening and prayed to Danu for a break, just this once. After long enough that her feet and legs numbed from lack of movement, she tried again, more because she couldn't think of anything else to do than because she thought it would work.

"Titania!" rang in her mind. It shocked her so, she bolted upright and nearly fell over because she couldn't feel her feet.

Even though she wanted the comfort of conversation with Oberon, she held herself back. It would work in their favor if the demons had no idea they could communicate.

The Unseelie closed around her. "They heard you." Sperrin was practically dancing, he was so excited.

"Ssht." Titania placed a finger over her lips and bent low over the hole again. *"Have you located us?"*

"Yes, thanks to your distress call. Do nothing to antagonize them before we can get to you."

"No more talk." Ronin cut in, sounding so stern Titania could have hugged him. She and Oberon had chosen well when they'd made him the Sidhe leader.

She straightened and motioned with her hands for the Unseelie to draw near so she could whisper what she'd heard.

"...and in the meantime," she added, "it could scarcely hurt for us to keep chipping away at that hole. We may need a route to channel our magic."

"If it gets big enough, all of us working together could blast this infernal tower into ruin." Moire grinned viciously and flashed two fingers in a victory sign.

～

"ARE YOU CERTAIN IT WAS HER?" Ronin curved a hand around Oberon's arm, but the king didn't shake him off.

Watching from his vantage point near the changelings and witches, Tristan expected fireworks, but Oberon was apparently so grateful to have a solution present itself, he didn't chide Ronin for his familiarity. They'd teleported to where Aedan thought he sensed the kidnapped Unseelie, but it had been some sort of Irichna trick. Where they currently stood was the third place they'd tried, but it had turned out the same as the first two. A dry well.

No Titania and no Unseelie.

"Yes," Oberon grunted. "I'd recognize my wife's telepathic voice anywhere."

"Maybe not," Aedan cut in. "It might be another Irichna trick."

"It's not."

"How do ye know?" Aedan pressed.

Oberon did shake Ronin's hand off then. He drew himself up and faced Aedan. "I am not used to being questioned. You will just have to take my word. If that isn't good enough for you, I suggest you take your contingent and leave. The last thing we need is this continuing current of ill will."

Erika stalked to Aedan's side. "Oberon's right," she said. "Either we swallow our discontent, or we should go home."

"I suggest you do more than swallow it." Oberon scrunched his eyes into stern slits. "Find a way to let it go." He pressed his lips together. "I know because it's the same battle I've been fighting."

The conversation continued, but Tristan had stopped listening. Tempers were growing even more frayed than when they'd been at Ronin's manor house. Krae had gone so far as to announce the witches and changelings weren't going anywhere else unless and until they had better intel.

"All we're doing," she'd said, "is leaving a track a mile wide for the Irichna to figure out a way to unravel our magic."

As it was, Tristan felt his powers weakening. It was gradual, but noticeable. At the current rate, he figured they had a few more hours at best before they'd have to leave, or they wouldn't have enough magic to teleport back to Earth. The one positive spot was Jenna. She and the other two witches were bright, funny, and optimistic, cracking black humor jokes when they ran up against one dead end after another. For the first time, he understood how they'd kept going when their kin died off one by one. The more time he spent around Jenna, the more he admired her spunk and her courage.

It was counterproductive, because their situation was only a few steps shy of dire, but his mind had turned more than once to the time they'd spent together in her bed. His body came alive at the thought of her firm curves pressed hard against him. She was so ardent and responsive, part of him hated to share her with Kiernan, but a bigger part wanted her to be happy and joyous and fulfilled. He'd seen her body's response to both of them in her fantasy. More than that, her spirit had welcomed him and Kiernan...

Kiernan elbowed him hard. "Blast it, Tristan! I've been talking to you, and you haven't heard a single word."

"Guilty as charged." He eyed Kiernan. "Tell me again."

The other Sidhe glanced away. "It wasn't important. I was floating plans for where and how we'd live once we get back."

"Um, don't you think that should be a three-way conversation?" Tristan tossed a warm glance Jenna's way and got an answering smile in return.

"I thought it would go better if we ironed out any differences we might have first and then presented a united front. We can always fine tune things depending on what she wants. Anyway, my house is more centrally located, and I have an entire empty floor if you wanted to move things from your place. Not that we wouldn't use your house as a country retreat..." Kiernan's voice trailed off. He gazed at Tristan and drew his brows together. "I fail to see what's so funny."

The corners of Tristan's mouth threatened to break into a smile. "Where have you been keeping yourself these past couple of centuries?"

Kiernan squeezed his brows even closer together, looking affronted. "I've been using my magic to keep us safe and training our acolytes."

"It was a metaphorical question." The smile that had threatened broke through. "You have a treat in store—and a bunch of surprises. Modern women are assertive. They don't let us tell them what they want anymore. You and I could spin the most amazing castle in the air, and she might tell us she wants to go back to Alaska."

"What?" Kiernan looked thunderstruck. "There's nothing there but ice and snow and primitive dwellings. Polar bears and reindeer."

"I believe there's a little more than that. Besides, it is her home."

"Tristan, Kiernan. Over here," Oberon commanded.

They joined their king, and Tristan said, "We're lending our power to the changelings and witches."

"No." Oberon narrowed his eyes. "From here on in, we're a unified command. This won't work with the changelings running one war and us another. Even Aedan finally came to that conclusion."

"Sire." Tristan inclined his head.

"Have you noticed your magic dwindling?" Oberon asked. At Tristan's nod, the king went on. "Everyone has, which is why we must move quickly. We will teleport to where I know Titania is and deploy every tactic at our disposal to move her and the Unseelie to safety. Once they're en route, we shall leave. Questions?"

Tristan shook his head. "Would you like me to let Krae and the witches know?"

"We heard," Krae called.

"Indeed." Roz chuckled. "Witches have excellent ears too, especially when we augment our senses with magic."

A muted crackling caught at the barest edges of Tristan's hearing. He might not have noticed, but it repeated itself. He twirled, raking the still, dead air of the borderworld with his augmented senses.

Kiernan mirrored his movements and mouthed, "I sense something too," just before all hell broke loose.

Fiery portals blazed into being all around them, and Hell's minions streamed through. Irichna, goblins, trolls, lesser demons, and the undead mingled with creatures Tristan had never seen before. Hundreds of fell beings surrounded them and moved between them, making it impossible to create a group ward.

Instead, Tristan warded himself and felt Kiernan do the same. They were too far from the witches and changelings to help them. Tristan tried to angle back that way and found the path blocked by at least thirty trolls. Their enormous, squat bodies were partially coated in dark brown scales, and they swung cudgels over their heads, flinging them into the air and howling with delight. It looked as if Abbadon didn't let them out very often, but they'd be a deadly enemy once they got over their elation over being free.

Tristan hesitated, unsure quite what to target first, and was buried in a pile of goblins that drove him to the ground. Adrenaline knifed through him, and he mobilized defensive magic like a madman. The goblins were trying to crush him, rather than using magic to annihilate him, but the end result—millennia in the *Dreaming*—would be the same. He thrashed about, struggling to get up, but failed. Fury and fear drove him, and he funneled killing power, desperate to see something other than the ground and goblin flesh. Tristan spat dirt while he gouged out eyes, created magical garrotes to cut off breath, and even kicked one particularly loathsome creature right in the balls. It worked; the goblin grunted in pain and fell backward.

Tristan saw his chance and grabbed it, lurching upright. He spewed power in an arc, twirling so everything within a few feet of him fell. Normally, he avoided killing, preferring to banish his enemies to off-world locations, but that wasn't an option here because it took more power, and they were badly outnumbered.

Once he'd cleared breathing space, he glanced about and took in a scene from Dante's Inferno. Dark power scorched the earth and sparked nastily when it ran up against theirs. Thick smoke roiled from the portals or from magic colliding with other magic. There were so many demons and minions, he couldn't do a head count of those on either side. When he sucked in air, his lungs burned from demon taint.

A form rocketed toward him through the murk. He raised his hands to kill it, had almost released power, when he realized it was Kiernan. "You shouldn't do that, mate," he panted as he reined in his magic.

"Never mind." Kiernan struggled for breath too. "We've got to do something. The changelings and witches are gone."

"Nooooooo!" Tristan barely recognized the desolate howl that rose from him as mortal, let alone coming from him. "Were they taken?"

Kiernan ran a hand down his face and left a sooty track across one cheek and his chin. "I don't think so."

"That means they've gone after Titania and the other Unseelies."

"Did Oberon ever say exactly where they were?" Kiernan asked.

"No."

"Doesn't matter." Kiernan grabbed Tristan's arm, but he jerked it away and sent power chasing after a phalanx of undead that were converging.

"What are you doing?" Tristan demanded after Kiernan grabbed his arm again. "I need to fight."

"We're going after the witches and changelings. I can track their route, but if we wait too much longer, my magic may not be strong enough."

Tristan held back, remembering Oberon's exhortations to stand as a unit. Kiernan stopped tugging on him and said, "I was just in your head. Oberon's wishes don't count at the moment.

The barn door's already open, and the cow is gone. I'm leaving with you or without you. Are you in?"

"We can't leave our king."

"I agree we shouldn't, but Oberon has Ronin, Duncan, and a bunch of Sidhe warriors, plus the Unseelie. They should be fine. We won't be gone long. Either we'll find them and free them, or…" He let his words trail off, but it wasn't hard to fill in the blanks. Kiernan clearly wasn't done because he forged ahead. "Look. The outcome here is…uncertain. We can remain where we are and possibly be trapped, overpowered, and run our magic down to ground zero, or we can split our forces in a way that makes sense. The way things stand, the witches and changelings may not make it, and this group may not, either. At least if we try to help the weaker link, it might even the scales."

"Did you see this in a vision?"

Kiernan's face twisted, and he spat the word, "Yes," so it eddied between them. "Parts of it."

Tristan knew the other Sidhe wouldn't say any more. He felt torn, but the witches and changelings needed help. They were fearless, but not always wise. Only the witches and a few changelings had formal training in battle strategy.

"I'll come with you—" lunging to one side, Tristan killed another goblin, "—but I'm letting Oberon know what we're doing."

"I already did," Kiernan jerked his chin upward in annoyance. "I'm not a total turncoat. Lace your power with mine, and we'll be out of here."

Misgivings riddled Tristan as the battlefield paled and disappeared. Magic crackled nastily, and he hoped to hell Kiernan knew what he was doing.

As if he'd read his mind, Kiernan muttered, "A couple more seconds now."

Tristan gathered power to cushion his fall, but he still hit harder than he would have liked. The smoke-choked air was exactly like what they'd left. "Goddammit! You led us in a circle."

"I did no such thing," Kiernan yanked him upright. "You think there's only one battle allowed at a time on any given border-world? We're smack in the center of another one. Now let's figure out where our queen is, so we can get the witches and changelings out of here."

CHAPTER 16

Fury filled Jenna as she watched demons and their spawn pour out of blazing portals. The attack had come so suddenly, it took her a moment to wrap her mind around what was happening. And another much-too-long moment before she sent a blast of lethal power chasing after misshapen creatures she'd never seen before. Massive like trolls, they sported two heads covered with greasy orange hair and four arms. Long, curved black talons sprouted from their hands. Just looking at them sent an unpleasant chill down her spine. What other treats did the Irichna have in store for them?

"At least this explains what they've been up to," she muttered.

"No shit!" Colleen said.

"I thought it was much too quiet." Roz's full mouth split into a wild, untamed grin. "I say we get 'em." Power crackled from her upraised hands, and a group of goblins exploded.

"And I say this is perfect cover for us to go after Titania and the others," Krae said. "I plucked the location from Oberon's mind, and no one will even notice we're gone. This crew will be much too busy defending themselves to stop us—even if they did notice us sneaking off—let alone do anything about it."

Jenna eyed rapidly thickening smoke. Krae's suggestion was more than tempting. She'd been annoyed when Oberon began ordering them about. From the sour expressions on Roz's and Colleen's faces, she suspected they felt the same. Of course, they were duty bound since their husbands answered to Oberon, but Jenna had no such obligations—yet.

"What do you think?" She looked from Roz to Colleen.

"It beats sticking around here." Colleen swung her head from side to side. "We're already badly outnumbered, and they just keep coming."

"They won't quit, either." Niall sidled to Colleen's side.

"How do you know?" Colleen asked her familiar.

"Because of all the times we've fought them." Niall drew himself up. "They want to get rid of you, all three of you, and they'll never have a better chance. They muffed it last time you were on their world. They won't make the same mistake twice. Not if they can help it."

"He has a point," Roz said.

"Of course he does." Krae exhaled sharply. "Are we going to talk this to death or leave?"

"Let's go," Jenna said.

Krae gathered the changelings. Magic flashed around them, but they only huddled for a few moments before Krae beckoned to the witches. "I've done what I can to buy us enough time to leave."

Jenna linked arms with Roz and Colleen and mouthed, "We're ready." She sensed Colleen's resoluteness and Roz's steadfastness and thanked Danu for the thousandth time for such remarkable companions.

"Girl power." Colleen squeezed her arm.

"Nope, witch power. Witches rule, and don't you ever forget it." Roz squeezed her other arm. "Let's get out of here before Ronin pitches a fit."

"Don't forget Duncan." Colleen made a snorting noise. "If he knew what we were up to, he'd lock us behind wards."

It was a fluke that Tristan and Kiernan had left their side, but Jenna didn't see any reason to mention it. The smoky battlefield flickered and then faded. Because they weren't going far, she barely had time to blink before the stale aspect of the borderworld reformed around her, musty with decay. This time, the unending plain of flat, packed dirt with mountains in the distance was broken by a crumbling castle.

Towers studded its corners. The occasional window dotted the front of the structure, but the side walls rushed upward without any breaks. Built of dreary gray stones, it was enormous with rambling wings jutting off in several directions. Jenna twisted her neck from side to side as she gazed wildly about in search of something to mask their presence. Unfortunately, trees were in short supply. She drew an invisibility spell, but its magical signature stuck out like a lion in a sheep's pen, so she gave it up. Even her new magic wouldn't last forever here, and squandering it wasn't wise.

"No chance for stealth." Roz pressed her lips into a thin, determined line.

"I agree." Krae drew close. "Speed is our friend. They're in the left hand tower farthest from us."

Jenna considered asking if Krae was certain but bit her tongue. She'd never known the changeling to be wrong. "Do we just storm in through the front door?"

"If we teleport into the tower, we might be snared in whatever caught them," Colleen pointed out.

Krae favored her with an approving glance. "Let's see if we can find a back door, or something closer to where they are." She switched to heavily shielded telepathy and called, *"Titania!"*

No response. "Maybe she's afraid you're an Irichna setting a snare for her," Jenna murmured. "Let me try. *Titania, it's Jenna. We're close.*"

After a pause that lasted so long they'd already set off for the castle's perimeter at a brisk lope, a faint whisper brushed the edges of Jenna's hearing. *"Prove it."*

"You brought Oberon back from the Dreaming after Irichna attacked at Colleen's wedding."

"You'll have to do better than that." A suspicious laugh crackled.

Jenna ransacked her brain for something Irichna wouldn't know. *"My magic is…different because apparently my father was over half Sidhe."*

Hissing breath rattled through Jenna's head. *"Holy godhead. I didn't know that. Who all are here?"*

"Me, Roz, Colleen, and the changelings."

"We're in some kind of tower—"

"Sorry to be rude," Jenna cut in, *"but we already figured that out."*

"Can you help us at all?" Krae spoke over Jenna.

"Yes." Titania sounded as fierce as Jenna had ever heard her.

"Do all you can. It's quiet now, but they're not just going to let us waltz in, spring you, and leave. No more talk." Krae's mind voice was edgy with pessimism, as if even she dreaded the next span of time.

As they closed the hundred yards to one of the castle's side walls, a deep trench filled with murky water became visible. "Where's the drawbridge?" Roz joked.

"Yeah, and the portcullis. Didn't these old places have those too?" Colleen chimed in.

"Shut up!" Krae jabbed a forefinger at the black-tinged water. "Look there."

Movement beneath the water's surface held a menacing aspect. Jenna stared because she couldn't look away. A huge triangular head broke the water and stared back. The thing opened its mouth to reveal triple rows of two-inch teeth. "Jesus Christ! It's the Loch Ness monster." Jenna raised her hands to send power auguring into it.

"Stop!" Krae shouted. Lowering her voice, she added, "It's illusion and an early warning system—for the Irichna."

Jenna froze and dragged her gaze from the sea serpent. It wasn't easy, almost as if the thing generated compulsion. "How will we get to the castle if we don't kill it?"

"One problem at a time." Krae broke into a run, heading for the back wall of the castle with the changelings strung out behind her.

Jenna caught up, along with Roz and Colleen. "This has an Alice in Wonderland feel to it," Colleen muttered.

"Do you suppose the white rabbit will show up to eat us?" Roz smirked.

Jenna wasn't in a joking mood. Maybe running off like this hadn't been wise, and they should leave while they still could. If Krae's plan blew up in their faces…

"Jenna!" Roz closed a hand around her arm and shook her. "Irichna! They're in your head. I can feel them. Shield yourself."

"Gawk! No wonder all these negative thoughts bounded in out of nowhere." Between Roz's touch and a magical assist, Jenna sensed Irichna lurking at the threshold of her consciousness. Fury boiled hot, and she slammed better wards in place to protect herself. "If they could do that," she panted, "they know we're here."

"Crap!" Roz skinned her lips back from her teeth. "Get ready, girls, we're about to have company."

In an instant replay of the scene just before they'd left Kiernan and Tristan, blazing portals morphed into being all around them. Irichna poured through. At least this time, it was only Irichna. No minions.

Only Irichna. That's rich. Since when am I thankful to be facing demons by themselves? They're far more lethal than anything else that crawls out of Hell.

Jenna stopped thinking. Power thickened the air, and it crackled and sputtered around her as the changelings channeled magic for her to use. Roz and Colleen stayed close, adding their castings to the mix as Jenna lobbed blast after blast of death at the demons. She hit a few, but most erected shielding she couldn't power through.

"This isn't going well," Colleen mumbled.

"No shit." Roz shoved hair that had escaped from her braids out of the way, but some caught fire and smoldered anyway.

They'd reached the back of the castle before the Irichna attack. Jenna made out a ground level door swathed in layers of illusion. It would get her inside, provided she could reach it. Since stealth had ceased to be important, she estimated what it would take to get across the twenty feet of water.

"Krae! If the sea serpent's a deception, does that mean I can swim across the moat?"

The changeling blew out a long, hissing breath. "I don't know."

"You are not going in there alone," Colleen told Jenna.

"It's better that way. I can move faster, and if something goes wrong, some of you are left to free Titania and the Unseelie."

"If you go, we're all going," Roz said and spun to target another Irichna. Jenna added a magical boost, and it exploded. Roz fist-pumped the air. "Die, you sorry bastard!"

Jenna sidled to the water's edge. Proximity to the dank, slimy water made her skin crawl. Even the brief time it would take to swim twenty feet to the castle side would be so miserable, she was certain it would haunt her dreams for a long time. She hunkered low and placed an experimental hand in the water.

Niall and Llyr rushed her, knocking her out of the way just before the serpent's head burst out of the water with its multiple rows of fangs bared. Jenna rolled away from the water, but not far enough. The creature sprayed her with a combination of spittle and the loathsome water. It burned where it contacted her skin, and she funneled magic to counteract whatever poison etched into her hands and arms like strong acid. Her clothing smoked where droplets touched it.

So much for swimming across the moat.

"I thought you said it was illusion," she shouted at Krae.

"Sometimes I'm wrong. Get up," the changeling barked. "We need to regroup."

~

TITANIA LAY on her belly with her ear plastered to the hole in the floor. It was the only way she could follow the battle raging outside. Sperrin had positioned himself right next to her, listening intently too. After Jenna yelled at Krae for being wrong about whatever abomination the Irichna set as a guard dog in the moat that ringed their prison, he said, "We have to do something."

"I agree." Titania pushed to a cross-legged sit. "The demons will keep them so busy, they'll never get inside, and even if they did, there's no door into this room."

"If they got close enough, they could decimate the wall with magic, but it's a moot point," Moire said. "How big is that hole?"

"Maybe six inches across," Titania replied.

"I still believe we could blow up this tower," Moire said. "Only problem is, it will require split-second timing. We have to be on top of the exact moment the binding in the walls that's muting our magic dissolves…"

"…because if we don't jump on it and use our magic to teleport out of here, we'll be buried in rubble," Titania finished for her.

"Where are we teleporting to?" the Unseelie male in blue jeans asked.

"Aye," Sperrin nodded. "Do we stop here first or go to where Oberon is?"

"We do both." Titania spoke firmly. "One or two of us must alert Oberon's group that we are free so they can abandon this borderworld. The rest of us will do as much damage as we can here before we leave."

"I'll let Oberon and Ronin know," the Unseelie male offered.

"Aye, and I'll go with him," the Unseelie woman who'd spoken up earlier said.

"Excellent. We have that part mapped out." Titania narrowed her eyes and met Moire's green gaze. "There's only one chance to get this right."

"Och, tell me something I doona know." Moire jerked her chin at Sperrin. "Ye and I will tap the dark half of Faerie, Titania the bright half. Once our power is woven together, we set it within the hole and give it everything we have pressing outward."

"It should work." Sperrin smoothed his hands down his robe. His smoke-gray eyes tracked from one Unseelie to the next. "Be ready," he cautioned.

"What about you?" the Unseelie woman with red hair asked. "Your magic will be tangled with the unmaking spell. Can ye draw it back soon enough to escape?"

Sperrin flashed a jaunty smile. "Thanks for the warning. We're about to find out."

Indeed we are. Titania envied Sperrin's ability to summon humor in the midst of desperate straits.

If I get out of this, I'll work on that.

Titania knelt over the hole and held out her hands on either side. Sperrin took one, Moire the other. No words were exchanged; they didn't need any. Titania reached deep, threading power from the roots of her being into the Unseelies' spell. It felt right somehow. As if the magic had languished for want of its mirror half.

At first the rim of the hole glistened wetly, and then it shimmered into a rainbow of colors before turning bright red. Moire's and Sperrin's hands tightened, and Titania gave a mighty heave with her mage gift. The red rim of the hole flashed so brightly, it burned an afterimage into her vision she feared might be permanent. A brisk, cracking noise was followed by another. The stone floor beneath her body swayed alarmingly, rippling like an unquiet sea.

"Keep going." Sperrin spoke as if the words cost him. "We need more."

Titania plumbed the well and found more magic, knowing she'd pay for running so much voltage through herself. Even if she ended up in the *Dreaming* forever, at least she would have gone out in a blaze of glory. It felt invigorating to be buried to the teeth in something worth fighting for. She breathed in the heady feeling and sucked it down like vintage mead. Fine dust filled the air, and the cracking sounds intensified, as brittle as automatic rifle fire.

She never knew what alerted her, but she shouted, "Now. We have to leave now," to Sperrin, Moire, and the others.

Breath rattled in Titania's throat, and her body was soaked with sweat. She redirected her power just as the opening in the floor burst outward, showering what was left of her teleporting molecules with huge blocks of stone. Tense moments passed before she tumbled onto stone-studded earth in the middle of smoke so thick she couldn't see anything. The rumble of at least part of the castle catapulting into ruin shook the earth beneath her. She clung to a boulder—or maybe it was part of what had been the castle—sucking air, still not believing she'd escaped.

"Sperrin! Moire!" she yelled, but her voice came out a feeble croak. She sucked saliva from the dryness of her mouth, swallowed, and tried again.

"Here," sounded off to her left, the voice so raspy she couldn't tell who it was.

Because the air was clearer next to the ground, Titania crawled toward the voice and found Moire. The Unseelie focused her green eyes on Titania. "Where's Sperrin?"

"I don't know."

"Have ye seen anyone else?"

Titania shook her head. "In case you hadn't noticed, no one can see much of anything." She took stock of what magic she had left. Not much. "How's your magic?"

"How do ye think?" Moire made a sour face. "Drained."

"I'll have to do this the old-fashioned way." Titania struggled to her feet, trying not to breathe too deeply because the air was so smoky and choked with particles. "We need to hunt for the others and let the witches and changelings know we're free."

"Wait!" Moire held out a hand, and Titania tugged her upright. "I'm going with you. We can help each other."

CHAPTER 17

Kiernan ducked as a chunk of castle flew by his head. It had imploded with a deafening roar not two minutes after their arrival. Air that had been smoky before was so clogged with dust and debris, it was impossible to see anything. He diverted a trickle of magic to clear the air before he breathed it in.

"I'm guessing Titania and them got out," Tristan said.

"It's a good guess," Kiernan agreed. "I'm assuming they survived. Have you tried to find her?"

"Yes, but she's not answering."

"Humph." Kiernan peered through the gloom. "She probably doesn't have enough magic left to power a mage light, which means we need to do something beyond telepathy to locate her and the Unseelie group."

Tristan cracked a broad grin. "Let's get moving. I want to find Jenna. Once we've located everyone, we need to teleport out of here, pronto."

Kiernan dropped a heavy hand onto Tristan's shoulder. "I agree about leaving, but we are going to dish out maximum destruction before we go. I never want to deal with these bastards again. Ever."

Tristan spat on the ground and wiped the back of one hand across his mouth. "Good luck with that, mate. I don't, either, but even if we blew this borderworld back to Hell, we wouldn't make much of a dent."

Should I?

Kiernan hesitated a beat because he rarely shared his visions.

"Whatever it is, spit it out," Tristan said. "Whoever's left here needs us."

"The seat of Irichna power is here. It's where their princes dwell. If we did *blow this borderworld back to Hell*, it would make a huge difference."

Tristan cocked his head to one side and narrowed his eyes in thought. Soot and grime streaked his face. "And you know this how?"

"My visions. All those years when you were figuring out modern women, I was sequestered in one cave or another reading the future of our people. I've seen today—in all its iterations. It's why we're here—and not back with Ronin and them."

"What exactly does that mean? Magic is where I live, but you're giving me the creeps with all this precognitive mumbo-jumbo."

Kiernan moved his hand. "Doesn't matter. Let's round up who's here and see if the demons stuck around after their castle exploded."

Tristan shot him an odd look. "Seems like you'd know that part."

Two figures stumbled toward them out of the murk. Kiernan sensed Titania's energy and raced toward them. "My queen." He bowed low and extended a hand to stabilize Titania, who swayed on her feet.

"Never mind that." She swatted his hand away. "Where's Oberon?"

Kiernan swallowed hard. There wasn't time to soft-soap the truth. Even in her depleted state, Titania would know if he lied to her. "He's with Ronin, Aedan, and a group of our people and Unseelie, fighting demons. The witches and changelings went after you. I thought they might need help, so Tristan and I followed them."

"Enough talk." Moire shook her head as if to clear her mind. "Sperrin is missing. Ye still have power. Please. Help me find him."

"And the other four Unseelie?" Tristan asked.

"Two went to alert Ronin and Oberon," Titania said. "Hopefully, they'll leave this accursed place, but I fear they won't leave without me."

Kiernan looked away to lessen the odds Titania would read either his mind or his face. Her part in today's battle was over, but the day—and its losses—was far from done. "I'm going to find the witches and changelings," he muttered and took off at a brisk trot, crunching over castle debris as he went. He sought witch energy with his mind and switched direction.

An Irichna stepped square in his path wearing its true form. Kiernan blinked and forced himself not to look away. He was used to seeing Irichna in borrowed human shapes. It came as a shock to see one that looked like a demon, complete with horns, hooves, and a tail. Its eyes glowed like banked coals, and fangs closed over its lower lip.

"Out of my way." Kiernan stepped to one side. The demon mirrored his movement and released power, but it bounced off Kiernan's warding. "Your days are nearly done," Kiernan said. "Now move unless you wish to die sooner than the rest of your people."

"You don't frighten me, Sidhe." Fire shot from the Irichna's hands. Kiernan's clothing smoldered where sparks landed.

"What's this?" Tristan chugged alongside. "Immobilize it and be done with things." Before Kiernan could answer, Tristan launched power at the demon. It grunted and doubled over.

Tristan landed a booted foot in its gut and started to draw more power.

"Good enough. Leave it. We have to hurry." Kiernan loped toward the witches with Tristan right behind him.

A high, keening wail pierced his soul, and he knew what he'd find. He'd hoped maybe, just maybe, he'd arrive in time to push the hands of fate askew, but that hardly ever worked. The murk thinned, and a scene he'd seen countless times in trance states spread before him. Krae lay on the ground in a spreading pool of blood. Jenna and Roz worked frantically, trying to save her, but Krae's spirit hovered above her body, anxious to move on. Colleen, Niall, Llyr, and the other changelings stood guard, ringed in an outward-facing circle, their faces as grim as the death that stalked them.

"Do something," Jenna exhorted Roz. "All this new magic of mine isn't worth a damn for healing."

"I've done all I can." Roz raised haunted eyes and bloodstained hands. "She's lost too much blood. Beyond that, she hosts demon bits. Removing them is beyond my ability."

"Then we need to teleport her to a Sidhe healer." Jenna bent low over Krae. "Hang on, goddammit. You can't leave us. More to the point, you can't leave me. I'll carry the guilt for the rest of my days."

A low, piteous moan bubbled past Krae's lips, and Kiernan hastened forward, kneeling next to her. The changeling's green eyes flickered open. "Sidhe man."

"Yes. It's me."

"Tell them…" Blood spurted from her mouth and dribbled down her chin. When she spoke again, he had to bend close to hear, "…my role is done. Let me go."

He gathered her to him, cradling her slight form against his chest. Kiernan looked from Roz to Jenna. "Sheathe your power. It's all that's holding her on this plane."

"But she can't die. Your magic is strong. Do something. Save her." Tears pelted down Jenna's cheeks, and her face contorted with grief.

"My magic isn't that strong. Besides, this was foretold. She's already dead. Your magic is all that's tethering her spirit. She's in a great deal of pain. You have to let her go."

Roz laid a hand over Jenna's. "Listen to Kiernan."

"Irichna are massing," Colleen said. "We need you, Jenna. You can mourn later."

Jenna bent and kissed Krae's forehead. "I love you for the doors you opened for me."

"I love you too, witchy girl. Remain true to all within you. Never doubt—" A fresh gout of blood shot from the changeling's mouth, cutting off further words and staining the front of Kiernan's shirt.

"Jenna. Now!" Colleen sounded desperate.

Jenna shot upright. She and Roz joined Colleen. Niall kissed Krae's forehead and motioned to the other changelings. "This one's for Krae," he snarled. "Let's wipe those bastards off the face of this world."

As Krae's body relaxed against him with the bonelessness of new death, Kiernan closed her eyes. Summoned by the changelings, power roiled around him, simmering like a live thing. Tristan stood behind the witches, lethal magic streaking from his hands. Kiernan laid his cheek against Krae's forehead. "Farewell, little sister. You fought well."

"You knew." Her spirit's voice in his mind was very faint. He just nodded. *"I knew too,"* Krae struggled on. *"Jenna was my last task."* She paused so long, he thought she was truly gone, but her spirit managed one last thought. *"Take care of her."*

"I promise."

When Kiernan looked up, Jenna was glowing like an otherworldly statue. Power soared through her, shooting from her hands in waves. Ranks of demons dissolved into nothingness. Off to his right, the air took on a numinous quality. Kiernan got to his feet, still holding Krae in his arms. He knew this next part too.

The dream guardian shimmered into being and walked forward. Kiernan handed Krae to him. When he looked into the ever-changing collage of images in the guardian's eyes, he saw the changeling's final resting place and bowed. "Thank you. It means I can visit her and pay homage."

The guardian inclined his head. "We are nearly done here. Take your people and leave."

Kiernan narrowed his eyes. "I have seen more than one ending for today."

"What happens next is out of your hands. Take your people and leave," the guardian repeated.

Titania and Moire stumbled forward. "May she rest undisturbed." Titania laid a hand on Krae's body, nestled in the guardian's arms.

"Please." Moire cast her hollow-eyed gaze at the guardian. "Do ye know where Sperrin and two more Unseelie are? We've looked everywhere, and now that my magic has recovered a bit, I canna feel their energy."

His stern aspect softened. "You cut your exit from the tower much too close. They were lost in my traveling ether, but I saw them safely home."

Moire's face crumpled; tears of relief stained her cheeks, making tracks through the grime. Titania folded her into her arms. Her gaze met the guardian's over the Unseelie's head. "Someone must tell my husband you expect us to leave."

"I tried." The corners of the guardian's mouth twitched. "He is one stubborn man. Once he lays eyes on you, he'll stage a retreat. He told me as much."

"I'll take care of things here," Kiernan told Titania. "Do you have enough magic to teleport to the other side of this ill-fated borderworld?"

She nodded. "That I do. See you soon. We'll be at Ronin's."

Moire untangled herself from Titania's embrace and looked pointedly at the guardian. "If ye're certain we're not needed, I'll be on my way."

"Quite certain." He screwed his face into a disgusted moue. "Normally, I don't interfere, but I want to finish things. Rid this borderworld of demons and dark taint, so it can recover enough to support life again. You must be gone before I proceed."

"Understood." Magic sparked around Moire, and she vanished. Titania gave a thumbs up sign and disappeared too.

Kiernan strode to Tristan's side behind the witches. Power flowing through them was so potent, it drew him into its spell. Irichna still fought back, but feebly. He raised his voice to make certain everyone heard him. "The guardian is here. We must leave."

Earth magic ebbed. Niall and Llyr trotted over and faced him. "Does the guardian have Krae?" Niall asked. At Kiernan's nod, the changeling smiled sadly and said, "He will see her memory is honored."

"You will too." Colleen turned to Niall and knelt so they were at eye level. "It's like with all the witches I've known who died. They live here—" she pointed to her head "—and here." She moved her hand to her heart.

Jenna knelt too and held out her arms. Niall walked into them. "Aw, sweetie." Jenna hugged him. "We'll never forget her."

"No, we won't." Niall wriggled out of her arms. His face contorted as he held back tears. "You stink like demon."

Jenna straightened, along with Colleen. "Thanks. You do too, bud."

"Sounds like it's past time to leave," Roz said. "I overheard Titania and them, so there's truly nothing left to do here."

Kiernan walked to Jenna and draped an arm around her. She leaned into him. Tristan moved to her other side and did the same. "Not that you need our magic," Tristan said, "but let us take you home."

"Wonderful idea," Kiernan seconded. "It will make us feel like old-time knights, protecting our woman."

Jenna snorted. "You two are impossible. The worst part of it is, you probably were old-time knights back in the day."

"Damn!" Tristan chortled.

"Yeah, she's got our number." Kiernan grinned. He'd seen this day in so many variations for so many years and dreaded it. All in all, what had unfolded wasn't nearly as devastating as some of his visions had predicted, and relief filled him.

"I'm waiting." Jenna looked from one to the other. "All this talk of gallantry, and I'll be forced to fall back on my own magic after all."

"Erk!" Colleen crinkled her nose. "Duncan's going to read me the riot act when I see him."

"So's Ronin." Roz shrugged. "If he'd wanted compliant, he should have married a Sidhe."

Kiernan and Tristan burst out laughing, and Roz rolled her eyes. "Okay, so maybe your women aren't particularly submissive."

"Leave!" The guardian's voice boomed.

"I'll round all of us up." Llyr sprinted away and was immediately swallowed by murky air.

"Will you need help teleporting?" Jenna shouted after him.

"No," floated back. "There's enough residual demon energy here, we could teleport to the moon. See you at Ronin's."

Kiernan summoned magic, tested it, and called up more. "We really do need to get out of here," he muttered. "Something about demonic power doesn't play well with ours."

Tristan nodded. "It never has, which is fine by me. I'm not sure I'd want it to."

Roz and Colleen's forms flickered and winked out. "We're almost gone too," Kiernan said. He felt Tristan's magic braid itself with his own. Jenna pushed hers into the mix. "Let us take care of you," he protested.

She leveled her hazel gaze at both of them. "I know what I said about gallantry and all, but I'm making up for all those years I couldn't teleport my way out of a closet."

"You heard the lady." Tristan grinned.

"Not the lady, *our* lady." Kiernan grinned back as the miserable, smoke-filled atmosphere of the borderworld dropped away.

He'd picked the front hall of Ronin's manor house as a target and was instantly sorry. Changelings raced about, regaling anyone and everyone with what had happened. Moire and Sperrin were locked in each other's arms, kissing fervently. Titania and Oberon stood near the front door with their hands clasped. The Unseelie —Aedan's group plus the four who'd arrived with Sperrin and Moire—sprawled on the floor sucking down mead from bottles that had materialized from somewhere. Roz and Ronin were nowhere to be seen. At first he thought Colleen and Duncan were MIA too, but they walked briskly in from the main hallway.

Duncan made his way to Oberon and Titania, with Colleen sticking to his side like a shadow. "I put in a request for the kitchen crew to make buckets of food." He looked at Colleen with his heart in his eyes. "Unless you have another assignment for me, we're going to clean up."

Kiernan peered close, using his enhanced senses, and saw worlds of worry in Duncan's green eyes. Fear he'd lost his beloved to demons sparred with poignant relief she was still alive.

"Nothing more just now." Oberon's tone was solemn, but his amber eyes sparkled. "Take care of that bride of yours. You're just barely married."

"Tell me something I don't know." The severe lines of Duncan's soot-streaked face relaxed into half a smile.

"Bubba!" Colleen called to her familiar and then slapped her forehead with an open palm. "Niall. Sorry, so sorry."

"It's okay." He skidded to a halt in front of her. "What?"

"You need to clean up too. We all stink of Irichna, and our clothes can probably hit the incinerator."

"Fine by me." The changeling grinned broadly. "Clothes were always your idea, not mine."

Kiernan stopped listening and drew Jenna more firmly against him. She was still in his arms since they'd teleported that way. He wanted to be alone with her and Tristan, but he felt unaccountably awkward. This would be easier if they'd made love before. Right now they were filthy, and Colleen was right about everyone reeking of the rotten egg, sulfur, and road kill mix that made up demon stench.

Almost as if she'd been inside his mind, Jenna ducked from beneath his arm. Her hazel gaze moved somberly from him to Tristan. "Give me about an hour," she said. "I want to bathe and say my good-byes to Krae."

Understanding cut like a knife. The changeling had been elemental to Jenna discovering who she was magically. "Jenna." He placed a hand on her shoulder and sought her gaze. "If you'd like more time..."

"...all you have to do is tell us." Tristan's silver eyes reflected grief he'd no doubt plucked from her heart with his empath gift.

She nodded. A small, sad smile crossed her face. "Thank you. I'll let you know when I'm ready." Jenna kissed Tristan's cheek and then his. The skin between her brows furrowed in thought. "Don't take this wrong," she patted Tristan's hand, "but I need a little bit of alone time with Kiernan before we all get together."

"I understand." Tristan smiled warmly.

With a wan nod, Jenna started up the stairs.

Kiernan drew Tristan into a nearby sitting room. "Thank you."

The other Sidhe shook his head. "You don't need to. The only way this will work is if we respect one another's needs. I had time alone with her. It's unrealistic to expect the three of us will always be together. Go clean up." Tristan elbowed him. "You want to be ready when Jenna's gotten past the freshest part of grieving for the changeling who became her friend."

"I'll miss her too," Kiernan said. "I hadn't met her before the night I met Jenna, but I saw her in so many visions, I felt I understood her quite well."

Tristan cocked his head to one side. "We all knew you spent time in trance states, but I guess I never thought much about what it meant. You'll have to tell me more about them—if you can, that is."

Kiernan considered it. "Maybe it's time," he murmured. "I've been alone with the fate of our people for a long time."

Tristan held out a hand, and Kiernan clasped it. "Any way I can ease the burden, just let me know."

"I will." Kiernan turned away. He detoured through the kitchen to pile some food on a plate and then trudged up the back stairs to his room.

The transition from isolated seer to support and understanding from not only Tristan, but also the woman they'd soon share, was quite a shift. It would take some adjustments, but Kiernan felt ready.

CHAPTER 18

*J*enna unlaced her boots, toed them off, and stripped off her stinking clothing. Colleen hadn't been kidding when she'd suggested the incinerator. Even if her pants, shirt, and jacket could be cleaned sufficiently so they didn't smell anymore, Jenna never wanted to see them again.

She still couldn't believe Krae was gone. The demon that killed her had streaked out of left field, striking before any of them could react and digging its lethal, poison-tipped claws deep into her chest. Just before it ripped out her throat, severing major vessels. Jenna had surged forward, killing the demon. She'd broken its sorry form in half pulling it off the changeling, but by then the damage was already done.

How the hell had the Irichna wormed its way through the changeling's warding in the first place? The more Jenna thought about it, the less she liked the only answer that made sense. Krae must have diverted power to support Jenna, which left her with less to ward herself.

That knowledge made things even worse. If Krae had truly martyred herself so Jenna could live, she didn't feel worthy of the sacrifice. As she plodded toward the shower, she caught a glimpse of herself in the bathroom mirror and rocked to a halt. She gripped the edges of the sink and just stared. Quite aside from her hollow, haunted eyes that looked like they'd been to Hell and back, her normally rounded face had settled into harsh lines that accentuated her cheekbones and jawline. The tips of her hair were charred, black wisps. She scrubbed the heels of her hands down her face, but all it did was rearrange the grime coating her skin.

"Why?" She demanded, not expecting an answer, but needing something to assuage her boatload of survivor guilt. Feeling like a fool on top of everything else, she bent to turn on the shower and set the temperature just shy of scalding. Warm clouds of steam settled around her, and she scrubbed until her skin burned, as if inflicting pain somehow evened the score that she was alive and Krae wasn't.

Still feeling perfectly wretched, but unable to justify using any more hot water, she stepped over the high rim of the tub and toweled herself dry. Wrapping a fresh towel around herself, she shook water out of her hair and opened the door to the cooler air of her bedroom. Kiernan lounged in a chair, obviously waiting for her. A protest that she wasn't ready for him or anyone else yet died on her lips when he shook his head.

"Look." He ran a hand down his jean and T-shirt clad body. "I'm fully dressed. I showered too, but then I put on clean clothes. I didn't let myself into your room to ravish you, but to talk." An uncomfortable look flitted over his face. "I probably shouldn't have done this, but I've been in your mind."

"Join the crowd." Jenna thought she should feel violated, but she didn't. "Everyone else helps themselves to my thoughts, why shouldn't you?"

He averted his glacier-blue eyes. "Um, would you like to put on a robe or something?"

She glanced down at herself and realized the towel had slipped alarmingly, exposing half her breasts. Heat crept up her chest, and she yanked a bathrobe off a hook near the bathroom door and ducked inside to trade it for the towel. Once it was securely belted, she returned to the bedroom.

"Have a seat." Kiernan gestured toward the only other chair in the room.

Jenna folded her body into it and gazed at him out of tired eyes. "What did you see in my mind that made you come in here?"

Rather than answering, he posed a question of his own. "Do you understand the role I play for my people?"

"Not totally." She crossed her arms beneath her breasts. "To be honest, not at all, other than you scry the future, and maybe the past too."

He nodded. "I foresee future events—past ones too if it's needed. Of course, I don't pick up everything. That wouldn't be possible. It would take more than one of me, and no one else has shown up in the past couple of millennia with my gift." He took a measured breath. "All Sidhe have some scrying ability, but it's rather like the difference between taking a pleasure walk and scaling Everest. What that means is the important things come to me whether I summon them or not. The more critical something is, the more frequently I see it. Does that make sense?"

"Uh-huh." Jenna motioned for him to go on because she had a feeling he was on the edge of revealing something important— and something she might not want to hear.

"When I see something often, I dig deeper. Sometimes my trance states last for days. I knew about today's battle on the borderworld—"

"How much of it?" she broke in, leaning forward.

"It's not like watching instant reruns on television, if that's what you're asking. Most of the time what I see is hazy. The people sometimes aren't clearly defined, but events are."

"Please don't walk around this." Jenna squeezed her eyes shut and then opened them. "I'm too done in to read between the lines."

He nodded. "All right. I saw the battle on the borderworld over and over again. I knew Krae would be a part of it and that she would die. I also knew witches would be involved. When I first met you, I got a kind of hit. It's hard to describe, but it's rather like a tingling deep in my magical center." He smiled wryly. "Actually, I felt a whole lot more than that, but I'm sticking with helping you understand my magic."

"Did Krae sacrifice herself for me?" Jenna set her jaws together, fearing his answer.

"It's deeper than that." Kiernan steepled his fingers in front of his chest. "Some of us, Krae being one, have direct communication with Danu and the dream guardian. Both of them dish out assignments, much like a modern general might. Krae knew she wouldn't make it off the borderworld alive." He paused and then said, "Look at me, Jenna."

She realized she was staring at her lap and slowly scraped her gaze upward until he caught and held it with his own.

"That's better." He smiled encouragingly. "Feel free to test my next words for truth. You were Krae's last assignment, and one she accepted willingly. Earth hung at a balance point. But that's something you and your sister witches already intuited. You coming into your power was a critical element on our side."

"Why didn't she tell me?" Jenna heard anguish beneath her words.

Kiernan tilted his head to one side. "What would you have done if she had?"

"Told her I wasn't in agreement, that I couldn't accept her life in exchange for my magic."

"Which is exactly why she said nothing."

"Oh." Jenna wrapped her arms around herself and shivered. A thought intruded, and she narrowed her eyes. "What did you see about us? You know, you, me, and Tristan?"

"Nothing." At the disbelief which must have been mirrored in her eyes, he added, "It's not allowed. I can't scry my own future. Danu would flay me alive."

"Does Tristan know about Krae?"

"Yes. We talked and decided I should tell you enough for you to understand."

"I wish you'd have told me all this before."

"I didn't for the same reasons Krae held her peace."

Even though it made sense, the truth made her feel odd and unbalanced. Because she didn't know quite what to say, she just dipped her head and studied her hands again.

JENNA LOOKED SO LOST and so vulnerable, Kiernan held out his arms and was surprised when she crossed the room and sat on his lap. He folded his arms around her. "Even if I'd told you, it just would have made things harder. We can't escape our destinies. You would have moved heaven and earth to keep Krae alive, and she would have died anyway. Who knows how many others might have been lost if your attention was focused on the changeling?"

She buried her head deeper in his shoulder. He expected tears, but maybe she was still too shell-shocked to have any. Tenderness filled him, and he stroked her singed hair.

"Who knew besides you?" she asked, her voice muffled against his body.

"Titania and Oberon. Obviously, the dream guardian."

"Is that all?"

He nodded, realized she couldn't see him, and said, "Yes. The Sidhe don't ask me questions about the future. Many of them have a limited version of my gift, but mostly they don't care. One of the curses of immortality is a laissez-faire attitude about tomorrow. There are so many tomorrows, one particularly good or bad day doesn't matter much."

Jenna pushed away, her forehead scrunched into worry lines. "What does my Sidhe blood mean in terms of my lifespan?"

A crooked smile formed on his face. "I was wondering when you'd get around to asking about that."

"That wasn't an answer."

"It's because I don't exactly have one. You're not immortal, but you could easily live thousands of years. We've never had a witch-Sidhe mix to study before." He cocked his head to one side. "It appears your mother was one, but I knew nothing about her before meeting you. She had far less Sidhe blood, so she might not be a good point of comparison. Your father was Druid and Sidhe. Again, not a good point of reference." Kiernan took a measured breath. "I'm guessing he kept a very low profile because I didn't know he existed, either."

"So do you Sidhe all know one another?"

He smiled sheepishly. "Pretty much. There aren't all that many of us, so it's not as big a chore as it might seem."

"I see. What about our children? Will they inherit your immortality?" She drew back, her mouth an *O* of surprise before she clapped a hand over it. "Ooops. Question was a bit premature."

Warmth began in his belly and radiated outward. Children. She wanted his children—and Tristan's. He twined a lock of her hair around his finger and smoothed it behind her ear. "Same answer. Immortality only comes with pure blood, but we'll all live so long, you'll find it ceases to matter." Kiernan stroked a finger down her cheek. "Would you like more alone time, darling? I've accomplished what I came here to do."

Jenna swallowed, her throat working with emotion as feelings played over her expressive features. "Thank you for telling me about Krae. I'm still sad, and blown away by her courage, but I'm not feeling quite as responsible."

"You're welcome." He continued to stroke her face, loving the feel of her skin beneath his fingers. He didn't want to leave, but he'd respect her wishes. Trapped between their bodies, his cock stiffened. He tried to hide it with magic, but there was no way she wouldn't notice something had shifted.

She laid her hand over his and leaned her cheek into his touch. "If you leave, I'll just wallow in feeling sorry for myself. Krae was an inspiration, something to cling to when I face dark times."

"Indeed she was." Kiernan shook his head. "We nearly blew it in a major way when we stripped the changelings of their power. Danu harangued me over that one, and I argued it with Oberon and Titania, and then just with Titania after Oberon got disgusted with the Sidhe and left for a long time. Neither listened until you witches showed up with a changeling in tow. I'd predicted that also, so I guess it commanded their attention."

"It's a little unsettling to see ourselves as pieces on some huge game board." Jenna bent forward and brushed her lips over his cheek.

"What do you mean?"

"If I'm reading you right, Danu plopped me, Roz, and Colleen into place just when and where we were needed. Niall too."

"I suppose that's one interpretation, but since that's the way the world has always worked, I don't think much about it." He wriggled his hips slightly, seeking a more comfortable position for his erection. "If you don't chase me out of here, you're likely to find yourself over there." He jerked his chin toward the bed.

She ran her lips down his cheek and nuzzled his neck, giving him an answer without using words. Kiernan tightened his grip and stood with her in his arms. He covered the short space to the bed in record time and laid her on it.

"I'm only a thought away," Tristan's voice echoed in his mind, and Kiernan grinned.

"Did you hear that?" he asked Jenna.

A soft smile curved her lips. "I did. What do you think? He had time just with me..." Her voice trailed off.

Well, what do I think?

"We'll have years and years together. To kick this off right, it should be the three of us."

"You'll have to help me," Jenna said. "Roz is the one with group expertise."

Tristan shimmered into being near the door. He snorted. "Does Ronin know that?"

Jenna laughed, and Kiernan's spirit soared. It was good she could laugh after what they'd just lived through. "I have no idea, but don't you dare tell him. Roz would be furious I wasn't more discreet."

"Never fear." Tristan moved toward them, leaving a trail of clothing in his wake.

Kiernan eyed him. "Looks like Roz isn't the only one with experience." He dragged his T-shirt over his head and unfastened his jeans, struggling a bit to free his hard-on so he could push his pants down his legs and step out of them. Fortunately, he'd had the presence of mind to forego shoes.

"Wow!" Jenna's gaze moved from one of them to the other. She rolled into a sit and reached a hand for each of their cocks. Her robe fell open, and her breasts, tipped by rosy, peaked nipples, popped free. Color splotched her chest, and she tugged gently on their penises. "Up on the bed, and then kneel in front of me."

Kiernan balanced on the bed, shoulder to shoulder with Tristan, and Jenna bent her head. Heat exploded upward from his balls when her mouth closed over his shaft, and he fought for control. She licked and sucked first him, then Tristan, and then back again. When she wasn't using her mouth, her hand took over urging him higher.

Somewhere along the way, Tristan's mind slammed into his. He felt the other Sidhe's lust as if it was his own, and it ratcheted his passion so high it was almost painful. He buried his hands in Jenna's hair and drove himself into her mouth. His balls snugged against his body, and his cock ached for release. Semen pooled, hot and ready, but he rode a ragged edge of control, wanting to go higher still. Her teeth grazed the edge of his glans, and she tickled his anus with a fingertip. Between the two bits of added stimulation, he groaned and gave in to sensation. Semen jetted out of him into her waiting mouth.

With his head tossed back and his neck corded with passion, Tristan worked himself with his hand atop Jenna's, showing her the rhythm he needed. Before he could finish, she transferred her mouth to him. Kiernan felt he was trespassing, but watching her mouth move on Tristan's ridged flesh was nearly as erotic as when she'd been doing the same thing to him. After only a few strokes, Tristan's cock exploded too.

Jenna lifted her head, a randy grin on her face. "I'm starting to appreciate the advantages—and the possibilities."

"Hear that?" Tristan elbowed him. "We've barely scratched the surface, and she's already a willing convert."

"I'm feeling that way myself." Kiernan stroked his still hard cock. "I have an idea."

"Shoot. Oh, I forgot. You already did that." Jenna's smile widened.

"Brazen hussy." He tackled her, tossing her backward onto the mattress. Tristan piled on, and they wrestled, trading kisses, strokes, and teasing slaps and pinches.

Kiernan maneuvered until he lay on his back. He spun Jenna so she straddled him and grabbed her hips to lower her over his waiting cock. The heat of her body nearly undid him, and he held her in place until he could ride herd on his control.

Tristan knelt behind her. "Would you like us both at once?"

Jenna nodded. She'd never looked more beautiful. Her face and chest were splotchy with lust, and her nipples tight buds of desire. She arched her back, and Kiernan felt Tristan's cock probe her anus through his mind link with the other Sidhe. It was all he could do not to pound himself into her, fast and hard. He wanted to come again, needed to. Instead, he moved a hand from her hip and rubbed her swollen clit. She shrieked her delight, and he rubbed harder. Her muscles tightened around his shaft as a climax rocked her.

Taking advantage of her passion, Tristan pushed all the way inside. Feeling Tristan's cock plunging alongside his own sent Kiernan higher than he'd ever been. He kept rubbing Jenna's clit while he thrust into her. Another orgasm shook her, followed by yet another. Control crumpling, Kiernan's body took over, and his cock juddered as semen burst from him in blast after blast of ecstasy. Just when he thought he was done, Tristan came, and his spasms pushed Kiernan over the edge again.

Panting and laughing, they collapsed in a puppy pile, sorting out arms and legs as they went. Jenna ended up cradled between them and said, "That was pretty damned amazing."

"We've barely gotten started," Tristan said.

"You're just full of surprises." Kiernan reached across Jenna and poked him.

"What do you mean me?" Tristan countered. "You came up with that last configuration."

"I'm not so sure about that. You were in my mind. Maybe you planted a subliminal suggestion."

"Stop it you two." Jenna snuggled closer. "Let's talk about the important stuff."

"What could be more important than what we just did?" Kiernan asked.

"Girls like weddings. Do I get one?"

"Of course you do," Tristan said.

"We'll have to discuss it with Titania," Kiernan cautioned. He couldn't remember their queen ever solemnizing joinings with more than two participants.

"Even if she's a pill about it," Jenna said, "I know witches who will marry us."

"Don't worry. We'll figure it out," Kiernan said. "For now, sleep. We'll take care of you."

"That we will," Tristan said. "I'll take first watch since I need to go rinse myself off."

Jenna stirred. "Keep watch? Isn't it safe here?"

"Probably," Kiernan said.

"We're not taking any chances," Tristan cut in. "You're too important to us."

Joy was such a foreign emotion, Kiernan barely recognized it, but it warmed him with hope for their future as he sank toward the waking dreams that passed for sleep. In a little while, he'd spell Tristan, and when they woke, they'd join the others and figure out what to do next. He was fairly certain the Irichna would lay low for a long while. Their most pressing problem was the fragmented relationship with the Unseelie. Even if Sperrin talked sense into Aedan, Locar and his splinter group were still running loose.

Because he couldn't solve anything until he rested, Kiernan nested Jenna against his body and let himself drift.

CHAPTER 19

Cradled between her lovers' hard-muscled bodies, Jenna woke so happy she was surprised joy wasn't spilling out her eyes. Tristan's even breathing suggested he was still asleep. Reaching out with her magic confirmed it, but when she sought Kiernan, his mind was busy. She opened her eyes and turned to look at him.

He smiled and placed a finger over his lips. *"Hey there, sleeping beauty."* He focused his voice only for her.

"Hey there yourself." She smiled back and shifted slightly to toss an arm over him. The feel of his skin beneath her fingertips made her heart beat a little faster. He kissed her forehead, and her smile deepened and turned inward until it illuminated her soul. *"I'm the luckiest woman alive."*

"Luck had nothing to do with it."

She curved her body against his, inhaling his spicy scent, redolent of rosemary and fresh-mown hay. *"Says the seer. I thought you didn't scry your own future."*

"I don't. All of us are taking a chance, making it up as we go, to borrow a modern expression. Luck's nowhere in the equation."

"If you two are going to talk, do it out loud," Tristan grumbled.

"I may not be able to make out your telepathic speech, but your magic buzzes so loud it doesn't matter."

"Sorry." Jenna wriggled so she faced him and planted kisses on both cheeks. "If you're still tired, we can get up and let you rest a little longer."

"Nah, it's okay. I'm hungry more than tired at this point."

"It's a bloody miracle we haven't received a summons from Titania or Oberon," Kiernan muttered.

"Now that you mention it, I wonder why not," Tristan said, sounding a little more awake.

"Maybe they're as wiped out as the rest of us," Jenna ventured. "Mmm, you guys feel so good next to me."

Tristan wove a hand around the back of her neck and pulled her face to his for a kiss. Kiernan cuddled her from behind, his rapidly growing erection pressing into her backside. Desire ignited, setting fire to her nether regions. Her nipples pebbled into points of sensation, and her crotch flooded. Maybe they could work in one more round of dynamite sex before they faced the others. If it were up to her, they'd retire to Fairbanks and surface sometime in the spring.

"Sweetie, hate to interrupt the honeymoon, but we need you." Colleen's voice sounded in her head.

"How about in an hour?"

"Now would be better."

"Come on, Jenna," Roz chimed in. *"You'll have years to screw them. So many, you might get sick of being fawned over."*

"Not very fucking likely."

"We'll have to hear all the nitty-gritty details." Roz laughed. *"Now get your ass downstairs."*

"We heard most of that," Kiernan said and flexed his cock against her bottom.

"Too bad." Tristan pressed his erection against her upper thigh.

Her breath caught in her throat. "You two are making it nearly impossible to leave, but the gals wouldn't have interrupted us if it weren't important."

"Kiernan!" Oberon's voice was so loud it rattled his brain.

"On my way. I'll let Tristan know."

The king chuckled and then added, *"You'll have to tell me all about,"* he paused delicately before adding, *"everything."*

"Christ!" Jenna wriggled out from between them and made her way to the end of the bed. From there, she got to her feet. "Everyone and their dog wants a blow-by-blow description."

Kiernan somersaulted off the bed, landing next to her. "Before you dash through the shower, how fast can you come?"

She rubbed up against him, arching her back like a cat. It felt empowering not to be ashamed of her body. No need to hide her curves ever again. "What a leading question."

"But a good one." Tristan materialized on her other side and announced, "I'll take her breasts."

"I've got her woman's parts covered." Kiernan winked broadly.

What began as a giggle morphed into a shrieking moan as Tristan took one of her nipples in his mouth and sucked. Kiernan sank to his knees and closed his mouth over her clit. Awash in sensation, she gave in to both men urging her on. A climax shot through her, followed by another that made her knees weak.

"Enough." She staggered away. "I want to collapse on the floor and take you both, but it will have to wait."

"We understand." Tristan licked his lips in a wonderfully lewd gesture.

"That was just for you," Kiernan said. He got to his feet and patted his hard-on. "This is too."

"Don't forget mine!" Tristan closed a hand around his wonderfully erect penis and waggled it in her direction.

"I'd say you're both pretty unforgettable." She made a dive for the bathroom before lust got the better of her. Jenna was still grinning like a fool when she came out of the shower and tugged on a pair of sweats. Both men had left, presumably to clean up in their own quarters. Still barefoot, she wrapped a towel around her hair. Once it had soaked up as much water as it could, she tossed it over a chair and padded out the door, finger combing her hair as she walked.

Jenna sent her magic spiraling outward to locate Roz and Colleen. They were on the first floor in the same small meeting room she'd been in the first night she arrived. Both women glanced up when she strode through the door, frank curiosity stamped on their faces.

"It was wonderful." Jenna gave a thumbs up gesture. "Now tell me what's up."

"We're having a meeting really soon," Roz said.

"Yeah, like in five minutes," Colleen added.

"Everyone has to be there, at least according to Ronin." Roz took over the conversation again. She rolled her dark, expressive eyes. "I hope he's not disappointed if the Unseelie have taken their marbles and gone home."

"Why would you think that?" Jenna asked.

"No one's seen them since we got back is why," Roz elaborated.

"There's lots of possible explanations for that," Jenna said. She liked Sperrin and Moire. Aedan had been a bit of an asshole, but he had good reason. "Does anyone know where Locar and his cronies are?"

"That problem's solved," Colleen said. "Duncan, Ronin, Oberon, and the Sidhe version of a posse flushed them out of a hidey hole on another borderworld, and they're back on Earth in Sidhe lockdown."

Jenna thought about it. "What will happen to them from there? Forever is a long time to jail someone."

"I asked Ronin the same thing," Roz said. "He tossed out a bunch of doublespeak, but what I think will happen is one of the Celtic gods will show up to mete out punishment. Locar and his cronies won't get to retreat to the *Dreaming* where they could thumb their noses at everyone for eternity."

"Oberon finally broke down and fessed up to the Celts?" Jenna quirked an inquisitive brow, and Roz nodded.

"Somehow Locar's and his buddies' punishment doesn't seem bad enough." Colleen shrugged. "I guess we should be happy there are *any* consequences. From what Duncan told me, Sidhe rarely make one another answer for anything."

"Kind of like witches. We need to get moving." Roz stood and led the way out of the small, cozy room.

Jenna followed with Colleen by her side. The other witch hugged her briefly. "I'm happy for you, sweetie."

"Thanks. Me too. Gosh, all three of us will be old, married women soon." She hesitated. "I know the guys are going to want to talk about nuts and bolts, like where we're going to live."

"That's already happened with Duncan," Colleen said.

"What'd you tell him?"

"That I plan to live in Fairbanks, at least part of the time. Roz told Ronin the same thing."

"Whew! I was worried we'd be stuck in the U.K. forever. It's nice and all, but I miss Alaska's wide-open spaces. Everything is so close together here."

"Um, you didn't ask, but the men weren't particularly thrilled." Colleen prodded her. "Hey. The meeting is this way. You must be hungry, you just turned toward the kitchen."

"I am, but food can wait. Hang on a sec." She grabbed Colleen's arm and spun her friend to face her. "If all of us take a stand about Alaska, the men will have to capitulate."

Colleen rolled her eyes. "They're Sidhe. I'm not sure capitulation is in their vocabulary."

Jenna drew herself up. "It may not be, but I'm spending my summers in Alaska. If I'm there by myself, so be it."

"You won't be." Colleen set her jaw in a stubborn expression Jenna recognized. "Roz and I will be right there with you, especially after the kids start coming. Besides, Bubba, er Niall, sees Fairbanks as his home too. Hell, even Roz finally got used to it."

"We'll have to move eventually, so people don't notice we're not growing visibly older," Jenna said, "but Alaska is a big place."

"There you are." Duncan trotted down the hall and joined them. "We're ready to begin."

"On our way." Colleen kissed his cheek. "Did the Unseelie surface?"

"Yes." Relief ran beneath the one word, thick and palpable. "Turns out they were here all along closeted with Oberon and Titania."

"Thank God," Colleen muttered and followed her husband's retreating back.

Jenna brought up the rear. The last thing she felt like was a meeting, particularly with the Sidhes' propensity to talk everything to death. A small, sad smile crossed her lips. Krae had said something like that. Jenna would miss the brash, outspoken changeling. At some level, she couldn't believe Krae wouldn't come bursting through one of the millions of doors in Ronin's manor house with her red hair trailing behind her. Tears pricked behind her lids, a reminder of how fresh her grief was.

She stopped outside the double doors that led into the large, first-floor meeting room and took a deep breath, following it with another. When she could arrange her face in neutral planes and swallow around the lump in her throat, she walked into the room and looked for Tristan and Kiernan. They stood in a group with Duncan and Oberon, their heads bent together and magic buzzing around them. Roz beckoned, and Jenna took a seat between her and Colleen. The Unseelie were nowhere in sight.

Titania swept through one of the back doorways in her usual jeweled finery. Her silvery hair was unbound, and it floated around her like a finely spun cloud. Moire walked by her side. Instead of her usual black jumpsuit, she was garbed similarly to Titania. Jenna wondered if she'd borrowed one of the queen's gowns.

"Oberon!" Titania snapped her fingers, and the king straightened as if he'd been caught with his hand in a cookie jar.

Jenna bit back a giggle. She'd love to be a fly on the wall in their household. Dollars to diamonds, Titania ruled that roost with an iron hand. No velvet gloves in sight.

"I'll see what's keeping them, dear," he said and hustled out of the room.

Jenna exchanged glances with Roz and Colleen, but both of them looked just as confused as she felt. Titania and Moire reached the dais at the front of the room. Titania angled her pale blue gaze around the room and announced, "It is time to seat yourselves. Leave space for your Unseelie kin."

Jenna did a quick headcount and came up with close to fifty Sidhe. Rather than bunching up, they spread out through the room. Oberon marched back inside with Sperrin and Aedan flanking him. The other Unseelie she'd met had been joined by at least twenty more. They all wore ceremonial robes set with jewels. Without any exchange of words, they fanned through the room and found seats among the Sidhe. Erika entered the room by herself and walked briskly to Aedan's side.

Oberon clasped his hands in front of him. "I believe we are ready. My dear." He extended a hand toward Titania, who took it and turned to face the assemblage, standing to the left of her husband. Almost as if it had been staged—and it may well have been—Aedan and Erika walked to one side of the King and Queen of Faerie. Sperrin and Moire placed themselves on the other.

"We are here today," Titania said in a clear, ringing voice, "to right an ancient wrong." She turned so she faced Sperrin and Moire, while Oberon did the same with Aedan and Erika. Titania bowed low. "On behalf of Faerie, I apologize for the hurts you suffered at our hands."

"I too wish to apologize." Oberon inclined his head. "The time has come for Faerie to be reunited."

"I accept your apology and offer my own for any hurts my

people may have caused." Aedan spoke formally in Gaelic. "I would once again offer my sword and my allegiance to the King and Queen of Faerie." He dipped his head, straightening quickly.

Sperrin bowed as low as Titania had. "I also accept your apology. I offer my sword and my loyalty to Faerie."

Aedan and Sperrin stepped forward and faced the group. "This will take time," Aedan said.

"Yes, and much discussion," Sperrin added. "Distrust willna die overnight, yet if those in this room set an example, others will follow."

Oberon plucked an ancient-looking bottle from the mantle behind him. He drew a knife from his robes and split the wax seal. "We shall drink to our commitment to be one people again."

Titania lifted a tray holding six cut crystal goblets off the ornate sideboard, and Oberon poured a small amount of amber liquid into each. Everyone standing in the front of the room took one. "To Faerie," Oberon said and drank. The others echoed his toast and drained their glasses.

In the meantime, Duncan and Ronin were circulating through the room armed with glasses and bottles. Jenna accepted a dram of liquor, which smelled like mead, and waited until everybody had one. Oberon poured more for those who stood on the dais. "I invite you to drink with me." He raised his glass.

"To Faerie," swelled through the room. Jenna, Roz, and Colleen joined in the toast.

"Thank you." Oberon's amber eyes shone. "To a new beginning for us all."

"What happened to the Irichna?" a Sidhe cried out.

"I'd love to say we got rid of them once and for all," Titania said, "but we didn't."

"What we did do was seriously cripple the borderworld they called home," Sperrin said. "No demons or minions are left there, and it will be long years afore that world can support life again."

"'Twas actually the dream guardian who finished off their

world." Moire spoke up. "More than anything, his participation in our affairs tells me how close we skirted to the end of days."

"What can we do?" an Unseelie woman with long, blonde hair asked in solemn tones.

"That is what we shall discuss," Titania said. "A meal awaits us in the dining room."

Kiernan moved to the front of the room. He'd traded his usual jeans for a dark blue silk robe, sashed in crimson. "If I could have a moment of your time before we share a meal, I'd appreciate it." After nods and murmurs of assent moved through the group, he continued. "The Sidhe know me. For the Unseelie present, I am seer to our people. My visions have always encompassed all of Faerie, not just the Sidhe portion. As we work together, there is something we must keep in mind."

He took a swallow from the glass in his hand. "Some of you won't like what I have to say, but hear me out. We won a major campaign against the demons on their borderworld, but Irichna exist everywhere, including the first eight circles of Hell, where they move about freely and are not contained behind a gate. We do not want to annihilate all of them."

"Why not?" a Sidhe Jenna didn't recognize called out.

Kiernan narrowed his eyes and raked a hand through his short hair. "Because every entity needs its opposite to survive. We—" he swept both hands wide "—had each other. Even through the years when we didn't acknowledge one another, we still existed. Dark to light. Sidhe to Unseelie. If one of us were to vanish from the Earth, the other would weaken and eventually die out. It's the same for us and any evil we battle. If we wiped out the Irichna, another evil would have to rise to take its place. If that didn't happen, our race would fade. Everything needs its opposite to exist."

"What are you suggesting?" Duncan asked.

"That our goal is to maintain the Irichna in a weakened state, not to kill every single one of them. Better the fiend we know than a new evil we have yet to meet."

Conversation rustled through the room with an unpleasant edge, and Kiernan raised his hands in front of him, palms outward. "Don't shoot the messenger. I warned you before I began talking that you wouldn't care for what I had to say."

"I agree with him." Sperrin projected his voice. "I scry for the Unseelie, and I have seen much the same thing."

"Would you care to elaborate?" Oberon asked.

Sperrin drew his brows together. "I assume it's much the same for Kiernan, but I see many iterations of futures. I never know which one will come to pass, but I am able to identify those I hope to hell never happen."

"It's the same for me," Kiernan murmured.

Sperrin went on, "I have seen versions of a future without Irichna, and the evil that rises to take their place is so hideous, I don't have words to describe it."

Because Jenna was focused on Kiernan's face, she saw a shadow cross over it. He made an instinctive sign against evil, and she figured he'd seen much the same thing. Even without knowing more details, a shiver cascaded down her back, and she wrapped her arms around herself.

Oberon raised his hands for silence, and the buzzing that had taken over the room died down. The king straightened his spine. "We may not like the implication in Kiernan's mini-lecture, but at least we have a direction. For what it's worth, he's been harping on the same thing for years to Titania and me." A corner of his mouth twisted into a wry smile. "Maybe we're finally in a spot to listen. Is everyone ready to eat?"

Amidst a chorus of *ayes* and *yesses*, the group walked slowly from the room in groups of twos and threes. Jenna noted Sidhe and Unseelie walked beside one another, and it made her heart glad. Kiernan and Tristan caught up to her, one on each side. "That went reasonably well," Tristan murmured.

"Better than well," Kiernan agreed.

Jenna linked arms with her men, proud to have them by her side. "Once the dust settles," she told them, "we can go home."

"But, darling," Kiernan said, "we are home. Or very nearly. My manor house isn't far from here."

"I meant my home." She looked from Tristan to Kiernan to gauge their reaction.

"Isn't it terribly dark there?" Kiernan asked and stopped walking.

"And cold," Tristan added. "Dark and cold."

"Yup, it's all those things," she agreed cheerfully. "But I'll be there, at least through the summers when it's neither. Frankly, maybe we could find somewhere more tropical to spend our winters. The U.K.'s not exactly cheery through the dark months, either."

Tristan kissed one cheek and Kiernan the other. "No worries, sweetheart. We'll figure it out."

"Indeed we will," Kiernan said. He lowered his voice, "Let's get through this ceremonial meal so we can pick up where we left off earlier."

"You mean in my bedroom?" Jenna cast an innocent look his way.

"That's precisely what he means," Tristan said.

Niall, Llyr, and a phalanx of changelings charged past. "We may have missed the meeting," Niall called over one shoulder.

"But we never miss a meal," Llyr said.

Jenna started laughing. "I really, really miss Niall when he's not front and center every day."

"Maybe we can adopt one or two of them for our household," Tristan suggested.

"Grand idea," Kiernan seconded. "I'll troll for volunteers over brunch or lunch or whatever the spread of food in the dining room might be called."

"I thought you Brits called the midday meal dinner," Jenna said.

"You're mixing cultures," Tristan said. "That was from your American west in the nineteenth century, where lunch was dinner and dinner was supper."

"If the conversation doesn't get more interesting than this, I'll retreat to my scrying cave," Kiernan said and grinned.

"You'll do no such thing." Jenna tugged on him. "Come on. I'm starving. If you want more of what we had earlier, I need fuel."

"You heard the lady." Tristan started walking again. "Actually, I'm half-starved myself."

Jenna leaned into both of them as they entered the dining room, which was set formally with linen, silver, and crystal. Light from chandeliers reflected off the stemware. Her eyes widened. "It's beautiful."

"Titania and Moire outdid themselves," Kiernan agreed. "That way." He pointed at a table in the front of the room. "Oberon already demanded our presence at the head table."

"I'd tell him to piss up a rope," Jenna murmured, "but since he's your king, we shouldn't keep him waiting."

"Wise witch." Tristan ruffled her hair with his free hand, and they headed for the front of the large room.

"Yes, the beginning of wisdom is picking your battles." Kiernan hip-butted her, and Jenna jostled him right back.

"Are both of you going to spend the next thousand years lecturing me?" She bit back a giggle.

"Probably." Tristan pulled out a chair for her, and she slid into it.

"No doubt about it." Kiernan sat on her far side and rested a hand on her knee. Not to be outdone, Tristan grabbed her other knee. She did giggle then. This was going to be a very interesting meal. Too bad she hadn't thought to wear a skirt.

"Yes." Kiernan leaned into her, obviously having been in her mind. "Skirts have definite advantages."

"What do you say?" Tristan teased. "Shall we buy her an entirely new wardrobe?"

"Now just a minute." Jenna glanced from one man to the other. "I am not giving up a say in what I wear."

"We weren't suggesting that," Kiernan said.

"Not really." Tristan moved his hand higher up her leg. "Of course we'd have you along to select things."

"Enough." Oberon sent a pointed glance their way. "An important conversation is about to begin, and I would prefer your minds were clear enough to participate."

"Yes, my liege." Tristan inclined his head, as did Kiernan. Both men angled their hands to the inside of her leg and squeezed her thighs.

Jenna laid her hands atop theirs and squeezed back, arranging the tablecloth to hide her lap from view. She met Oberon's gaze with a cheerful smile and wondered just how long the Sidhe and Unseelie would talk this time.

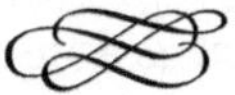

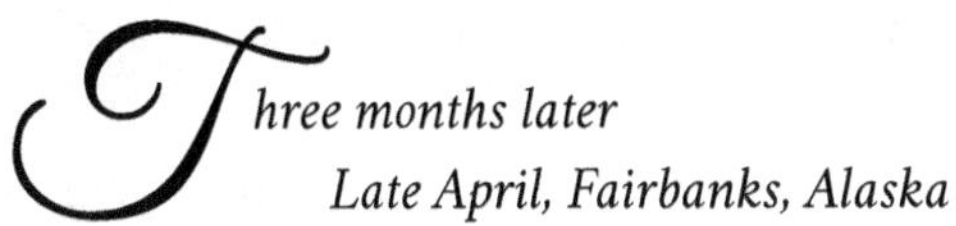

Three months later
   Late April, Fairbanks, Alaska

JENNA DUMPED a bag of potatoes into boiling water and jumped back to avoid being splashed. She chucked the potato bag into the trash and settled her hands on her hips. She, Roz, and Colleen had teleported to Fairbanks, along with a few changelings, the week before, and the men were due to arrive any moment.

Roz trooped into the kitchen. "Anything I can do?"

Jenna made a choking sound. "Other than firebombing our house and starting over? Nah, can't think of a thing."

"Aw, sweetie." Roz walked briskly to her side and gave her a hug. "It will be fine. I worried myself silly Ronin would take one look at our humble abode and storm out, but he didn't."

"That helps. I guess." Jenna nibbled her lower lip. "It's just after weeks of food always being ready and Kiernan's house basically cleaning itself, I'm afraid Kiernan and Tristan will be…disappointed by how we live."

"Did you spend any time at Tristan's home?" Colleen

wandered into the kitchen, turned a chair around, and sat on it. "We've been so busy sanitizing this place, I never thought to ask."

Jenna nodded. Everyone had spent time at Kiernan's, so Colleen wouldn't need to ask about his manor house, which was every bit as old and elegant as Duncan's or Ronin's. The time between when they'd returned from the demons' borderworld until now had been spent in a round robin of traded social events, mixed with interminable discussions, at Ronin's, Duncan's, Kiernan's, and the Unseelies' homes.

"What does a nod mean?" Colleen crooked two fingers her way.

"Tristan has a slightly smaller place on the eastern coast. It's charming, maybe eighteen hundreds vintage." Jenna shrugged. "They all live so luxuriously, it's hard not to want to make apologies for this place."

"Oh no it's not." Roz slapped a lid on the potato pot. "We've done pretty damned well. No bills, no debt. We live within our means."

"Spare me. They do too, but their wealth pushes things to a whole new level." Jenna took two steps to the refrigerator and peered inside. "What should we have along with the potato salad?"

"We could grill burgers," Colleen suggested. "It's almost warm enough to uncover the picnic table."

"Great idea." Jenna switched to the freezer and hauled out a few packages of frozen meat.

"Fooooood," Niall cried and catapulted into the kitchen, followed by Llyr and Kara. Kiernan had made good on his promise to see if some changelings wanted to join their household, and Llyr and Kara had volunteered. A distant relative of Krae's, Kara was younger than many of her kin and had a dreamy, thoughtful demeanor. Her dark hair was pulled back in a ponytail, and her dark eyes shone as she dragged a stool over so she could peek inside the pot.

"Yum," she announced. "I love potatoes. We need to cook more."

Jenna snorted. "Probably so."

"I'll get a bigger pot," Roz said. "Or we could add a second one."

Niall straightened and cocked his head as if he were listening. A broad grin split his face. "The men. They're almost here," he cried and jumped up and down.

Jenna finger-combed her hair and smoothed her red tunic over black leggings. Her heart beat a little faster. Despite the months they'd been together, Tristan and Kiernan excited her beyond words. "Maybe we should have waited another month before the men came to Alaska," she ventured, feeling nervous they'd take one look, make excuses, and run like hell.

"Nonsense." Colleen got to her feet, her pale blue eyes glowing with anticipation. "It's us they want, but Alaska is a huge plus."

"Just because we see it that way," Jenna murmured, "not everyone else does. It's like Herman Hesse's *Magic Theater*. Not for everyone."

The air thickened, pulsed, and the men stepped through a gateway. Ronin scooped Roz into his arms and headed out the kitchen door, presumably for her bedroom. Duncan pulled Colleen into such a heated embrace, the air around them shimmered with desire. Jenna blinked to clear her vision, but the space where they'd been standing was empty. She grinned, knowing they'd teleported somewhere private.

Kiernan closed on one side of her, Tristan the other, and they engulfed her in hugs and overwhelming maleness. "We missed you something fierce," Kiernan murmured against her neck. "Longest week of my life."

"But we talked every night," Jenna protested. She threaded her arms around the men, thrilled by the acres of hard muscle flexing beneath her fingers.

"It's not the same. Show us the house," Tristan demanded, "so we can get to the important stuff."

"Nah, just show us your bedroom." Kiernan winked lasciviously. "The house will still be here afterward."

"What about our dinner?" Niall demanded, pushing his way in among them.

Jenna laughed. "Excellent point."

"I'll watch over it," Kara said. "But we do need to make more potatoes."

Tristan eyed the changeling. "Do we have your word on watching over it, rather than eating it?"

"Absolutely." She grinned engagingly and then added, "Well, maybe. Depends how long you're gone."

"It doesn't matter." Kiernan pulled Jenna closer to him. "We can always go out, or order in, or figure something out."

"Hear that?" Llyr crowed. "If we eat the potatoes, we get to go out."

"Second dinner." Kara grinned. "I like it."

"Okay." Jenna got a second pot out, filled it at the sink, found another sack of potatoes, and set the whole mess on another burner. "There you go." She beamed at Kara before turning to her men. "I had an idea."

"So long as it involves getting naked, I'm all for it." Tristan pressed an obvious erection into her thigh.

"There's a glade not far from here on the Chena River. Remember our wedding night when I told you both about a special place I wanted to make love?"

"Sweetheart." Kiernan nuzzled her neck and pressed the length of himself against her other thigh. "I'll never forget a single detail of our wedding day or night."

"Me, either," Tristan cut in. "Especially Oberon hammering on the door and shouting suggestions."

A laugh bubbled past Jenna's lips. "As I recall, some of them were quite creative. Wonder how he came by his knowledge."

"He and Titania got around quite a bit," Kiernan said and moved a hand to her breasts where he tweaked her nipples through the fabric of her tunic. "What's your pleasure, my heart?"

Jenna sent them an image of a sheltered glade next to a broad, flat river. "I know there's still a bit of snow, but we can figure things out."

"What are we waiting for?" The air glistened as Tristan summoned magic. "I'll take us all."

"Don't let the potatoes burn," Jenna called to Kara as the kitchen dissolved around them.

Tristan's magic ran true, and they emerged dead center in a place Jenna considered her own. It was where she went to think about things and to feel closer to Danu and the natural world. "I was hoping the two of you would agree—" she felt herself blushing "—so I made us a bed through there in the tussock grass. Even used magic to dry things out a bit."

Jenna disentangled herself from their embrace and led the way through shoulder height foliage into a sheltered nook with a view of a bend in the river. She settled on a thick mat of grass and held out her arms to the men she loved. Kiernan and Tristan joined her, cradling her body between theirs and trading off kissing her neck and mouth. The air around them warmed from body heat mixed with lust and magic.

"Tell us what you want," Kiernan said, his voice rough with desire while his hands played over her breasts.

"We're never letting a week go by without you again," Tristan said and placed a hand between her legs.

"We would have shown up sooner—" Kiernan tugged her top upward and twirled her nipples between his fingers "—but Oberon had other ideas." He lowered his mouth to her breasts, suckling them in perfect sync with what she needed.

Jenna arched into his touch and moved her legs apart for Tristan, who knelt and tugged her boots off so he could slide her tights down her hips. "You're not cold, darling?" he asked.

"How could I be with the two of you radiating warmth?" She

wriggled her hips and sat to pull one leg out of her tights. Because she was within easy reaching distance, she unzipped Tristan's pants and angled a hand inside to free his cock, running her fingertips up its length.

"Do mine too." Kiernan angled closer to her fingers. He wore the lace-up breeches, which he preferred, but they were actually easier to unfasten. She fondled his penis, and her heart slammed into overdrive. Two amazing men, two unbelievable cocks, all for her.

"God, but I love you both." She let her gaze linger on Kiernan's face, then Tristan's.

Tristan made a satisfied male sound as he drank her in from her face to her breasts to her toes. "By the goddess! You are the most beautiful woman in the world."

He slithered down her body and closed his mouth over her pussy, tonguing her sensitive nub into an exquisite point of sensation. Jenna lay back, enjoying the hell out of his talented tongue.

"Beautiful and ours," Kiernan growled from where he laved her breasts. "I love you, darling."

Tristan sucked harder and moved two fingers inside her, touching a place that made her crazy with need. Heat gathered in her belly, a pool of molten possibility. Locked between her lovers' hands, her body bucked in the throes of a climax so intense it developed a life of its own as spasm after spasm shot through her.

She caught her breath, opened her eyes, and gazed at her lovers, feeling inexpressibly tender. She never knew what would happen next, but it was all so passionate and creative, the choice between hands, tongues, pussy, or cocks scarcely mattered. At first she'd worried about choreographing their lovemaking, but Kiernan and Tristan were endlessly inventive. They linked magically while loving her and were eerily accurate at anticipating her needs.

"On your knees, love," Kiernan's voice was full of hunger, and she loved how he sounded when he wanted her.

Tristan moved his mouth and hands and stretched onto his back with his cock jutting skyward. "Straddle me."

Joy ricocheted through her, and she rolled to a sit, her body still humming from her climax. "How about this first?" She closed her hand around Kiernan's erection where he lay propped on his side and lowered her mouth onto Tristan's. Both men groaned hungrily. She'd gotten to know their bodies well in the months since they'd joined their lives. Their excitement fed her own, and she'd come many times while fondling them.

She moved her mouth on Tristan's shaft—licking, nibbling, biting—and milked Kiernan with her hand. Tension grew in his ridged flesh, and he uncurled her fingers and moved behind her. She felt his cockhead at the entrance to her body and repositioned herself to make it easy for him to sink inside.

In her wildest imaginings, Jenna hadn't anticipated what two men would truly mean. Lust so profound it blotted out everything else in the world pushed her so high she couldn't get enough. Tristan's cock swelled in her mouth, and Kiernan fucked her harder from behind. She dissolved into a series of orgasms. Tristan shuddered and came, crying out in Gaelic that he loved her. Kiernan rode a desperate edge. She felt him scramble for control just before his penis jerked inside her.

With her breath still coming fast, Jenna licked every last drop of semen before sliding up Tristan's body to lay her head on his shoulder. Kiernan stayed inside her and lay atop them both. "Ooph," Tristan said once their breathing had slowed. "She can use me for a pillow, but you're heavy."

"Complaints, complaints." Kiernan rolled off the pile and set his clothing to rights.

"Not fair." Jenna sat and twisted her tights so she could get them back on. She plucked a handful of tussock grass and blotted herself with it. "All you have to do is tuck yourselves back inside your pants, while I have to actually get dressed."

"Remember our conversation about skirts?" Kiernan got to his feet and extended a hand to her. She grabbed it and clambered upright. He stabilized her while she got back into her boots.

"Ah yes, skirts. They're quite convenient." Tristan stood too and covered himself with clothing, zipping up. Stretching his arms over his head, he rotated his torso and looked around. "It really is lovely here. A bit chilly, but lovely."

"Late May is better. And the wildflowers start in June. Along with the mosquitoes, but they're no match for magic." Jenna strode to his side and hugged him. She held out an arm for Kiernan, who drew next to her other side. "I know I've said it a hundred times, but I love you both so much. Thank you for making this easy." She twisted her head and looked first at one man, and then the other. "I had serious doubts. Figured we'd get mired in petty jealousies, but there hasn't been any of that."

"You missed the time I lost it after you and Tristan first made love." Kiernan's blue-green eyes sparkled. "I felt like an ass and made a few decisions."

"So did I," Tristan murmured. He tightened his arm around her. "Loving someone means being invested in their happiness. I knew you needed us both—"

"—so we made a commitment to do whatever we had to." Kiernan angled his head and brushed his lips over her cheek.

"It's been easy for us too," Tristan said. "I'm happier than I ever imagined I'd be."

"We all are," Kiernan seconded.

Jenna watched the river flow by. "I almost hate to bring this up, but I still can't believe this much time has gone by without an Irichna attack."

"Believe it," Kiernan said. "They'll return, but it will take years."

"How are you doing with missing Krae?" Tristan moved until he faced her and tilted her chin so she had to look at him."

Jenna pressed her lips together and rubbed the side of her face with her open palm. "Some days are better than others, but there's not one where I don't think about her."

"That's true for me too." Kiernan's voice rumbled against her ear.

"I didn't know her as well as you two," Tristan said, "but she was the epitome of courage. I don't know many Sidhe who'd march into battle knowing they'd die a hero's death. Of course they'd end up in the *Dreaming*, but there's not much difference between that and death."

Jenna nodded. "I remind myself of Krae's bravery all the time, especially whenever I feel uncertain or scared."

"We never want you to feel that way," the men said with close to a single voice.

"Of course you wouldn't, but that's not realistic." Jenna gazed fondly at the men who loved her. "You can't lock me in a tower and protect me from life."

"Not any more than we can convince you to wear skirts," Tristan joked, probably in an attempt to lighten the moment.

"Come on." Jenna took the path leading back to the river's edge. "Let's walk a little, and then we'll go home."

"I'm looking forward to it," Kiernan said.

"Yes, despite our grousing, we're prepared to embrace Alaska," Tristan cut in.

Jenna turned and smiled at them. "I just realized something pretty basic." She spread her hands in front of her. "It doesn't matter where we are because no matter if it's London or Penrith or Alaska or Timbuktu, we're a family. We'll love and support each other no matter what."

"Aw, darling." Emotion made the air around Kiernan glisten, and love glowed in the depths of his eyes.

"Couldn't have said it better myself." Tristan wrapped an arm around her and patted her bottom. "Alaska, wench. Show us Alaska."

"I will, but we should go home at least long enough so the others aren't worried about us."

"Duncan and Ronin will never notice we're not there," Kiernan pointed out.

"Yes, but the changelings will. You'll be here for months. We'll see a lot of Alaska in that time."

"And even more of each other," Tristan said. "Maybe by summer's end there'll be a child in the offing."

"Twins." Kiernan smiled shrewdly.

"I thought you weren't supposed to scry your own future." Jenna stared at him, trying to wrap her mind around incipient motherhood.

"I didn't." His smile broadened. "Ronin told me."

"Nice to know you guys aren't above cheating."

"Cheating?" Kiernan deadpanned and shot a meaningful look Tristan's way.

"Not us," Tristan deadpanned right back. "Never. We leave the underhanded dealings for lesser creatures."

"You two are impossible, but I love you to pieces." Jenna mock slugged them both before she wove the happiness pouring through her into a spell and took them home.

THIS IS the end of *Witches Rule* and the end of the Demon Assassin books—at least for now. If you enjoyed the story, you might like another of my witch trilogies, the Coven Enforcer Series. A sample from *Blood and Magic*, first of the Coven Enforcer books follows.

ABOUT THE AUTHOR

Ann Gimpel is a national bestselling author. A lifelong aficionado of the unusual, she began writing speculative fiction a few years ago. Since then her short fiction has appeared in a number of webzines and anthologies. Her longer books run the gamut from urban fantasy to paranormal romance. Once upon a time, she nurtured clients, now she nurtures dark, gritty fantasy stories that push hard against reality. When she's not writing, she's in the backcountry getting down and dirty with her camera. She's published over fifty books to date, with several more planned for 2018 and beyond. A husband, grown children, grandchildren, and wolf hybrids round out her family.

Keep up with her at www.anngimpel.com or http://anngimpel.blogspot.com

If you enjoyed what you read, get in line for special offers and pre-release special reads. Sign up for Ann's newsletter on her website or her blog.

BOOK DESCRIPTION: BLOOD AND MAGIC

Magic didn't just find Luke Caulfield. It chased him down, bludgeoned him, and has been dogging him ever since. Some lessons are harder than others, but Luke embraces danger, upping the ante to give it one better. An enforcer for the Coven, a large, established group of witches, his latest assignment is playing bodyguard to the daughter of Coven leaders.

Abigail Ruskin is chaperoning a spoiled twelve-year-old from New York to her parents' home in Utah Territory when Luke gets on their stagecoach in Colorado. A powerful witch herself, Abigail senses Luke's magic, but has no idea what he's doing on her stagecoach. Stuck between the petulant child and Luke's raw sexual energy, Abigail can't wait for the trip to end.

Unpleasant truths surface about the child. While Abigail's struggling with those, wraiths, wolves, and dark mages launch an attack. Luke's so attracted to Abigail, she's almost all he can think about, but he's leery too. The child is just plain evil. Is Abigail in league with her? It might explain the odd attack that took out their driver and one of their horses. In over his head, he summons enforcer backup.

Will they help him save the woman he's falling in love with, or demand her immediate execution?

BLOOD AND MAGIC, PROLOGUE

A VILLAGE WEST OF BOSTON

1 *830*

LUKE RAN as if the devil dogged his heels. Breath caught in his throat. His lungs burned. Running and crying weren't a good mix, but Ma was dead and he couldn't help himself. The thing Ma had turned into danced behind his eyes and filled his mind with terror. His foot twisted sideways into a pothole and he nearly fell. Panting, he came to an abrupt halt and sucked air hard into lungs that had forgotten how to cooperate. When the world quit spinning, he straightened and rubbed his eyes until Ma disappeared and all he saw was the rocky, pitted road, slimed with mud from the rain.

"Good thing I stopped," he muttered. The turnoff to Aethelred's was behind him—not by much, but any time wasted wasn't good. Luke always avoided the town wizard with his long, white hair and penetrating dark eyes that looked right through you, but today was different.

Pa's words rang in his mind. "Run like the wind, son. Bring Aethelred. He's our only hope…"

Luke shoved strands of wet black hair out of his face and started up the steep hill to the school where some of the village youth studied mage craft with the wizard. Branches grabbed at his damp wool clothing almost as if the trees were alive. Shudders wracked his body. Magic made him uncomfortable. He didn't trust what he couldn't see.

Darkness closed as he huffed up the hill, and Luke's heart stuttered in his chest. Was it night already? If it was, then he was too late. He twisted his head wildly about. Trees were blocking what little light the gray day provided.

Thank Christ! I still have time.

He winced and tried to take back the *Christ* word since he wasn't supposed to swear. Once his Ma would've scolded him, but not anymore.

The hill ended abruptly. At the far side of a clearing stood an imposing stone house with smoke curling from one of its chimneys. Shutters covered the windows. The air around the house shimmered, but Luke ignored what felt like a warning to stay away. He pelted across the scrub grass and up the front steps. Before he could knock, the door creaked inward.

Aethelred eyed him shrewdly. "Well don't just stand there with your mouth hanging open, lad. Did you finally come to your senses about your magic?" The mage quirked a brow, his black robes fluttering about him.

"Pa sent me, he…" Luke choked out, but his tongue had taken root and refused to form words. He tried again. Wizard or no, Aethelred couldn't read his mind. Or maybe he could. Luke cringed away from the uncomfortable thought and forced his next words. "Pa said you've got to come. There's trouble—"

Aethelred drew his brows together into a thick, white line. "Wraiths. I see them in your head. Tell me quick, lad. Who'd they get?" He blew out an annoyed-sounding breath. "Your Pa's a right fool to send you off so close to dark. Is he wanting to lose his only son too?"

"Ma. They took Ma." The words burst out of him. Luke squeezed his eyes tight and bit down hard on his lip.

"Get inside." Aethelred yanked on Luke's arm and slammed the heavy oak door behind him. "What'd your Pa do?"

"Nothing yet. He said we had to burn her. That you'd have something to add to the fire so she'd, uh, stay dead." In a burst of brazenness he didn't know he possessed, Luke tugged at the wizard's sleeve. "Come on. We've got to hurry."

"You should've arrived earlier. They walk at night." Aethelred shrugged Luke's hand off. "Too late now, lad. We'd never make it back to your farm in time."

Luke ran for the door, intent on flight. If the wizard wouldn't help, he needed to get home, be there for his Pa and sissies. He pulled the latch, but it wouldn't open. Aethelred's arms closed around him from behind.

"Damn you," Luke cried, struggling to get free. "I've got to warn Pa and the girls. We never had wraiths before. Pa, he didn't know. He thought he was supposed to let Ma rest through two nights."

To his shame and horror, great gasping sobs tore out of him, leaching the air from his lungs. Luke didn't want to be fifteen anymore. He wanted his mother back, wanted the world to be right again, where your parents knew what to do. Where whether your family lived or died didn't rest on a half-grown kid's shoulders.

"It's not fair." Aethelred apparently read his thoughts easily, which amplified Luke's discomfort a hundredfold. "But if you go back to your farm, your Ma will get you. You'll end up one of *them*."

"Come with me."

"I think not." Aethelred released him and turned away.

"But you know magic…" Luke's voice trailed off.

A very large raven perched on a rafter squawked, "Know magic, know magic."

Luke startled. He hadn't noticed the bird until it spoke.

The wizard snorted. "Of course I know magic. It's a precarious magic, though—and not within my ken—that'll save someone from wraiths once they've risen."

"I can't abandon my family."

Aethelred looked hard at him. Luke tried to meet his gaze, but couldn't. It was as if the old man was sifting through his soul, hunting for something. "You have talent for magic," the wizard said. "I've told you that before. I could train you, but you must welcome the call to waken your power." He hesitated for a long moment and then asked, "Are you willing?"

Luke shook his head. "No. The answer is still no. I've got to go home. Try to help." His shoulders slumped. "I still wish you'd come."

Aethelred sighed. "It doesn't work that way, lad. If we go, you'll be the first one your Ma singles out."

"Not you?"

"Not me," Aethelred agreed, then added, "I'm not her blood."

"If you can protect yourself, do the same for me," Luke demanded, anger edging out fear.

"It doesn't work that way," Aethelred said sadly. "You're her blood kin. Blood calls to blood from the other side."

Luke moved a few steps farther into the wizard's home and paced in a restless circle, his hands clasped behind him. Mercifully, Aethelred let him be.

It didn't take long to solidify his decision, and Luke stomped forward until he stood dead center in front of the wizard. He forced himself to meet the man's dark gaze. Despite being taller, it was painful to hold his ground. Power fairly oozed from Aethelred until the air thickened with the feel of it.

"I'm going home," Luke said. Terror ground at the edges of his sanity, eroding it one filament at a time. Looking at the wizard hurt his eyes, so he gave up and dropped his gaze to his boot tops. "Is there something—anything—I can do to protect myself?" Luke's heart hammered against his ribcage. His breath came fast and hard.

The wizard blew out an annoyed-sounding grunt and muttered, "I suppose I can at least do that much for you." He unfastened a heavy gold chain from about his neck. "Take this. When you run into trouble—and you will—grasp the stone and call for the goddess. She may help you. Other than that, light a torch. Wraiths avoid fire, unless they've summoned their own to hurt you." He pursed his lips into a hard, flat line. "They have to be wraiths for a while before they learn to call upon fire of their own, so you're likely safe on that front."

Luke gazed at the smooth, dark stone hanging from the chain. Something warm and inviting glimmered in its center. His fingers shook so hard he had trouble with the clasp, but he finally managed to tuck both stone and chain beneath his wet top. They felt soothing against his skin. "Thank you," he managed through suddenly chattering teeth. "I've got to leave now."

Before I lose my nerve and can't go at all.

The door behind him opened, scraping against its hinges, even though no one had touched it. Spinning sharply, Luke ran for all he was worth out the door and down the steps.

The raven's cries of, "Fool, fool, foolish lad," followed him until he was well into the trees.

Panting and with a stitch in his side, Luke didn't slow until he was almost home. So much time had slipped away, it was long past full dark. He'd puked up what little was in his stomach hours before, but the taste of sickness lingered in his mouth. Leaving the road, he crept along a familiar path that led to a cave he went to when he wanted to get away from everyone. Some of the straw there might make a torch—if it wasn't soaked through.

It had been tough to manage his fear while he'd been running. Once he slowed to wend his way under low-hanging evergreen boughs, terror threatened to paralyze him. What if his cave was some sort of channel the wraiths used to emerge from their underground lairs? What if…?

Stop that, he chided himself. *I could've stayed with Aethelred. I didn't.*

Luke bit the inside of his mouth until he tasted blood. The coppery tang broke through his inertia and he surged forward, pulling rushes and tree limbs away from the cave's hidden entrance. A faint, wavery light shone from within. Horror gripped him, tightening his gut, and he spun on his heel to flee.

"Pa? That you?" His sister's thin voice surprised him. Tamra sounded terrified, as if she was barely hanging on.

Yanking more of the cover back from the cave's entrance, Luke called, "No. It's me."

"Luke!" she exclaimed, followed by, "Where's Pa?" Her seven-year-old voice shrilled with fear.

"Don't know."

Gotta be careful, they might've gotten her…

Luke paced the length of the cave. Warily, he watched his sister and the smoky fire sputtering next to her. Aethelred said wraiths avoided fire, so maybe, just maybe, Tamra really was his sister, not some undead horror in sister form.

"Luke—" She gazed up at him out of eyes the same bright blue as their mother's. "Hold me," she whimpered. "I'm s-scared."

Unable to deny his littlest sister—not when she sounded like *that,* so anxious and so alone—he swallowed his dread and knelt next to where she huddled under a tattered blanket. The minute he was on the ground, Tamra threw herself against him, mewling with fright.

"Hush, hush," he murmured, smoothing her hair and reassured by the all-too-human warmth of her small body. Ma had been cold as death after the wraiths took her. "Tell me what happened."

Tamra pushed herself slightly away from him. Her wispy,

blonde hair stuck out at odd angles, and her eyes shone with tears. "We—well, Pa—was waitin' for you to get back…"

"Waiting," he interrupted, and then he kicked himself. What earthly difference did her grammar make now?

"You been to school, I ain't."

He hugged her. "Go on, Tam. Sorry."

"It was gettin' dark." Tamra cleared her throat. "Pa, I think he figured it'd been wrong to send you off so close to dark and all. And he was just pacin' up and down the cabin somethin' fierce. Then…then…" Her voice trailed off. "I can't," she mumbled and squirmed back against him.

"You have to. I need to know."

Her small head nodded against his chest. The rest of her body trembled. Voice muffled against him, she went on, her words halting. "Ma, she walked into the big room just like always, even though she'd been laid out dead in the bedroom all day. She was smilin' and she sort of sidled up to Pa and put her arms 'round him. He had this…look on his face. It was awful. He screamed at me, told me to run.

"I…" Her voice broke. She tried again. "I wanted to go to Ma. So bad. But I did what Pa said."

He tightened his arms around her. "Where're Lilly and Marta?"

"Pa, he sent 'em to the Waverlys' farm so they'd be safe. I was supposed to go too, but I didn't want to leave Ma. So I snuck back."

My sisters. They're all still alive. Thank the goddess I came back.

"Did you ever tell anyone about this cave?"

She shook her head. Tamra had followed him one day, tracked him without him knowing. Lilly and Marta weren't nearly as adventurous, preferring to spend their time spinning, cooking, and sewing when they weren't in school. Because Tamra was youngest, their mother kept her home, saying she'd be lonely if all three girls were gone. Tamra had chafed at Ma's edict, and Luke planned to tutor her once the winter crops were in. Suddenly that felt like another world.

Was it safe to spend the night here? Maybe, if he stoked the fire… When dawn came, they could head for the Waverlys' house, half a league away. Tamra wriggled in his arms.

"We need to build up the fire, sissy. Where'd you get something dry?"

"Didn't. That's why it's smokin'."

"What'd you light it with?"

"My flint."

"I've got to get some tinder in here. Do what you can to keep it burning till I'm back."

Tamra let go of him. "I understand," she said, her quavering voice solemn.

Luke's heart went out to her, and he swore he'd do whatever he had to, if it meant keeping her safe from harm.

He stayed within a few paces of the cave. Every rustle in the thick undergrowth made him jump. He longed for a torch, but darkness was his friend. As soon as he was back inside, he whittled strips of wood, paying them into the fire. Tamra wrapped herself in the ragged blanket and fell into an uneasy sleep, twitching and moaning.

He tried to stay awake, but the fire warmed the cave, and he caught himself dozing a time or two. When he woke again, his mother and father stood on the far side of the flames with bodies like tall, thin puffs of smoke, their eyes gleaming unnaturally bright.

"Luke," Ma cooed, holding out her arms. "We found you. Come here so I can hold you, son of mine. I'm lonely."

Mouth agape, Luke glanced from one to the other. Pa's eyes were strange, tracking in opposite directions, and they weren't blue anymore, but a muddy charcoal. Luke looked closer. Ma's eyes were the same red-rimmed smoke shade and both his parents had long, blood-red claws where their fingers used to be.

Luke's stomach clenched. If it hadn't been empty, he'd have vomited.

"Your Ma, she told you something," Pa said, his voice gravelly and odd-sounding.

Out of the corner of one eye, Luke saw Tamra edge toward their parents. "No," he cried sharply and snaked out his arm to grab hold of his sister. "You have to stay on this side of the fire." When he pulled her close to him, she was shaking, her eyes round as small moons.

"I-I think I was knowin' that," she whimpered. "It's just…"

"Hush," he said. "I understand."

Luke's hand crept under his woolen tunic. He grasped the amulet and called for Danu, mother goddess of the Earth. Aethelred just said to call for the goddess. Since he hadn't said which one, Luke hoped against hope Danu could help them.

A hissing intake of breath from the far side of the fire shocked him. "I'm your ma. You pay attention to me." The wraith didn't sound nearly as friendly this time. Nor anything like his mother.

Closing his eyes, Luke sought Danu again, begged for her protection—and her wisdom. He thought he felt…something from the amulet, but he could've imagined it.

The things that had been his parents roared their fury from the far side of the fire pit and reached out with spectral arms. Tamra made another run for Ma, and he dragged her back. Nerves on edge, frayed like old rope, he finally turned away since he couldn't bear to look at what had become of his parents any more. Tamra tried to talk to him, but he shushed her. He didn't want to disrupt what had become an internal litany as he pleaded with Danu for help.

Hours passed. Luke paid out the wood, a bit at a time. He maintained a thin line of flames between them and the wraiths, but the feeble fire flickered ominously. Could it last through until dawn? That was looking less and less likely. Fear for his other sisters nagged him, but he reasoned if Ma and Pa were here, they weren't at the Waverlys' farm, so Marta and Lilly should be safe. He added them to his prayers as a hedge against a phalanx of unknowns.

Luke cast a desperate eye about for something else to burn, but didn't see anything. Tamra had used up the straw to get the fire going. Only a couple chunks of wood remained, and it was still black as pitch beyond where Ma and Pa had planted themselves.

"We're runnin' out," Tamra whispered, clutching his arm and pointing to the few remaining shards of wood.

The husks of his parents leaned closer, their mouths curved in feral grins.

They're practically salivating. They've figured out there's not enough wood. Soon as the fire wanes, they'll be on us.

Luke cursed himself for a fool, his anger flaring. All his prayers had done was keep him from coming up with a real solution.

Tamra twisted and stabbed a grimy finger in front of her. "What's that?"

An odd light, all colors, and yet no color he could name, oozed through the rocks at the rear of the cave. "I don't know," he muttered. As he stared, mesmerized, the otherworldly glow grew to such a brilliance it hurt his eyes. The amulet, still clutched in his hand, warmed and began to throb.

The fire made a wet, gurgling noise and guttered. Like a hunting dog on red alert, his father jumped the pit, grabbed Tamra, and hauled her toward the mouth of the cave. His sister wailed piteously, writhing and kicking in Pa's grasp.

"No!" Luke screamed. "Noooooo…" He let go of the amulet and lunged after the pair, grabbing Tamra's feet and yanking as hard as he could. Tam screamed louder. Luke kept on tugging. As Ma lowered her face for the kiss that would steal Tamra's soul, the amulet turned red hot against his chest.

The brightness coming from the rear of the cave pulsed with energy.

His father cursed, words he'd never used before spewing from him, but at least he loosened his grip on Tamra. Luke sprinted toward the rear of the cave holding his sister close. His mother shielded her own body with her hands, but the light curled around her, creating noxious-smelling smoke.

The brilliance was so intense, Luke had to shut his eyes. When he pried them open, Ma and Pa were gone—and so was the mysterious light. The cave sat empty, except for him and Tamra, who was dangling from his hands and still screaming.

Repositioning his sister, he cradled her against him. "Ssssh, hush," he murmured over and over.

"I wet myself," she sobbed, face buried against him.

"Never mind. I would've too, if it'd been me."

"Put me down so I can get my drawers off."

A burnt smell, different from the fire pit, rose and he realized it was his own flesh, scored where the amulet rested against it. He rubbed at his breastbone, but that made it hurt more.

"They're gone," Tamra mumbled from somewhere behind him. "You saved us, Luke." She was still snuffling, but seemed in control of her fear.

Luke readied himself to sit out what remained of the night. He'd just settled against a damp, curving wall when an unpleasant thought struck. "The wraiths. We ran them off here, so they've likely gone after Marta and Lilly." He recognized the ring of truth as soon as the words were out.

A dim version of the curious light in the cave returned, almost as if it agreed.

"If Ma and Pa are truly gone," Tamra sounded much less scared than she had earlier, "we might could take the horse to the Waverlys'."

Of course. Why didn't I think of that?

"Great idea." Luke realized he should've taken the horse when he went after Aethelred—not that it would have altered the outcome. But Abel was a plow horse and rarely ridden, so it never occurred to him.

He pushed heavily to his feet. "Let's go get Abel. We'll toss a blanket over him. In fact, bring that one." He pointed to hers, wadded in a heap near the wall.

Nodding, she scrambled up. "Think it's safe?" she muttered and peered at the odd light, still suffusing the cave with its comforting warmth.

"Truth?"

"Yes, I'm wantin' the truth." Tamra drew herself tall, a solemn light in her eyes.

"I don't know how safe it is." He swallowed hard. "Probably not safe at all, but we have to warn the Waverlys." He hesitated. "There's something in this cave taking care of us. Let's hope it follows us out of here." He took Tamra's hand. "Come on."

It was black as pitch outside. And cold, but at least it had stopped raining. A slender thread of the multi-hued light floated out of the cave and wrapped itself around the two of them, rather like a length of shimmery rope. Its soft glow was welcome, and Luke managed not to stumble as he led the way to the moss-coated shed where Abel was tethered.

Clucking softly to the horse, Luke tossed the blanket onto his broad back. He untied Abel's halter, and then boosted Tamra up. She ducked to avoid the shed's low-hanging roofline. Luke led the horse out, vaulted onto its back, and turned its head toward the Waverlys' farm. They bounced unpleasantly once he whipped Abel into a ragged trot. When he looked down, Luke was surprised to find his free hand still clutching Aethelred's amulet.

A lighter gray painted the far horizon, and pink streaks formed, pale as seashells. "Hurry," Luke urged, gripping Abel with his knees. "Hurry." Tamra's small body, rigid with determination, pushed against him. He stared down the deserted road, willing the Waverlys' farm to appear.

The glowing rope unwound itself and stretched outward into a straight line.

"I think it means for us to walk from here," Luke muttered, not understanding how he could possibly know that, but knowing it all the same. He wrapped his arm around Tamra and jumped down.

"Abel's leaving," Tamra whispered urgently.

"It's all right. He knows the way home." Luke looked around nervously and followed the ghostly light's trail, with his sister clinging to his side. The amulet warmed again in his hand. He clutched it so hard it cut into his flesh, and blood trickled down his palm.

The road turned a sharp bend. Light shone from the windows of the Waverlys' rambling, two-story farmhouse. Folks used lanterns sparingly because it took a lot of work to render the fat to fuel them. Did all that light mean Ma and Pa were somewhere close? The fine hairs on the back of Luke's neck stood on end, and he combed the dark for any sign of the wraiths.

Tamra gasped, "Luke! Look there," and clung even tighter to his hand.

Outlined in the light of the coming day, Ma and Pa grinned at them from the far side of the Waverlys' front yard. They weren't as...solid as they'd been in the dark of the cave, but they leered and beckoned, calling for their four children.

"Blood knows its own," Ma crooned, her voice simple and terrible. "I birthed you all. Come to me now." The farmhouse door opened, and then thudded shut. Luke heard raised voices inside and understood one of his sisters tried to go to Ma, but had been pulled back. His parents shambled toward the farmhouse, their eyes glistening brightly.

"Go," he hissed at Tamra. "Run onto the porch and get inside." He placed his body between his sister and his parents. Acid curdled his empty stomach and tears stung his eyes. He wanted Pa to be, well, his Pa again. And Ma... She'd fed him, cared for him... How could she have turned into the atrocity advancing across the yard?

Tamra's footsteps pounded as she raced for the porch and

safety. Another slam of the door told him she was in the Waverlys' capable hands. With the glowing rope of light in place around him, and apprehension chewing a hole in his guts, Luke shut out the rest of the world and faced the wraiths.

"You shall leave here," he called out sternly, except it wasn't his voice. Someone else spoke through him. It terrified him, but that didn't matter. What did was sudden understanding he'd been picked to kill the wraiths that had been his parents—or be killed trying.

His head whirled, but power humming through him kept him on his feet. Things grew disjointed after that. Pa leapt toward the porch. Before Luke could react, Ma jumped him and he had to push her chill weight off himself again and again. Then it was Pa he grappled with, and then Ma again. In a distant corner of his mind, Luke wondered which was worse: killing his parents or letting them kill him.

He struggled to his feet for the hundredth time, or maybe it was the thousandth. He'd lost count. His head pounded, and his heart ached as if he'd been stabbed.

The amulet grew hot, blazing hot, and the shimmering cord tightened about him. Fire erupted from his outstretched hands, but his parents—and something else he couldn't quite make out— were finally fading, scattering in the light pouring off him. In moments, they'd be gone.

"Ma, Pa," he moaned, surprised to hear his own voice. "I love you. I'm sorry, so very sorry…"

Something constricted his throat, choking off his air, and the other voice took over his vocal chords again. "You are banished from the light," it shouted. "You shall not return. Not ever."

After that, saying anything became a struggle because the magical cord cut off his wind. The stench of his own burning flesh filled his nostrils, gagging him. Gasping for air, he collapsed in the wet mud of the yard.

Shaking long, gray hair out of her lined face, Clare echoed, "Yes, it's the least we can do."

"I couldn't let you," Luke protested. "My family's my responsibility."

"Go, son," Joad said. "Soon as you're strong enough. Things will be all right here."

A strange desire mingled with Luke's grief. It was so foreign it took him a few moments to sort it out, to realize he wanted to learn about magic, *needed* to learn. Just like he needed to eat and breathe. Whatever he'd awakened in the cave called to him, sang to him, dared him to pluck the strings holding his inner knowledge captive.

"I feel it too, lad." Weariness creased Aethelred's forehead, yet his eyes shone with hope. "It won't go away. You have no choice after tonight. The call, it comes to each of us in its own fashion. The way your magic found you, well, it was harsher than most." He exhaled softly, his dark eyes full of warmth as they rested on Luke. "Rest now. There's time yet before we must leave."

Luke's eyelids felt suddenly heavy and he let them close. The warmth stealing about him was probably Aethelred's doing, but he didn't fight it. Burned, weary, and heart sore, he called up images of his parents and sister. Once he'd bid them farewell, he let the wizard's spell carry him away.

entral Overland Stage Route, East of Salt Lake City
1860

THE UNMISTAKABLE STENCH of spoiled meat, mixed with fresh excrement, wafted into the stagecoach. Abigail Ruskin knew that smell. She covered her nose with her handkerchief, but it was just as saturated with dust and grime as everything else and she sneezed.

The coach swayed alarmingly, rocking on the leather straps that dampened its lateral motion.

She thrust the heavy leather window curtain out of the way, so she could see how bad things were outside. Usually wraiths left you alone in the daytime—but not always. There'd been a time when they did, but dark magic fueled them these days, making them more dangerous than when they'd just been shades of the dead.

"Damn!" The word escaped despite her effort to stifle it.

"What is it, Miss Abby?"

"Nothing dear." Abigail patted Carolyn Giraud's hand. She was only twelve, and there was no need to alarm her about the wraiths. Without magic, Carolyn wouldn't be able to see them anyway—at least not as anything but gray shadows. Unfortunately, that wouldn't stop them from killing her.

"I want to look." Carolyn craned her neck, but Abigail slammed the curtain back into place. "I really did want to see." Petulance rode beneath the girl's words, reminding Abigail just how privileged and spoiled she was. "My parents employ you. You have no right to tell me *no*." Pain blossomed in Abigail's arm, and she realized the girl had pinched her…hard.

"Now, now. We'll have none of that, young lady." It took all her forbearance not to haul off and slap her young charge.

Abigail settled Carolyn firmly back into her seat and pushed the girl's blonde hair out of her blue-gray eyes, arranging it behind her shoulders. Curves were just starting to show beneath layers of finely woven woolen clothing. Maybe incipient womanhood was responsible for the girl's foul temper—and near inability to follow directions.

"Naught to look at," Abigail said, rubbing her arm. "I must've been half-asleep when I pulled that curtain aside. I'm sure we'll be on the other side of this mountain range in no time and in Salt Lake tomorrow or the day after that."

Unless the wraiths decide to attack. That could push our schedule back quite a bit.

She arranged her mouth in an approximation of a smile to settle her apprehension. The boning from her stays poked uncomfortably into her sides. Abigail did what she could to alleviate the pressure, which wasn't much with the man sitting across from her staring.

"I don't like you." Carolyn crossed her arms over her chest and glared at the floor.

Abigail blew out an exasperated breath. It had been clear from the first day of their long journey from New York City that Carolyn's parents denied her nothing. Gifted witches in Abigail's

Coven, they'd hired her through the Coven network to chaperone their only child cross-country to their new family home in Utah Territory. The journey had been quite an odyssey, and it wasn't over yet. They'd traveled by train—three different rail lines—to St. Joseph, Missouri, and then gotten on the Central Overland Stage.

If the goddess kept a kind eye out, the elder Girauds would have their little darling back in short order.

Good thing too, or else I'd kill her.

Abigail's instructions had also included providing tutelage in the magical arts, which was probably why the elder Girauds hired her and not some non-Coven-linked governess. She'd tried, but Carolyn had absolutely zero aptitude, not even enough ability to light a candle. Strange, given how powerful her parents were, but not unheard of since witchcraft didn't follow genetic patterns of inheritance.

Abigail shook her head. She wasn't looking forward to being the one to tell the Girauds their daughter didn't even have a future as a hedge witch, let alone a stronger practitioner. In truth, she was surprised they hadn't already figured it out on their own.

"Like me or no, you'll be rid of me soon enough." Abigail aimed for a cheerful tone. "I'm certain your folks will be delighted to be reunited with you."

"Unless those danged Indians cause more problems," the other occupant of the stagecoach spoke up.

Luke Caulfield was a fortyish gunslinger, who hadn't said much since introducing himself when he boarded back in Sterling, Colorado. Twin colts graced his hips, and rows of bullets crisscrossed his broad chest in leather bandoliers. Black hair fell straight as a stick past his shoulders. Unsettling green eyes stared right through her, almost in invitation to reveal her ability. At times, she'd caught him fairly vibrating with power. Others, no matter how hard she looked, he was as unremarkable as a rain-washed windowpane—at least in terms of magic.

No living, breathing woman would ever consider Luke unremarkable in any other way. Muscles bulged under his form-fitting leather clothing. He was so masculine he made her squirm, and Abigail pressed her thighs together, suppressing thoughts of what she'd like to do with that leather-clad body.

She laced her fingers tightly in her lap, thinking she'd be damned glad to get off this stage and away from both Carolyn and Luke. The child was a pain in the rump and the man too sensual to even consider. He probably had women in a dozen cities across the country drawing straws to see who got to warm his bed. Not that she wouldn't like to be one of them, but he was a complication she didn't need right now.

"Oooh, Indians would be exciting," Carolyn trilled. "Do you really think they might attack us or something?"

"Of course not." Abigail jumped into the breach and shot what she hoped was a meaningful look across the small, enclosed space.

"Do you have to ruin everything?" Carolyn snarled, and reached out with pincer-like fingers.

Abigail anticipated her, though, and caught the girl's hand before she could strike.

"If you try that again," she snapped, "I'll tie your hands behind your back."

Or feed you to what's outside this carriage.

"You wouldn't dare—"

"Oh yes, I would. It's what we do to young ladies who refuse to behave as such."

"I'd tell."

Abigail grabbed the girl's chin, forcing her to look up and meet her gaze. "Yes, and so would I. I scarcely think your parents would be pleased by your behavior." That earned her a sulky silence. When Abigail glanced at Luke, the corners of his mouth were twitching. "Ever raised one of these?" She waggled a finger toward Carolyn.

"No ma'am. Can't say as I have." He chuckled. "Not looking like a very attractive proposition, watching you."

The stage ground to an abrupt halt, throwing her forward and then back against the seat cushions. The hum of brass gears, which worked as an assist to the horses through rough terrain—and that she'd been powering with a steady stream of magic—fell ominously silent. Luke tensed his jaw into a worried line. One of his guns found its way to his hand so quickly, Abigail didn't see him draw it.

She quirked a brow, but he shook his head and said, "I don't know why we stopped. We're not due at the next station for an hour."

"I'm going outside to look," Carolyn announced and lunged for the door latch.

"The hell you are, youngster." Luke's other hand closed around Carolyn's wrist, and the girl yelped. She tried to draw her hand back, but Luke held fast.

Carolyn wailed. Abigail, edgy because she had a bad feeling about what was happening, grabbed the girl's shoulder. Not hard, but enough to get her attention. "You will be quiet," she hissed. "Do you want to advertise your presence to whatever's out there?"

"What'd you see outside?"

Luke's question was so quiet, she wasn't certain she'd even heard it. The shriek of a horse whinnying filled her ears. It sounded like it was dying. The stagecoach canted crazily from side to side as the horses pulled against their harnesses. Luke tapped her leg with his pistol.

"Quick. Tell me."

"Wraiths."

He drew his lips back from his teeth in a snarl. "Figured as much from the smell. You need to help me or none of us'll get out of this."

"What are wraiths?" Carolyn sounded more like a frightened child than a surly almost-teen.

"Never you mind," Luke shot back. "Didn't anyone ever teach you to stay out of grownup conversations?"

"What do you have in mind?" Abigail asked, ignoring his question to Carolyn. She felt power pour off him, and wondered why he bothered with his six-guns. The horses started shrieking again.

"You and I are going out there to take on whatever's stopped us. This isn't a time to hide what you are."

"Carolyn." Abigail kept her voice low. "You will stay inside the coach. No matter what. Do you understand me?"

The girl hesitated before stammering, "Y-yes."

"I don't want to have to explain to your parents that you were killed because you didn't do what I told you."

"All right. I'll stay here," the girl muttered sullenly. "Just go outside and get rid of whatever it is."

Child always has to have the last word.

"Ready when you are." Abigail reached deep, down to the reservoir that held her power. Thank the goddess she'd eaten and rested. Magic was persnickety. It knew when she was worn down.

"I'll take this door." Luke gestured. "You go out the other one. Blast the holy crap out of 'em. Watch out for the horses. Sounds like we only have three left."

"Were the horses how you knew about my, um, abilities?"

He rolled his eyes. "As if I couldn't hear the gears whirling. Driver didn't have a lick of power. 'Sides, most coaches need six horses to pull these grades. We only had four. Now get the hell out there, woman, before we lose another horse."

His door slammed open, clunking against its stops. The last thing Abigail saw before she leapt out her door was Carolyn cowering as far back as she could get against a seat cushion.

Good! Hope the little bitch stays there.

Cursing her long skirts and cumbersome petticoats, Abigail used magic to skip the coach steps. Power blazed from her hands before she could see what she was aiming at. She was afraid if she took even a few seconds to hunt for a target, something would get her. Being dead wasn't desirable, but it was better than the other things wraiths could do to her. Those turned her blood to ice chips.

With her booted feet planted firmly on the ground, Abigail finally got a good look at the wraiths. She drew magic from deep in the earth and sent it chasing after them when they jumped sideways to evade her magic. Insubstantial as tall, thin puffs of smoke, they had glowing charcoal eyes. Long, blood red claws graced what passed for hands. Binding their victims with fiery strands was a favorite trick—just before they sucked your soul right out of you, leaving a handy vessel for one of their masters to occupy. Wraiths used to feed only on the living, making them into new wraiths. They'd been bad enough then, but now they functioned as hired thugs for practitioners of the Black Arts. It lent them the ability to operate in broad daylight. Abigail wondered which group of sorcerers this crew worked for. The Alchemical Council? Black Magick?

Good God but there were a lot of them. *Why?* Surely they weren't interested in the contents of the coach, which only carried mail and Carolyn's substantial luggage. Ducking and spinning to escape being entwined in a blazing net, she thought about the girl's steamer trunks. Abigail only helped pack two of them. The third had been locked and ready to go. Could that possibly be what the wraiths were after?

She shut off her thoughts so she could focus. The ragged sound of her own panting thrummed loud in her ears as she chucked one killing blow after another. Bolts of blue-white light flared from both hands. No point in running anything less than wide open. For each wraith she obliterated, three more showed up to take its place. Her chest ached from breathing sooty air and wraith stench.

Heat seared her back. Damnation! Her skirts were on fire. Abigail funneled magic behind her to quell the flames, but it didn't work. Smoke stung her nostrils. Fire had already eaten a long gouge in one of her hands. If she dropped to the ground to deal with her burning clothes, the wraiths would pounce. Terror licked at her along with the flames.

In spite of her brave thoughts earlier, she didn't want to die. Not here. And not like this. She cursed her corset. It was hard to get a decent breath. If she'd known she was going to have to fight—

"Keep after 'em," Luke growled from behind her. "I have your dress under control." She felt him drape something heavy around her shoulders—a lap robe he must've snatched from inside the coach—and press it close against her with his body. Gratitude wrapped warm tentacles around her. Having him right next to her made her already pounding heart do flip-flops, but she forced herself to focus on something other than all those rock-hard muscles jammed against her back.

"Are they all on this side of the coach?" she wheezed, still struggling to breathe. Between the smoke, her stays, and Luke's body so near, it was a losing battle.

"Pretty much. Guess they want you more than me. Actually, they've been trying to get to the trunks up top."

A discordant warning note sounded in the back of her mind. What the hell was in the girl's luggage that would draw wraiths? Her back wasn't hot anymore, so she assumed the fire was out.

That fire, maybe. The one inside me is just getting going...

She squirmed from more than the smoke and struggled not to turn around and press the front of herself against Luke. They had bigger problems than his undeniable charisma. Luke didn't seem to be in a hurry to move away, though. He remained front to back with her, and she absorbed power flowing from him. Damn, but he was strong. What she wouldn't give for that kind of magic.

It would help if I could breathe...

With difficulty, Abigail forced her mind away from Luke's charms. "The driver?" She hadn't been round to the front of the wagon to check.

"Dead."

"Ever driven one of these things?"

"Concentrate on killing, woman. If we can't get shut of the wraiths, 'twon't matter a diddly damn."

Anger flashed through her at Luke's highhandedness. She stepped away from him, and the lap robe slithered to the ground. Raising her hands, she pulled magic and killed three more wraiths. It was convenient they didn't hang around. They just sort of winked out once hit. For all she knew they weren't dead at all, just returned to some sort of central depot for reanimation. A flash at the edge of her vision set off alarms, but her reflexes were sluggish, and she was a hair too late. A wraith closed, slashing deadly nails down her already-burned hand. Abigail howled with pain. Luke's gun roared, making her ears ring, and a hole opened in the wraith's chest that got bigger and bigger until the thing folded in on itself.

"Thought you couldn't kill them with bullets," she gasped, staring at the place the wraith had been.

"Silver does the trick. I mix it with iron in my gunpowder, just to be on the safe side." Taking aim, he fired again.

Her breath came in little pants. She had a stitch in her side. Her face burned, and her injured hand was gashed so deep bone showed. Wraith fire was deadly like that; once it gained a toehold, it could burn a body to cinders. Thank the goddess, the flames attacking her were all extinguished. She twisted her head from side to side and looked for more wraiths, but couldn't find any.

"They're gone. Must not have liked the odds." Luke holstered his guns.

"Bravo. Nicely done." Clapping came from one of the open stagecoach doors.

Abigail looked toward the coach through eyes that were hot, gritty, and stinging from smoke. Carolyn sat on the floor of the stagecoach with her legs dangling. Something inside Abigail snapped. She raced to her charge and grabbed a fistful of her blonde hair with one hand, wanting to slap her. Hanging onto

Carolyn made her wounded hand ache something fierce, but she didn't let go.

"You ungrateful little girl," she snarled. "What do you think this is? A sporting event?"

Blue eyes huge as pinwheels, Carolyn twisted in her grasp, trying to get away, but Abigail held tight. "You've needed your behavior reined in for years. While we're at it, what's in your luggage?"

"Good point," Luke muttered from somewhere close behind her. "We should take a look in there."

Carolyn screamed epithets no well-bred child should even know, and shock slammed Abigail in the guts. "If you don't stop that right now," she gritted, "I'll use magic to bind you." The threat seemed to work because the girl shut up.

Abigail stepped back from her and eyed a stream running by the road. She stumbled over to it, knelt, and threw water on her face and hands. It felt good, cooling the places her skin was charred and split. She pulled the pins out of her hair, bent forward, and soaked the singed, sooty strands. They floated in the current like exotic, dark red seaweed. What she really wanted to do was loosen her corset, but she'd need to strip down for that. Not something she could do in front of Luke.

"I won't look," he said.

Giving her hair a final dunk, she pulled it out of the creek, and wrung as much of the water out as she could manage. She straightened and met his gaze. "You have the mind reading gift?"

"That and other things." He turned away from her. "Go ahead. We've got some hard work ahead of us. It'll help if you can get a straight breath into you."

Unbuttoning her dress, she pulled at the laces holding her stays. She'd planned to just loosen them, but once they were undone, she let the whalebone-reinforced undergarment slip under her skirts where she could just step out of it. She inhaled all the way to the bottom of her lungs and smiled grimly.

Yes. More like it.

"You took your underthings off in front of a man." Carolyn sounded scandalized—and fascinated.

Abigail stomped back to the coach and tossed her stays inside. "And you just cursed a blue streak. We need to have a talk, but not right now."

Her wet hair soaked through the bodice of her dress, but at least the day was warm enough it didn't matter. She twisted and looked over both shoulders assessing just how damaged her dress was. The thick linen fabric was singed, but not so badly she couldn't still wear it. Good thing, since she'd only packed three others. She focused a few strands of magic to dry everything and moved to the front of the coach.

One of the horses was, indeed, dead. Drawing a knife from her belt, Abigail cut it free from the others with a great deal of difficulty. The remaining three pranced, eyes rolling as they attempted to distance themselves from their fallen companion. She tried to soothe them enough so they wouldn't kick her. When that didn't work, she reached into their minds with a strong suggestion they settle down. *Now.* While she waited for the horses to stop snorting and pawing the ground, she diverted a trickle of magic to patch up the worst of her injuries. There wasn't time to truly heal herself, but she did take a bite out of her pain. She also retrieved the lap robe and stuffed it back inside the coach.

"How should I hook them up?" she asked Luke, finally satisfied she could approach the horses safely.

He'd already pulled the driver off the box and was piling rocks over his body. "One in front, two behind. I'll help you once I'm done here."

As Abigail worked, she speculated just how much more magic it would take to run the gears that powered the wheels and helped the horses over the steep parts. That had been one of the attractive parts about this journey: getting paid twice. Once for shepherding Carolyn, and again for helping with the stagecoach. Still panicked, one of the horses nipped her with its broad, flat teeth. She thwacked the side of its head and wondered what was keeping Luke.

As if in response to her thinking about him, Luke materialized by her side and started tightening the leather straps. "Looks like you've about got it."

"Thanks. Same thing I thought. Should we open her luggage?" Abigail feared what they'd find.

He laid a comforting hand briefly over one of hers. "Nah, let's wait until we're well clear of this spot." Luke jumped onto the box and gathered the reins. "Get inside with the hellion—ah, I mean the girl." He laughed, but without much warmth. "She's not what she appears, but there's not time to talk about that right now."

www.ingramcontent.com/pod-product-compliance
Lightning Source LLC
Chambersburg PA
CBHW071236190726

48292CB00007B/2322